Sand Cove

Sand Cove

Niyah Moore

www.urbanbooks.net

Urban Books, LLC
300 Farmingdale Road, NY-Route 109
Farmingdale, NY 11735

ISBN 13: 978-1-62286-197-2
ISBN 10: 1-62286-197-3

First Trade Paperback Printing September 2019
Printed in the United States of America

10 9 8 7 6 5 4 3 2 1

Distributed by Kensington Publishing Corp.
Submit Orders to:
Customer Service
400 Hahn Road
Westminster, MD 21157-4627
Phone: 1-800-733-3000
Fax: 1-800-659-2436

Sand Cove

Niyah Moore

Acknowledgments

I thank God for everything he has blessed me with this year. I thank my husband, Malcolm, and my children, Cameron, Ciera, my angel in heaven, Londyn, and Miles for being so loving and caring.

To my grandparents in heaven, my parents, my siblings, my aunties, uncles, and cousins, I love you guys.

Thank you to my huge network of friends that I have accumulated over the years, new and old.

To my literary family, you guys rock. To my literary agent, N'Tyse, thank you for believing in my writing talent. Straight to the top—no ceilings.

To my ReadMoore Crew, thank you so much for reading and enjoying my work. It's been a blessing to be able to share my work with those who take the time to "Read Moore."

Stay blessed. Stay encouraged. Dream big.

Niyah

Chapter 1

Alohnzo

The sweltering sun set hours ago, and the sky had become a thick, dark curtain of silk as I sat on a white lounge chair in front of my pool from the deck of my beach house. I drew in a deep breath of the salty air and could hear the gentle waves of the ocean caress the sand back and forth the way a man's hands stroked a woman's curves. The song of the waves lulled me. My backyard was among one of the most desirable beaches in Southern California, and whenever I wanted to go to the beach, it was only a staircase away.

Sand Cove was a small community of four beach homes lined up in a straight line; our secret haven tucked away. Our beach was entirely off-limits to the public. Though it was against the law to claim a beach as private property, the designers separated the houses with tempered glass fences, trees, and ceramic potted plants so that it was impossible for unwanted guests to touch any parts of the sand. The only way to the beach was through invitation.

While enjoying a few glasses of Rosé, my glossy eyes continued to stare out at the beach that was shaped like a shepherd's hook of gold. I was on the brink of being tipsy, but I wasn't drunk. I wasn't celebrating anything special. I drank champagne often for no reason at all. I worked long hours during the week as one of the head advisors for my father's financial company, so drinking champagne was one of the things I looked forward to at the end of my day.

Though it was dark, I could vaguely see Tru and Noble Mason holding hands and walking, taking advantage of some free time while their 4-year-old fraternal twins were sleeping. The young African American couple lived in the very last house of the row. They were some of the most genuine people I had ever met. They were successful entrepreneurs, and the love they had for each other was resilient. One day, I hoped to have what they had—*real love*.

The moon was full and shining brightly. Underneath the moonlight, I could make out Tahira walking toward the shore. She lived in between my house and the Masons'. Her robe became one with the sand before submerging herself into the ocean. Disappearing beneath a wave shortly, she popped back up. The 21-year-old actress was born in the UK and married to 55-year-old Luca Moretti.

I hated to admit that I was slightly jealous of Luca, and I wasn't the kind of man who wanted anything or anyone who belonged to another man, but Tahira was everything I would want in a woman. I had never seen her act crass or rude to anyone.

With Luca and Tahira's thirty-four-year age difference, I wondered what she saw in him other than his money. With all his wealth and status, I was sure plenty of thirsty women wanted to walk in her Red Bottoms.

Who was I fooling? I wasn't *slightly* jealous. I was *insanely* jealous. He was too old to know what to do with a woman like that.

As soon as I heard the sliding door of my dining room slide open, I tried to act like I was fooling around with my iWatch.

Kinsley stuck her head out and asked, "When are you coming inside, sexy?"

Kinsley and I were sort of, kind of, in a situation. She wasn't my girlfriend, and I wouldn't say we were working toward that either. Kinsley had been working for Amos Kelly Advisors for ten years, but we had only been fucking for two weeks. She was a few years older than I was and much more aggressive. She was bad in her own right—light creamy-brown skin, dyed red hair that resembled the color crimson, and natural hazel eyes that sparkled each time she looked at me. This was complicated because it wasn't my intention to mix professional business with pleasurable nonsense. Sex was going to happen because she wanted it to happen. I usually was good at ignoring sexual advances from the women I worked with, but Kinsley's sexual advances were strong, like a mad bull, and irresistible like a favorite treat.

I glanced at the time on my iWatch. It was getting late, and I needed to get to bed. Taking the last drink of champagne, I let the taste linger in my mouth before swallowing.

"Did you hear me?" Kinsley asked with her lips out in a pout.

"Give me a minute," I replied without turning to look at her.

Kinsley lingered for a couple of seconds. Once she realized I would come in when I was ready, she left the sliding door open as she walked away.

I smirked.

She may have had a bit of an attitude when she didn't get my attention right away, but she did all the right things to turn me on. I was going to give her exactly what she wanted, but not right now.

I returned my eyes to my guilty pleasure while I poured some more Rosé into my glass. The moon gave me some light to see enough of Tahira. The way she swam made the water look warm and inviting, but it was colder than an Alaskan Eskimo's rosy cheeks. Once she was done swimming, she looked up toward my house and waved warmly.

I waved back.

She picked up her robe from the beach and walked toward me.

I got up from the chair and walked around my pool. I rested my arms on the tempered glass encasing the pool to peer down at her. When it came to showing off her plump breasts, her tight tummy, her slender legs, and her hips that accentuated her ass in that black bikini, she wasn't shy. It was hard for anyone not to look. Nothing was wrong with looking. I mean, looking was all I was doing. Tahira was mouthwatering, like a perspiring glass pitcher of lemonade.

She said in her British accent, "I decided to come over and say hello. How are you tonight?"

She was intoxicating when she spoke with that British accent, and whenever she flashed that cute grin, I would feel all crazy inside.

I kept my cool, though, as I replied, "I'm good, you?"

"I'm well. It feels so good out tonight, yeah?"

"It does. How was the water?"

"Bloody cold," she said with a slight little sexy laugh, though she wasn't shivering.

"Well, you definitely don't make it look like it's cold."

"Oh, that's because I'm used to it . . ."

The air between us became thick like our sexual tension was rising. I could feel it, but could she?

"What are you drinking?" she asked.

Even in the dark, I could see her curious chestnut-brown eyes shimmering the same way the moon's reflection danced upon the ocean.

"Ace of Spades. You want some? It's nearly gone, but I can go grab another bottle from inside."

"No, thank you. I'm trying to give up liquor for a few weeks . . . Well, I gotta get up early. You have a good night."

"Same to you, Tahira."

She smiled, turned, and slowly walked next door. Her hips swayed from left to right the way a series of swinging spheres did inside of Newton's cradle. All the blood rushed to the top of my head, and the hairs on my body stood straight up. I had to shake this feeling off and quickly. I finished my glass before heading inside because my thoughts were starting to get too carried away.

Inside, the house was tranquil. I closed the sliding door behind me, placing the bottle and flute on the dining room table. Only one light was on above the stairs leading to the second floor, and I couldn't hear Kinsley moving around. It was funny how after just two weeks, she took it upon herself to spend the night without an invitation. The only reason I didn't say a word or ask her to leave was that I hated to be alone. I had gotten used to her warm body being with me.

I turned off the light after I made it to the top of the stairs. Once in my bedroom, Kinsley was underneath the covers, cuddled up, and naked. I admit that Tahira had me aroused. I got out of my clothes, leaving them on the floor before getting underneath the covers with her. I scooted to Kinsley's backside. She moaned, sounding aroused by my presence. I rubbed her breasts. She wrapped her arms around my neck to pull me down on top of her.

Chapter 2

Tahira

I removed the wet bathing suit and placed it on the master bathroom counter. Staring at myself in the mirror, naked and natural without makeup, I examined myself. All the makeup and airbrushing my stylists did for hours to make me look fabulous on screen was strictly for the cameras. I wished I could wake up looking the way I did in pictures on a regular. Tyra Banks said it best when she said that she wanted to wake up looking the way she did in photo shoots. *Hell, me too.* When someone called me pretty or beautiful, it was hard for me to believe it myself. Call me insecure, but I didn't *feel* beautiful.

My mum always told me that it wasn't the makeup that made me beautiful. She said I was beautiful because of who I was, but how come *I* didn't see it? People needed to see these dark circles and bags underneath my eyes that my husband so often nitpicked. Luca had an extensive list of things he didn't like. My hair was too short, so he demanded that I wear hair extensions and wigs. He paid for D-cup breasts and liposuction in my fatty areas performed by the very best plastic surgeons. Daily, Luca was applying more pressure for me to look impeccably faultless. I spent a lot of time in the mirror picking at myself, finding flaws before he could so it wouldn't make me feel as bad when he pointed them out.

Yawning, I ran the water hot for a shower. Thoughts were skipping through my head. *Am I happy?* I asked myself. I didn't know if I was. I wanted so much more than the life I had, and I wasn't talking money either. I had plenty of that. I didn't have any children, and my husband didn't want any because he already had two daughters that were older than I was. Because of my acting career, he said that children wouldn't be good for me, so I quit nagging and focused on my career. He made sure to go with me to my appointments to watch me get the birth control implant to make sure that I wasn't going to get pregnant behind his back. I wasn't a sneaky person, but he was going to make sure of it.

Luca was money-driven and one of the best directors, producers, and screenwriters around. He was older, but he was youthful, adventurous, and had a net worth of a little over $2 billion. I knew what people thought when they stared at us. He was white. I was more black than white because my father was biracial. The age gap made people believe that I was nothing but a gold-digging black whore. They couldn't have been more wrong. What was all this black and white nonsense anyway? I wasn't a stranger to dating outside of my race. Growing up in London, interracial dating wasn't anything out of the ordinary. It was more common than uncommon. I thought things would be the same in America, but people were so fucking judgmental.

The only people who didn't seem to mind were our neighbors. They loved us, and we loved them. I didn't feel self-conscious when I was with them, and that was one of the many reasons why I loved them so much.

We were the very first people to buy one of the four homes in Sand Cove three years ago when we got married. The Masons moved in on the right side of us a few months later, and Alohnzo moved in on the other side of us a year after them. The first house of the row has never been occupied.

Tru Mason had become my best friend, and her husband was close to Luca. We had dinner dates as often as possible. Tru and Noble gave excellent marriage advice that I valued. I don't think Luca appreciated it because he figured since he was older, he was wiser. Tru had this gorgeous dark skin. Noble and their twins even shared the same rich cocoa complexion. They were a beautiful-looking family.

What would Sand Cove be without Alohnzo? Now, he was handsome. His hair was neat and lined up to perfection. His five o'clock shadow never grew out a full beard, but I bet he would look just as handsome with one. His skin was a smooth, creamy caramel. For a single man, I didn't see many women come in and out of his home, which was something that Tru and I couldn't believe. It was no wonder why I felt the way I did. It started with a crush, but lately, I had been feeling like I was falling for him. Whenever he was around, I had the kind of butterflies that flapped around in my stomach. The feeling was scary; yet, it felt good . . . but it was also nerve-wracking.

I had his number in case of an emergency if anything was going on at his house while he was away, but I didn't dare use it. For two years, I kept my feelings for Alohnzo to myself. I found myself Facebook-stalking him. I told myself that I was only going to check out his profile for a few seconds, but an hour later, I would still be looking at his photos.

I stepped into the shower, and the steam instantly rose from the tip of my white polished toes to the top of my head. Allowing the water to cascade down my face, I reached for the shampoo. The top was already removed, so I squeezed the thick, silky liquid into my hand and rubbed it into my scalp. Working up a rich lather, I massaged the shampoo thoroughly into my hair before rinsing it out.

Why am I not happy anymore? I was back to that thought again.

Maybe it was because my husband had been cheating on me since the beginning of our relationship. I mean, I did not have any proof. After three years of marriage and six months of dating, I should've had one piece of solid proof, but I had nothing. I was going to have my evidence one of these days. Naturally, Luca was a flirt, and he thought it was harmless, and I used to think it was harmless . . . before I realized he wasn't going to change. My husband was fucking everything walking. I heard the rumors, but I thought they were just rumors. The vibes I got from other women were suggestive, but when I asked him, he would shrug it off as if it were no big deal. To be honest, I was terrified to know the truth. It was easier to ignore the problem than confront it because I hated confrontation.

I conditioned my hair before I washed and rinsed my entire body. Then I got out of the shower, dried off quickly, and slipped into my white cotton robe. Wrapping my hair in a pink towel, I turned off the bathroom light and walked downstairs to my husband's office to see if he was ready to come to bed. Most likely he would be working on his new script until the wee hours of the morning. When he wasn't at home, he was shooting a film that was supposed to be his biggest film yet.

He made me audition for the leading role and said that if I got it, it would be the role that would turn me into a star. I was so excited, but then someone else got the part. He said the casting director didn't think I was a good fit, but I knew he was lying because it is always the decision of the producer and the director who was cast. I was disappointed that he would lie and expect me to believe that he didn't have any power when he was the director.

His office door was partly opened, and I could faintly hear his voice. He was talking low. I didn't have to open the door completely to see him talking on the phone because it was opened enough. He was pacing, smiling at whatever the other person was saying. His hair was black on the top and white on the sides, cut with a razor by his barber. His pencil-thin mustache made him look as debonair and as dashing as the actor, Vincent Price.

He used to be so kind to me, or I thought he had always been good to me. I wondered how long he had been seeing other women and if he had any intention of stopping. I was straining to hear, concentrating so much that I accidentally bumped the door open. He turned toward me and ended the call without telling the person goodbye.

"Fuck, Tahira! You scared me," he said.

"I'm sorry. I wasn't trying to startle you."

"When did you come in from your swim?" he asked.

"Around twenty minutes ago . . . I took a shower and came down here to see if you were ready to come to bed."

"No. I have to finish writing this scene." He hardly looked at me before he walked over to his desk and sat down. "I hate it when you sneak around the house like a fucking mouse."

"I wasn't sneaking around the house, Luca. You probably didn't hear me because you were on the phone." I thought of asking who he was talking to, but I was too afraid.

"Go dry your hair. I hate it when you get the pillows wet."

I replied, "Of course. I'm going up to blow-dry my hair right now."

"Close my door all the way when you leave."

I bit my bottom lip to stop myself from cursing at him. I was getting sick of the way he treated me. If he wanted to be able to do what he wanted, why didn't he leave?

I closed the door until it shut and walked upstairs. Fighting my tears, I thought, *I'm going to have to find a way to get back to my own happiness.*

I plugged the blow dryer and removed the towel from my head. After twenty minutes of replaying what happened in my mind, my hair was thoroughly dry. I stopped the dryer, turned off the light, and walked into our bedroom. Luca wasn't in bed. I wasn't surprised. My heart used to sink into my stomach, but now, I was numb because I was used to this.

Chapter 3

Tru

"Trudee, I'm leaving you in *two* minutes," Noble said, fixing his tie in the mirror behind the door of our walk-in closet.

He stood a little over six feet. Noble had the physique of an NFL defensive linebacker, and I was still head over heels as the first day he swept me off my feet three years ago.

He rubbed his freshly shaved chin as he watched me struggle to pull my hair out of the spiral rods that I had slept in. I was dressed for work, but I still needed to do my hair and makeup.

"Let's go," he demanded again as if I didn't hear him the first time.

I fluttered my eyelashes, looking at him as if he were crazy. "Do *not* rush me, Noble Mason."

"I'm leaving right now."

We went through this back-and-forth dialogue in the mornings. It didn't make any sense to me. I wanted him to wait for me because I didn't want to drive. Beauty took time, and he knew this already. It was his fault why we were running late in the first place. He wanted to have sex as our alarm clock went off. Asking me to hurry up while getting ready for work was like asking him for a quickie. He hated quickies.

"You're not going to leave me, Noble," I reiterated. "Besides, it's Friday. We can stand to be late for once in our lives."

He looked at the time on his gold Rolex. "No, I'm never late. You know that. I'm leaving in two point five minutes."

"You don't love me if you leave me," I said, trying to lay it on thick.

He laughed a little. "Don't be silly. I'll see you once you get to work. Don't forget that we have a scheduled meeting at eight o'clock sharp. At least if I'm there, it won't make everyone else's schedules fucked up."

I removed a roller. "Yeah, but—"

"You think I should wait for you to finish playing with your hair and risk showing up late?" He grabbed me by my waist and pulled me toward him in a playful manner while biting his lower lip.

"Noble, you better quit. See, *this* is why we're late in the first place. Look, if you must leave, then go. I'll be there before the meeting is over."

He studied my eyes, not letting go of my waist. After kissing my forehead, he let me go. "You need to do whatever it takes to get there no later than thirty minutes. I don't need anyone talking crazy."

I rolled my eyes. "Maybe we shouldn't have sex in the morning before work."

His eyebrows furrowed, looking as if I were talking like a crazy woman. "You know how grouchy I am if I don't get my fix."

A grin graced my face, and I stared at him in the mirror. "Mmmhmm. I'll talk to you later."

Noble strutted out of our master bathroom, looking refined in his suit and tie.

I opened my makeup case and took my time putting on my makeup. I wasn't going to rush. Since he left me, there was no need to hurry. As soon as I was done, I went downstairs, made some coffee in my Keurig, and put it in a travel mug before kissing the kids.

I turned to our new nanny and said, "Ximena, make sure that they eat more vegetables today because they're not getting enough. We should be off work before seven."

"No problem," Ximena replied with her thick Spanish accent.

I made my way to the garage and eased into my red, 4-door Mercedes-Benz C63. Putting my briefcase in the passenger seat and my coffee travel mug in the cup holder, I backed out of the driveway, pressed the button to close the garage, and headed toward the highway.

Traffic was horrific, long lines in each lane, but I expected it to be this way. I turned up the satellite radio and bobbed my head a little to the smooth R&B tunes while sipping my coffee. My iPhone rang. I turned down the radio, and since the phone was automatically synced whenever I got into the car, I hit the answer button.

"Yes, baby?"

"Tru, where are you?" Noble asked with an attitude.

I looked at the time. I was close to forty-five minutes late and was stuck in traffic.

"I'm on the highway, Noble."

"I told you to be here within thirty minutes, right?" he barked.

I rolled my eyes and replied, "I know, but I wanted some coffee, and I had to make sure that Ximena knew what to do with the kids today."

"Woman, you're driving me crazy. I was hoping you could've been here to go over some things."

"I'm sure you did your thing up in there."

He exhaled as if he had been holding his breath. "I did what I had to. Hurry up so we can talk about our plans. I hear someone is moving into the house next to Alohnzo today. Are you going to invite them, or will you wait until next year?"

The bonfire was something Tahira came up with three summers ago and had been doing it ever since. This year, I volunteered to host.

"This would be a clever way to welcome them to Sand Cove. Do you know if it's a family or a single person? Male or female?"

"I don't know anything about them other than I saw the for-sale sign coming down on my way to work. Now, hurry your sexy ass to work."

"I'm coming."

"I should bend your ass over as soon as you get here."

I shook my head slowly. He was always ready to make love, but I didn't have time to be fucking my husband in his office all day. We could've stayed home for that.

"I'll see you when I get there."

"Hurry but be safe."

"I will."

I ended the call and turned my music back up with a smile forming. Noble loved getting his hands on me whenever he could.

Constantine Enterprises was a cosmetic corporation we launched together named after Noble's grandmother. We started it from home, and together, we worked hard and devised a plan that turned our company into a billion-dollar business in a few short years.

As I strolled down the corridors of the building with my head held high and sunglasses on, I didn't show any signs of being remorseful for being late or missing the meeting. Noble had everything under control and was being dramatic.

Our receptionist, Sam, greeted me, "Good morning, Mrs. Mason. Mr. Mason said to make sure that you go to his office, once you are settled in, of course."

He was a petit gay male standing at five foot four with thick brown hair, who wore the most adorable professional outfits to work. He had plans to make his way up to executive assistant soon. I was ready to promote him as soon as his first year as a receptionist was up because he deserved it.

I removed my sunglasses and smiled politely at him. "No problem. Would you mind getting me my usual from the café?"

"No problem."

"Oh, and I'm sure Mr. Mason has yet to eat breakfast, so can you also make sure that he has his usual?"

"He already ate. Yvette brought bagels and coffee for the meeting this morning."

I was shocked. Noble was just as much of a picky eater as I was.

"Okay. Thanks." I walked to my husband's office because once in mine, I would get swathed in work.

As soon as I got into his office, he wrapped up his call and stood up. I closed the door. He buttoned his blazer and walked over to me. As soon as I was in his personal space, he pressed his body up against mine.

I smiled at him. "See, I knew this was a setup."

"I'm going to punish you right now." He paused for a second as his eyes traveled from the top of my head to my toes. "You look beautiful. I love your hair like this."

"Cut it out. My hair is the reason why I was late, and you were mad about it earlier, remember?"

Noble kissed me with so much passion that I moaned. He was smudging my lipstick. With my eyes closed, I enjoyed my husband's passionate kiss.

"I want you so badly, like right now," he said, biting down on his lower lip.

I put up my hand in front of his lips. "Save it for later, boo."

Noble sighed but tried to pull himself together. "You make it so hard for a brotha."

I laughed at him. He was too much at times. "Anyway, hey, so I sent Sam to get me some breakfast, but he told me you ate already."

"Yvette brought bagels. I think there's some more in the break room. You want some?"

"No, thank you."

Noble smiled and nodded, but then changed the subject. "I have a few meetings off-site, so I gotta run."

"Okay. Tonight, after the bonfire, you and I have unfinished business."

A great charming smile graced his handsome face. "Ooooh, I like the sound of that."

"Go on. Get out of here." I strolled out of his office and headed toward mine.

Before I could sit in my chair, Sam knocked twice before walking in the room with my breakfast.

"Perfect timing. I'm starving," I said.

Sam nodded before walking out quietly. I turned on my computer to let it warm up.

Chapter 4

Alohnzo

It was six o'clock in the evening when I watched Noble start the fire from my bedroom window. The sun had another two hours before setting. Tru had hired a caterer the way that Tahira had before. Tru had a band setting up to play music. I nodded my head, feeling impressed. It was going to be interesting to see what other things Tru would do differently this year. Little Noble and Noelle were running along the shore, playing in the water, leaving their tiny footprints in the sand before they were washed away by the waves.

Glancing over at Kinsley, she was looking at herself in the full-length mirror in the corner of my bedroom, taking forever. She blew air from her lips and kept resting her hands on her hips, and then plopping them down at her side.

What is her problem? I thought.

I wondered if she was nervous. She shouldn't have been nervous because she had already met my neighbors before, but for some reason, she looked like she was on edge. She already changed her clothes three times before she ended up wearing a red summer dress, which looked astounding on her, but she was still dissatisfied.

"Everything makes me look fat!" she complained as she tossed her cinnamon-colored hair over her left shoulder. "I wish I had time to rush home or go shopping for a different outfit." Biting her lower lip, she seemed to be looking for me to say something. Only, I didn't know what to say.

Kinsley only weighed 130 pounds, and she was five foot five. The word "fat" shouldn't have come out of her mouth. Her hair and hazel eyes complemented that red summer dress perfectly. Even the tiny freckles on her nose were adorable. I went over and placed a gentle kiss on her neck.

Clearing her throat, she looked at me to say something.

I knew better than to agree with her. I knew women because my mother was the same way. These types of situations with women never went well. If I said she didn't look fat, she would most likely disagree. If I told her that she looked fat, which I knew better than to say that, she would be in tears.

"I don't know why you say those things about yourself, but it's annoying," I wound up saying.

Cocking her head to the side, she put those hands on her hips again. "Annoying? *Really*, Alohnzo? You think I'm annoying?"

"I'm not saying *you're* annoying. All I'm saying is that a woman as beautiful as you are shouldn't be complaining about her appearance. I like my women to be confident, so don't act that way. It's a huge turnoff."

She propelled air out of her lips and stared at herself in the mirror one last time. "Okay . . . I guess I'm ready to go down there in this."

"What's wrong with what you have on? You look good. I like the way the red complements your skin and your hair. Are you ready?"

She smiled instantly. She even blushed a little as she walked away from me. I was glad I could make her feel more confident.

I didn't understand women. I never stressed off what clothes to wear. I was wearing cargo shorts, a white button-up, short-sleeved shirt with a white tank top underneath, and a pair of teak-colored Olukai Hiapo flip-flops that I only wore on the sand; nothing too fancy. I was a sneakerhead, but I wouldn't dare to wear my sneakers on the beach. What I had on was perfect bonfire attire in my opinion. Even if someone didn't think so, I wouldn't give two fucks.

Kinsley put on her silver rhinestone-studded sandals, and we walked down the stairs. We went out of the sliding patio door before heading down the steps that led to the sand. Warm sand filled my flip-flops as it always did and was tossed out each time I lifted my foot to take a step.

Kinsley's nerves must've been getting the best of her because she started to trip over her own clumsy feet as she tried to walk. She looked up at me with a dazed expression, not sure of how she almost fell when sand was all that was in front of her. I had to catch her before she hit the sand face-first.

"Are you, all right?" I heard a male voice ask from behind us.

We turned around. The voice wasn't close enough to make out the shadowy figure, but someone had come out of the once-vacant house next door. I noticed the moving van earlier, but I couldn't tell who was moving in. As he got closer, I froze. I could not believe this. What was my brother, Alistair, doing here?

"Don't tell me you're my new neighbor," I said.

"Yup," he replied with a hearty laugh as he came closer. "I'm your new neighbor. Surprise, bro."

He never could stand to lose when it came to me. He was always so competitive. I should've known that when Mom asked me if the house next door was still empty that she was asking for him. She hated the beach, and Pop loved their home in Beverly Hills too much to move into a beach house.

Kinsley said, "Well well well. It's good to see you outside of the office, Alistair."

"If it isn't Kinsley Smallwood. Good to see you."

"Same here," she smiled.

Alistair's eyes landed back on mine. "You don't look all that happy to see me, little big brother. Fix your face. You look like you saw a ghost." Dressed in a navy, short-sleeved button-up and jeans, he stood in front of us.

"You could've told me you were interested in the house," I said.

"It's a beautiful house. Why wouldn't I be interested?" he answered. "I couldn't resist."

"You move in alone or with your family?" Kinsley asked.

"What family? I thought you knew I was single. It's plenty enough house for me, but one day, I'll be able to raise a family of my own here. That's the goal, at least, anyway."

"Have you met the other neighbors yet?" I asked, interrupting his bold-faced lie. He didn't want a family. He was trying to impress Kinsley. I saw the way he was looking at her.

"Not yet. Someone left a nice note on my door inviting me to a bonfire. That was thoughtful of them. Who is Tru Mason?"

"She lives on the end. She's married to Noble Mason," I said, making sure he understood that before he sought her out.

Noble was very protective of his wife. I didn't need my brother coming to my community, messing things up.

"You didn't have to say it like that," Alistair said with a laugh. "Dang, you're acting like I don't know how to conduct myself around women. I'm respectful."

"Whatever. Come on. I'll introduce you to everyone," I said.

I held Kinsley's hand so she wouldn't trip on the sand again as we walked.

The sounds of the Caribbean music were pleasant. The tinkling of the steel pan drums at once put me in a tropical frame of mind. The reggae beats told a story of Jamaica. The fire was blazing, and everything on the buffet table looked delicious. Noble was sitting at the head of the table that was dressed in a white tablecloth and candles. Tru had a glass of red wine in her right hand as she sat in the seat on the left side.

Tru said, "What do you think about the Calypso band, huh? I'll pat myself on the back."

"They sound incredible. Everyone, this is our new neighbor," I paused as I pulled out a chair for Kinsley to sit on the other side of the table. "This is—"

"Alistair Kelly," he interrupted me and smiled.

"Are you Alohnzo's brother?" Tru asked, taking a good look at both of us.

I didn't think we looked that much alike, but everyone else always said we did. They used to think we were twins when we were younger.

"Yes, I am," he said proudly. "His older brother."

I rolled my eyes. He always let everyone know he was older.

"Alohnzo, why didn't you tell us your brother was joining the community?"

"He didn't tell me either," I said dryly.

"I wanted to surprise him," Alistair replied.

"You're older?" Tru quizzed, glancing him over.

"I am," Alistair replied.

"Only by a year," I interjected.

"I am the little big brother," Alistair added with a slight snicker.

I was glad to be taller than him. Taking after our father's side, I stood at six foot three. Alistair took after my mother's side, and he stood at five foot seven.

"Welcome, little big brother. Glad to have another Kelly. I got an opportunity to meet your father, and he is a good man. I know we're safe with a Kelly. I see you got the note I left on the door," Tru said. "I assume you already know Alohnzo's *friend,* Kinsley. I'm Tru. This is my husband, Noble."

Noble stood up and said, "Nice to meet you. Welcome to Sand Cove."

"Thank you for the warm welcome," Alistair said, sitting in a chair on the other side of Kinsley.

Luca and Tahira were heading down from their wooden deck. Luca was wearing a black suit jacket with a purple ascot around his neck, slacks, a straw hat, and sunglasses. It was too warm outside for his old Hollywood glam, but it was Luca's style nonetheless.

Tahira's figure killed that white crop top and long, white, flowing skirt. Confidence exuded from her pores. Her hair was long, extensions I presumed. I preferred her short hair when she was swimming, but she looked good either way.

"Everything looks beautiful, Tru . . . Hey, everyone," Tahira said as she and Luca joined us.

"Hey!" Tru smiled. "This is our new neighbor, Alistair. He's Alohnzo's big brother."

Alistair waved with that cheesy-ass grin plastered on his face.

"I'm Luca Moretti, and this is my wife, Tahira," Luca introduced.

When Tahira sat next to Tru, her breasts seemed to be sitting upright in her top without a bra. I had to walk away to get a beer out of the tub of ice to play it off.

Tru said to Alistair, "We like to get together with a bonfire once a year at the end of summer. We do not invite any outside friends to this event, but if you want to bring someone next time, just let us know. It's just us neighbors having some good ole bonding time."

"Very nice. Do you mind if I help myself to the food?"

"No, help yourself. Let's get this party started."

Alistair walked toward the buffet table, and I sat in the chair on the other side of Kinsley. As I popped the top to drink, Kinsley's icy eyes were piercing through me.

"What's the matter?" I asked.

"You didn't offer me anything to drink."

She was acting as if she were too afraid to move.

"What would you like to drink?" I raised one eyebrow.

She was making me regret that I invited her. If she didn't feel up to hanging out with my neighbors, she could've just declined the invitation, but Kinsley wouldn't do that because she wanted to be near me at any given opportunity. I wished she would pretend like she was happy to be here.

"I don't know. What are my choices?" she asked.

Tru interrupted. "We have soda, bottled water, Cabernet Sauvignon, Riesling, and beer."

"Do you have diet soda?" she asked timidly.

"Yes, Alohnzo, why don't you get your friend one."

I got up and grabbed a Diet Pepsi out of the steel tub. I handed it to her and sat back down. I couldn't mask my irritation. I was never good at hiding my emotions. Feeling how tight my jaw was becoming, I took another drink from the beer and stared out at the water.

"Thanks," she replied unenthusiastically.

This woman was impossible. I wasn't going to fall into this trap. I wasn't the type to argue when I wanted to have fun.

"Noble, come talk to me for a moment," Luca demanded.

Noble nodded. "Sure, let's uh . . . go over here."

Luca walked beside Noble as they stood closer to the fire.

Tahira was laughing at whatever Tru said.

I started to get up, but Kinsley put her hand on my arm. "Wait," she started to say.

"Kinsley, you don't need to be all up under him," Tru said.

"Excuse me?" Kinsley asked with a deep frown.

"Come on, girl. You're acting like we're going to hurt you or something," Tru said.

Kinsley's hazel eyes looked worried as she stared at me with her mouth slightly parted open. She wanted me to save her.

I said, "I'll be right over there with the guys."

She cut her eyes at me as I walked away. I was glad Tru invited her to talk. Tru might've been direct in her approach, but she was a sweetheart, and Kinsley was going to find out how lovely these ladies were.

Noble cleared his throat as soon as he saw me, and Luca folded his arms across his chest as if he were irritated.

"Hey, I'm sorry. Am I interrupting a private matter? I can go back with the ladies."

"No, no, Alohnzo," Noble said. "How are you?"

"I'm good. You?"

"I'm feeling good tonight."

"You sure I didn't interrupt?" I asked.

Luca was still looking highly irritated by my presence as he sighed, but he waved his hand in the air as if he were swatting a fly. "You're fine. We're done talking. Hey, I just wrapped up the movie I was shooting."

"That's awesome. This one took nearly two years, right?"

"Yeah," Luca said.

Alistair walked up with a plate of delicious-looking Jamaican food. He had jerk chicken skewers, callaloo, fried plantains, and grilled pineapple. Tru did an excellent job with the menu. That was really no surprise because she was an excellent cook, and I was sure if she had time, she would've cooked the food for the bonfire all by herself. Tru invited me over for dinner plenty of times, and my favorite had become her grilled lobster tails.

A multicolored beach ball whizzed by us, and little Noble was running fast to get it.

The nanny was on his heels, calling after him in her thick Spanish accent, "Noble! Noble! Come back here!"

I couldn't help but notice that her body looked incredible in that one-piece bathing suit.

"Ximena, I think you should take the kids inside," Noble said. "The sun is going down. Bathe them and put them to bed."

"No problem, Señor Mason." Ximena took little Noble's hand while holding Noelle's hand in the other.

As she took them down the sand toward the Masons' home, Noble's eyes never left her ass. Luca's eyes were glued to her backside as well.

"Did you guys get to meet our new nanny, Ximena?"

Luca nodded.

Alistair shook his head.

I said, "Yeah."

Ximena was too attractive. I mean, Tru was a beautiful woman, but to have a live-in nanny that looked like Ximena, well, things could get sticky and awkward if Noble looked too hard. The Masons would've been better off with someone that looked like Mrs. Doubtfire.

"She's hot, right?" Noble said while making both eyebrows go up and down.

I swallowed my beer quickly before clearing my throat. *Did he just admit that aloud?*

"So, you *do* have eyes," Luca declared. "I was starting to wonder about you, Noble."

"No need to worry about me," Noble replied. "She's beautiful. That's the obvious thing."

"Is she single?" Alistair asked.

My brother and I were so different. He was single, but he fucked everybody. I was surprised he hadn't hooked up with Kinsley yet as much as he came down to my building at work. I didn't know why he came to my building so much when he had his own. I felt he did shit to piss me off intentionally.

Noble replied, "She's single and never been married. She doesn't have any kids of her own. Tru hired Ximena because she helped raise her siblings ever since she was 14 years old in Mexico. I wasn't home when Tru interviewed or hired her, but I approved. There's no need to look at me like that, Luca. You all know I love the hell out of my wife. Tru is a very confident woman and isn't intimidated easily, so I'm cool with having a hot-ass nanny as long as Tru is."

"I'm single too," Alistair replied with a coy smile, "but your nanny isn't really my type."

"You have a type?" I scoffed.

"I see there's so much you have yet to learn about me, little brother. Now that we're neighbors, you can get to know me. Yes, I do have a type. I like women that look like Kinsley, in fact. I guess that means we have the same taste in women." He smacked on the food as he chewed. "You all gotta taste this Jamaican food. It's so good. Noble, is Tru Jamaican?"

"She is," Noble smiled proudly.

"Nice," Alistair replied.

I heard him slide in there that his type of woman was like Kinsley, but I didn't let his comment get to me. We only had the same taste in women because he went after the women I had. He loved going after women I already had, and that was how it always had been. It wasn't like he couldn't get women on his own; he just liked to piss me off. I stopped letting that get to me when we were in high school.

"Did she cook this?" Alistair asked.

"No, although she could. She ordered it from this bomb little Jamaican restaurant called Ackee Bamboo. You guys hungry?" Noble asked.

"I'm starving," I said.

"Same here," Luca nodded as we made our way over to the buffet table.

"If you love Tru's cooking, then you'll love this because it's just as good," Noble added.

Alistair walked with us saying, "Let me see if I need to add anything else to this plate. I think I might've skipped a few things." He was looking over at the women, taking in his surroundings.

I watched his eyes land on Tahira a few times, and I felt the muscles in my body tighten. I wasn't going to show any signs that I was feeling jealous of the way he was staring at her. If I did that, Alistair would try to beat me to her. I smirked at the thought of the two of us competing for a married woman. I cared that she was married, but Alistair didn't care if a woman was married. Whatever he wanted, he went after, and there was nothing anyone could say to stop him.

"Luca, how do you keep up with your wife?" I heard him ask. "What's the age difference?"

Luca laughed and replied, "I can't tell you that, but I will tell you that ginseng and green smoothies are a part of my diet."

Alistair and Noble laughed.

Luca continued, "Our age difference doesn't matter much because I'm youthful. The question is, can *she* keep up with *me?*"

Alistair went to stealing looks at her again. The way Tahira's head tilted back a bit at that moment had him staring too hard.

"Yeah, okay . . ." Alistair laughed. "I'm sure you got a gun to keep a lot of men away from her."

"Not at all. She's faithful and knows how to handle herself around other men. I'm far from the jealous type."

"If she were my wife, I would be jealous as hell," Alistair said.

The way she twirled her hair in her fingers as her slanted, soft brown eyes sparkled had me wishing that I was hers. I wanted Tahira with each ounce of strength that I possessed. I wanted her, and it was starting to turn into this feeling as if I needed her the way I needed oxygen. I had a real desire for her. I wanted what I needed and needed what I wanted—Tahira. I felt the craving in the depth of my soul and the nerves in my body. This was lust, but it was starting to feel like something more. This was why my want had transcended into a need.

Luca didn't seem to be bothered at all that Alistair was staring at his wife. In fact, he looked proud because he knew Tahira was coming home with him at the end of the night. That was the reality. She could never be mine as long as she was his.

Chapter 5

Kinsley

Alohnzo's laughter was so infectious. I never heard him laugh that way. With his incredibly charming smile, I found myself giggling. I was on fire for Alohnzo, and I wanted him to know it. Everything about this man was captivating. However, he always played it so cool with me, and at work, he hardly smiled at all.

The Kelly men, Amos, Alistair, and Alohnzo, had a charming way with women. There wasn't a woman who worked for Amos Kelly Advisors who didn't feel the same way. The married women may have been ashamed to admit it aloud, but their eyes gave them away.

I started working for Amos Kelly Advisors when I was fresh out of high school. At 18 years old, I felt it was my destiny to be married to a Kelly. They were not only as fine as hell, but they were also smart and wealthy.

Out of the Kelly men, Alohnzo was the one I wanted to have the first time I laid eyes on him. After ten years of working for the company and being shuffled around to various positions, I was promoted by Amos as a financial administrator. I had the opportunity to show Alohnzo I was interested because now I was working directly with him.

Does he like me? I wondered. I couldn't tell because he was acting like I was getting on his nerves. I thought our chemistry was fantastic, and the sex—it was mind-blowing. Alohnzo was a thorough lover; liked to take his time. He didn't like me as much as he loved his neighbors, and that was what bothered me the most that night.

I always imagined and dreamed that the two of us would be in a relationship, not just sexual. After two weeks of fucking, Alohnzo chose to keep things professional at work. I tried to get him to fuck me on his desk or inside the copier room, but he wouldn't. I had to wait for him to call me on the way home. When we weren't having sex, Alohnzo liked to keep things brief; but with his neighbors, I saw a side of him that I had never seen before. He came to life, and I wanted to be someone that could do that to him, as well. They had a way of making him laugh and smile in a way that I couldn't. Getting to know Alohnzo was like trying to solve a Rubik's Cube, and I was frustrated.

A few weeks ago, I didn't think he would respond to my advances at work since I had been flirting with him for a long time. It wasn't until one afternoon when he cracked a smile at me as I said, "Are you holding the door just for me? Thank you, sexy."

I thought my flirting was going to land me in HR with sexual harassment papers. The next day, he invited me over to his place for a few drinks. Then, it evolved into what we were doing now . . . *friends,* as Tru said. I thought we were more than that!

While at the bonfire, I talked candidly to Tru and Tahira about celebrity gossip and fashion, but I really wasn't interested. I went to smile at Alohnzo because I loved watching him laugh, but he wasn't looking at me. I followed his eyes . . . and they were right on Tahira. As if everything was happening in slow motion, I watched for a moment. That was when I saw something else even more attention-grabbing. She was looking at him too.

What is going on? My thoughts were racing the way those cars were in *The Fast and the Furious.* The way she looked at him unnerved me. Now, I had never been married, but a married woman wasn't supposed to look at another man the way she was looking at him. I started looking for signs that would tell me these two had something going on. Maybe this was the reason why he didn't want to be in a sincere relationship. Was he fucking his married neighbor?

I worked too hard to get this man's attention, and it was all going down the drain only after a few fast-flying weeks. *What is happening?*

Tru switched subjects and started going on and on about how wild her sex life had become. She felt comfortable enough sharing that information in front of me, considering I hardly knew her. She and Tahira were the best of friends, and I felt out of place. I couldn't add to their inside jokes, and it was pissing me off.

The soda in my hand was empty. I needed a stiff drink to deal with this bullshit, but I wasn't sure if I was going to have to drive home for the night. Alohnzo hadn't invited me to stay, so I assumed that I was going home. At this point in our relationship, I felt like he needed to be the one to suggest or ask me. I didn't like imposing, especially when he always seemed as if I annoyed him.

I got up without saying anything to Tahira or Tru. Alohnzo hadn't noticed that I was walking toward him. He was too busy talking, laughing, and stealing looks at Tahira. By the time I reached the buffet table, he was walking with the men back over to the bonfire. He gave me a half smile as he walked by. He didn't ask if I was okay or if I was ready to go inside of the house or anything.

Alistair grabbed a beer out of the tub and gave me a warm smile as he said, "Hey, Kinsley. I haven't seen you in a while. You move departments again?"

"Yeah, I was promoted. It's been a minute since I've seen you, but I'm an administrator in Alohnzo's department."

"Ah . . . okay . . . So, you're my brother's girlfriend too?" he asked. "Must be nice to work with your boyfriend."

Was he trying to be funny? Looking at the smile on his face, he was smug. He knew good and well that I was not Alohnzo's girlfriend.

"You got jokes, Alistair. We're just friends—"

"Friends with *benefits?*" he cut me off.

That was one way to put it, and he was very blunt, but that was how Alistair was. Though he and Alohnzo resembled each other, he was much more arrogant and flashier. He was handsome too, but not quite as beautiful as Alohnzo. When I first started working for Amos Kelly Advisors, Alistair was so rude that I didn't care to speak to him again. The more he came around, the more I noticed that was his personality. He was always flirty with everyone, and he hit on me a few times, but since I wanted Alohnzo, I didn't pay him any mind.

I opened another can of diet soda. "I guess you can say we're friends with benefits."

I wasn't going to lie to Alistair, even though it was none of his business. Since he was the only other person I knew, I felt a little more comfortable talking to him than the others. My thoughts of the others weren't so kind. Luca was the typical old, snobby asshole, Noble thought he was God's gift to women, Tru was loud and obnoxious, and Tahira was a stuck-up bitch like her husband.

I didn't know what it was about them that made Alohnzo light up like a firefly. I didn't like the way he changed when around them. I didn't know any of them the way he did, and I probably shouldn't have had my reservations about them, but those were my observations.

Alistair smiled, and I noticed how deep his dimples were in each of his cheeks. Now, that was a nice trait on him.

"So, tell me a little bit about yourself. We've never spoken outside of the office before. I don't think we've even had a chance to talk at the Christmas parties," he said.

"That's because I don't go to the Christmas parties . . . I don't like to be around large groups."

That was only partially the truth. I didn't like doing any parties within the company to avoid their mother. She wasn't the most pleasant person to be around.

"Oh, okay. No wonder I've never seen you there."

I giggled a little. "Well, as you know, I've been working for the company for some time now. I'm from Baldwin Hills, so I've lived in Los Angeles all my life. I don't have any kids, but I have a cute little furry baby, my puppy. His name is Baskin Robbins."

He chuckled. "That's cute. How do you like working for my brother?"

"I love it."

"Really? I think you might like my department a lot better."

"What's the difference? I hear once you work for one Kelly, you've worked for them all."

"Sort of. We handle different departments of the business. My department handles contracts and accounting. Alohnzo's department handles the advising and planning. Hey, why did you stop being my father's personal assistant anyway?"

He sure was all up in my business. I looked over to see that Alohnzo was still watching Tahira on the sly. My jealousy grew. With Alistair standing right next to me and asking all these questions, I wanted Alohnzo to see that his brother was giving me the attention that he should've been giving me.

"I was actually recommended for the financial administrator position by your father," I said. "He felt I deserved a position that would pay more. The company paid for my tuition to get my bachelor's degree in business, and he thought it would be a promising idea to use it."

"Oh, okay. I didn't know that." Alistair stared at me as if he were trying to read my thoughts. "Anyone ever tell you that you have beautiful hazel eyes?"

I giggled, feeling my cheeks grow hot. "Thank you."

Alistair smiled handsomely. "You're welcome."

I couldn't help but notice that Alistair looked just like his father, Amos. He was a much younger, cuter version. I bet Amos looked just like Alistair when he was his age. Alistair was making it hard not to flirt. I guess you can say the Kelly charm hypnotized me.

Chapter 6

Tahira

Tru and I stared at Kinsley as she flirted with Alistair. She was giggling at everything he said and touching his hand between every other word. Not that it was any of my business, but she wasn't trying to hide her attraction to him. The only one who seemed not to notice or care was Alohnzo. Why didn't he care that the woman he was seeing was now in his brother's face? His nonreaction was interesting because I thought he and Kinsley were becoming an item. She had been spending nights with Alohnzo, and I believed their relationship was progressing to the next level. I was confused.

Alistair was showing off his dimples each time he smiled, and he wasn't acting like he knew Kinsley was involved with Alohnzo.

"Do you think Alistair is just a natural flirt, or do you think he is crazy enough to try to take his brother's chick?" I questioned, shaking my head.

"It's that bitch," Tru hissed to me. "A man will always be just that, a man. Seems to me like Alistair is having a 'whose dick is bigger' contest with Alohnzo, and I think Alohnzo is over it. Kinsley should know better, but a ho will always be a ho."

"Poor Alohnzo," I said, feeling a little sorry for him.

"I wouldn't say poor Alohnzo. He doesn't give a fuck."

"He probably doesn't, but then again, I think he doesn't want to show all of us how upset he is. When have you ever seen Alohnzo lose his cool?"

"Never, so you may have a point." Tru nodded her head as she stared at Kinsley and Alistair. Then her eyes went over to Alohnzo. "Maybe he doesn't really like her like that."

Kinsley was now looking at Alohnzo to make sure he could see her flirting with Alistair.

"There it is, Tru. She's trying to make him jealous on purpose." I smacked my lips loudly and hissed, "This is a hot mess."

"Fuck her. Hey, did I tell you I saw your new feature in *Hollywood Raw Magazine?* You looked fabulous as always," Tru said, changing the subject.

"You did? Aw, thank you. I enjoyed that shoot. It came out magnificent. I loved it."

"Girl, I had to get a copy to show off at work, like this is my bestie."

"You're too sweet, Tru."

"Have you ever considered modeling? You would be the perfect model since your husband won't cast you in any of his big-budget films. I'm still mad at him for that."

"The perfect role will come along. Besides, he doesn't want anyone to say that the only reason I got that part was because of him. He wants the world to know me for my talent."

"What? Are you serious? That's the way Hollywood works, honey. If you can't get a leading role from the man you're screwing—who happens to be the director—who else will take you seriously? They will say if you were good enough, your husband would give you a role just like that."

Everything Tru said were thoughts I had all the time, but Luca's way was Luca's way.

"Modeling and acting go hand in hand. I always said that if I didn't make it big as an actress that I would try modeling."

"I don't see any point in being married to one of the biggest directors if you can't use that to your advantage. You put up with too much of his shit to be crawling around at the bottom of the barrel. You're more than his arm candy. You can act."

I shook off what she said about Luca once again. Tru was right, though. I should've been cast in his film, but I wasn't, so there was no need to dwell on it.

"Thank you, Tru. You're always my biggest cheerleader."

"Hey, let's go over and get some of that yummy Jamaican food so we can hear what Kinsley and Alistair are talking about. I'm nosy."

I got up from the table and followed Tru to the buffet table.

The reggae music was upbeat and made me want to dance. Tru wiggled her hips to the rhythm as she walked and snapped.

Kinsley said to Alistair, "I never noticed how deep your dimples are."

He had this broad smile on his face that made them even more profound.

Tru's smile didn't exist, and neither did mine. We weren't going to pretend as if we approved of their behavior. We tried to like Kinsley, but this proved that our thoughts about her were correct. Alohnzo was too good for her.

I grabbed a plate in complete silence, eavesdropping on their conversation the whole time.

"Has Alohnzo told you about our family ranch? I have five prancing horses that I show off in expos and competitions."

Kinsley replied in a flirty tone, "No, he doesn't talk much. I've only heard a lot about it from your father. Alohnzo talks a lot about his planes, though."

"Has he taken you to his hanger?"

"No," she replied, sounding a little sad that he hadn't.

"You're not missing anything. I told him not to buy it. Aircraft hangers are unexpected pitfalls that trap people who aren't aware of them. I can take you out to our ranch sometime if you like. You like horses?"

I rolled my eyes at how he downplayed Alohnzo's love for his planes. My first impression of Alistair was that he was the jealous big brother who felt the need to compete with his little brother to prove that he was better than him. I was starting not to like him.

"I love horses. That would be incredible," Kinsley gushed.

"Do you ride?" The heavy flirting in his voice when he asked that question made me raise my eyebrow at Tru.

Tru smirked and rolled her eyes as she reached for some crushed pineapple.

Kinsley giggled before she responded, "Oh, I'm no stranger to riding. I'm a pro."

This conversation was heading in the wrong direction. Were they even talking about horses anymore? Neither one of them cared we were standing there.

"Is that right?" he asked, licking his lips.

"I can *show* you better than I can tell you," she replied in a tone that made me sick to my stomach.

I heard enough, and my plate was now full of ackee and saltfish, rice and peas, plantains, carrots, and green beans. I grabbed Tru by the arm so we could head back to the table.

"I like how you brought Jamaica to us tonight. The music, the food—everything is perfect, Tru."

She smiled. "You know I have to represent."

"We should all go on a trip to Jamaica."

"That would be nice. We'll plan something." Suddenly, Tru had a fire blazing in her eyes as she looked at Kinsley and Alistair. "I hope Alohnzo never invites her ass back again. I can't stand her ho ass."

"I bet after this, Alohnzo will never invite her again. He's looking over there now."

Tru saw Alohnzo's cold glare at Kinsley and put her fork into her plate. "He doesn't look happy at all. If she thinks this is going to get him to make her his girlfriend, she better try something else."

Luca caught my attention because he was spending time texting on his phone instead of engaging with the rest of us. I felt irritated. My eyes left my husband and rested on Alohnzo.

My heart skipped a beat. What I felt for him wasn't black and white. It was like this shaded gray area. Thoughts of him surged and filled me with magical feelings of happiness and bliss. I could not define what I felt.

I took a deep breath and stared at my food as I used my fork to play around with it.

"You okay, Tahira?" Tru asked, eyeing me closely.

I exhaled but smiled at her. I tried to play everything cool while scooping up some rice. How could I look in her eyes at that moment while having thoughts about Alohnzo? She was going to figure me out.

"I'm all right. It's been a long day," I uttered.

"I understand. You've been working hard lately with these photo shoots and interviews."

"I've been at it since five this morning . . . I can only hope that my arduous work will pay off one day."

Tru smiled. "It will. I know it will."

I nodded as the band played an up-tempo reggae beat. It wasn't long before Noble came over to get Tru to dance with him. As he pulled her to dance, I admired their winding Jamaican moves. I wiggled my shoulders a little offbeat. I didn't have any rhythm to save my life, but I loved to dance. Tru laughed at me all the time when I danced.

My husband sat next to me and complained, "I can't do the food. It's too damn spicy. I don't know why Tru didn't have other options."

Luca always had to say something negative. It was rare he could compliment anything without following it up with a negative remark.

"Jamaican food *is* spicy, honey, and I love it," I replied.

"Of course, you do . . . I'm starving and bored out of my fucking mind."

"I'm not bored at all. I don't see how you're not having fun."

"Well, for starters, I can't eat that spicy food."

"Everything isn't spicy, love. There's some fruit and salad. I'm thinking about getting some of that hot caramel to dip some pineapple slices in. Would you like me to get you some?"

"No. I'm going to go get a steak at Ruth's Chris when this is over."

I tried not to roll my eyes at how rude his tone was.

Alohnzo sat in a chair on the other end of the table, and Kinsley made her way over to him shortly after. I narrowed my eyes at her. I couldn't believe how comfortable she was with moving from one brother to the other so smoothly.

Alistair was now walking toward his house quietly without saying goodbye to anyone. What was up with that?

As hard as I tried to ignore Kinsley and Alohnzo's tension as they started to argue, I couldn't help but zone in on their conversation. Luca was now staring at them as well because their voices had escalated.

"If you don't want me here, I'll go home," Kinsley said with aggression.

"I think you should go home," he replied.

"Really?"

"Really."

Kinsley hopped up from the table and stormed toward Alohnzo's house with her arms swinging, marching like Sofia from *The Color Purple*. She jogged up the steps and disappeared inside.

Alohnzo sat there, calm and relaxed as if nothing happened. I was happy he put her in her place. Her attitude tried to ruin our party. He slightly nodded his head to the music while watching Tru and Noble dance seductively against each other. Thoughts of my own husband came to mind. How much longer could I pretend that I was still in love with my husband? Looking back at Alohnzo, I smiled a little as I envisioned dancing with him the way Tru and Noble were dancing.

Chapter 7

Kinsley

He wanted me to leave—so I left. If it weren't for Alistair entertaining me for fifteen or twenty minutes, I would've been bored out of my mind. I thought I would be able to spend time with Alohnzo, not sit there and watch him with them. I saw how Tru and Tahira came over to the table, pretending as if they weren't listening to Alistair and me talk. I also saw how they went back to the table to talk shit about me. If Alohnzo had been showing me any attention, I wouldn't have had to flirt with Alistair.

I used the bathroom, then changed into a pair of shorts and a T-shirt before I grabbed my purse to leave. I looked at my phone and saw that I had a couple of missed calls. All from men that I had pushed to the side because I thought Alohnzo and I had something special.

Though I was leaving his house, I told myself that Alohnzo would be calling me to come back as soon as it was over. He was just upset with me because he didn't like me flirting with his brother. I was going to give him his space until he was ready to see me again. I looked at his sliding glass door to see if he was going to stop me from leaving. I waited for about a minute.

He wasn't coming.

As I walked out of the front door and made my way down the driveway, I could still hear the steel drums and their laughter coming from the beach. Disappointment and hurt propelled through my blood. I felt tears welling up in my eyes. Before I could touch the handle of my black Mercedes, I was sobbing. I put both hands over my face and cried. Who was I kidding? I was in love with Alohnzo, and it hurt me that he didn't feel the same way. He used me the way all men used me. I wanted to be more than just a piece of ass. I wanted to be someone's girlfriend and wife one day. Wasn't I pretty enough, smart enough, sexy enough, to be more than his cuddy buddy?

"What's the matter?" I heard a deep voice call out to me.

I turned around and looked up to see Alistair coming down the steps of his porch.

Wiping my tears with the palm of my hands, I replied, "Alohnzo doesn't want me here, so I'm leaving."

He frowned with a look of concern. "He told you to leave?"

I nodded and sobbed, "I am so embarrassed. I don't belong here. These aren't my friends. They're his. They've been giving me a tough time ever since I met them."

He stood in front of me. "Really? They seem to be nice people. I didn't see anyone giving you a hard time."

"Well, they were," I snapped.

"I'm sorry. Alohnzo should be more understanding, but empathy has never been his thing. What if I said I want you to come back to the party with me? Will you?"

There was no way I was going back. Not after the way Alohnzo just embarrassed me.

"I don't want to be around them—"

"Well, we don't have to go back. You can come inside and chill for a bit. I have some things to unpack." He looked at me with wide and curious eyes.

"You want me to hang out with you?"

I didn't take any of Alistair's flirting seriously because I figured he was just playing around, but the sparkle in his eye let me know that he didn't care about my feelings for Alohnzo. He wanted the opportunity to give me the attention his brother didn't offer.

"I want you to do whatever you feel is comfortable. I enjoy your company, and since we both don't really know these people, we can chill inside and enjoy the rest of the night. Stay."

I smiled because a little part of me wanted to stay to get back at Alohnzo. I would've been happier if Alohnzo decided to leave the party to come inside with me, but that was wishful thinking.

"Okay, I'll stay. I'm sure Alohnzo is happy looking at Tahira's ass while her husband isn't looking."

"Oh, you noticed that too, huh?" he asked.

"You'd have to be Stevie Wonder not to." I paused, stopping myself from saying too much. "Never mind . . . It doesn't matter. Alohnzo and I are not together, though I would love to be."

"Well, this wouldn't be the first time a woman fell hard for him, but his high standards won't allow him to love anyone. I'm sure he only wants Tahira because he can't have her. Even if he could have her, she would be like the rest of these brokenhearted women. I feel like you deserve so much better. Come inside and have a drink with me."

I bit my lower lip while I thought about it. I could see what Alistair wanted from me in his eyes, but I wasn't going to go there. Nothing was wrong with a little flirting. Plus, I could remain close to keep an eye on Alohnzo.

"I really shouldn't drink since I have to drive home tonight."

"One drink won't hurt. I think it will help you to calm down. If you feel a little too tipsy, you don't have to leave until you feel okay to drive, no matter what time it is."

"All right. Do you think I should leave my car parked in Alohnzo's driveway?"

"It won't hurt to leave it there."

I shrugged and followed him across his driveway and up the stairs to his front door. Once inside, I took a good look around. I didn't see one box in sight. Each piece of furniture was placed in the proper place. "You sure you just moved in this morning?"

"Yeah, I had some movers help me out. They unpacked and set up as they brought stuff in. I gave them a tip of $100 each. I only have a few of my personal belongings to unpack."

Everything about his place felt so familiar. He had a lot of the same furniture pieces as Alohnzo. Either they had the same taste in furniture or Alistair tried too hard to be like Alohnzo. "This floor plan is just like Alohnzo's."

"You think so?" he tried to hold his laugh but couldn't. He chuckled as he shook his head. "The floorplan is identical down to the pool. We like a lot of the same kind of things, and that drives him crazy. I think it's pretty damn hilarious."

I shook my head at him. "Are you in a pissing contest with Alohnzo?"

"I wouldn't call it that. We have this brotherly rivalry going on. Come in and have a seat."

Walking toward the den, I could still hear the music coming from the beach. I went over to the window to look out. Even though I didn't want to be down there at the party, I wanted to see what Alohnzo was doing. I looked down at my phone to see if he texted me, but he hadn't. I could see Tru and Noble dancing and laughing. Alohnzo was dancing next to them while Luca and Tahira watched while sitting at the table. Alohnzo's dance moves were impressive as he two-stepped to the beat. See, if I were still there, I would've been grinding in front of him. He didn't have to dance alone. "Alohnzo doesn't care that I'm gone."

"Hey, forget about him. Alohnzo is doing what he wants to do. You don't have to cry or be sad at all. I know you have feelings for him, but if he can't appreciate you, then fuck him. What do you want to drink?" he asked, pointing at his nicely set up bar.

My eyes scanned his bottles. "Oh, um, let me get some Malibu rum. You got some pineapple juice?"

"Even better. I have some mango pineapple juice with a splash of lemon-lime soda."

"That sounds good."

"Let me hook you up."

While he fixed me a refreshing cocktail, I continued to stare out of the window. I should've listened to Alistair. Why should I care so much about Alohnzo when he didn't care about me? Alohnzo wasn't sad or upset that I left. He was laughing and looked like he was having more fun with me out of his sight. I didn't want to get more upset, so I turned away from the window just as Alistair was handing me the drink with a fresh slice of pineapple wedged on the glass.

"Thank you." I took a sip. "Mmmmm, this is good."

He lifted his and said, "Come sit with me."

I followed him over to his couch. We sat down, and I took another sip. I was fighting with my mind to stop thinking about Alohnzo, but it wasn't working. I couldn't help but think about how his hands and lips felt as they touched every part of my body.

"Can I ask you something?" Alistair asked, taking me out of my soft daydream.

"Sure."

"I hope I'm not too intrusive when I ask you this, but why are you so in love with Alohnzo?"

I wasn't expecting him to ask me that question. I could give him a million reasons why I was in love with his brother. He had the mind of a genius, he was an impeccable dresser, smelled so good like fresh, clean linen, his smile lit up a room, and he was more charming than a fantasy Disney prince. What was there *not* to love about him?

I played with the rim of my glass with my fingertips as I replied, "I love him for a lot of reasons, but now . . . I don't know . . . He doesn't feel the same way about me as I do about him, so what's the point of loving him?"

Alistair watched me drink the rest of my drink. He got up and brought a pitcher over to refill it. "Well, is he the only man you're seeing?"

"Once we got involved with each other, I quit seeing other men." I drank some more.

The more I drank, the more he looked just like Alohnzo to me. I relaxed because his eyes were kind, soft, and inviting. He looked at me the way I wanted Alohnzo to look at me. The way he kept biting his lower lip was igniting a fire. Something about Alistair made me want to show Alohnzo that his brother wanted me. Alohnzo was going to miss out on me. I was a good woman. I deserved to have someone give me the attention I needed.

"How long have you two been seeing each other?" he questioned.

"Going on three weeks. I don't want things to turn sour between us because I love my job too much, and I've been with the company for so long."

"Can I be honest with you right now?" he asked, staring intensely into my eyes.

"I like honesty." I felt warm all over, and it might've been the liquor that had me feeling this way . . . or it might've been Alistair's dreamy brown eyes.

"I think you are one of the most beautiful women I've ever seen. I mean, no shit. I love your hazel eyes, the color of your hair . . . the way you smile . . . I'm very attracted to you, Miss Kinsley."

The way his eyes smiled without his lips doing so made me throb between my thighs. Was he flirting with me to prove that he could have whatever Alohnzo had? Whatever his reason was, I didn't care. I was wrapped up in the moment and feeling very tipsy.

I put my glass down on the coffee table and scooted closer to him. "I'm attracted to you too," I heard myself say.

He leaned toward my face, and I saw the kiss coming. I didn't budge or move. His lips felt soft as he kissed me. I felt his hand move to the small of my back, and he held me there so I wouldn't be able to get out of his reach. As soon as we parted, we stared at each other, speechless.

The heat from Alistair's passion tunneled through me as he came back for more. This time, I moaned. We continued to kiss as he leaned me back on the sofa. Was it wrong that I was comparing his kiss with his brother's to see the difference? I admit that Alistair was the better kisser, and I say that only because Alohnzo had just kissed me once, and it was so brief that I can't remember if he used his tongue or not.

The more we kissed, the more we got turned on. He lifted my shirt and unbuttoned the top of my shorts. He traced my red lace panties with the tips of his fingers before removing my shorts and the panties. He kept his lips right on mine as he inserted his finger into me.

I gasped as his tongue glided in and out of my mouth. Placing his finger deeper inside of me, I clenched the couch's pillows with my hands. I started grinding up against his hand. Alistair held my waist firmly with one hand and didn't stop fingering me until I had an orgasm.

Chapter 8

Alohnzo

"Dance with me," Tahira said to Luca.

He was sending someone a text message from his cell as he shook his head. As she pulled on his arm, he snatched away from her.

She pleaded with him, "Come on, honey. I want to dance."

"I said no!" he snapped, continuing his message.

Her eyes looked a little sad as she turned away from him.

That was the first time I ever saw him snap at her, and I felt a twinge in my body. I rubbed the back of my neck so that I wouldn't look tense.

"Tahira, you should dance with Noble," Tru said as she moved in front of me. "I'm going to dance with Alohnzo."

Tahira gladly got up from the table and moved offbeat. Noble couldn't help but chuckle at her as he took her hand and tried to move her to the beat.

"Don't laugh at me, Noble," she said with a smile.

"I'm laughing *with* you," he replied. "You got this. Let's just two-step it out. Too bad this band isn't playing Rick James. Rick James gives everybody rhythm."

"He isn't lying," Tru said as she grabbed my hand and pulled me closer.

Tru and I danced before, and it was like dancing with my sister. We always had so much fun together, but my eyes were glued to Tahira. She was cute as she tried to roll her hips like Tru. Tru had to stop dancing with me to help her out because she wasn't doing it right. Noble and Tru sandwiched Tahira. No matter how many times Tru told her to close her eyes and feel the beat, it didn't work. Tahira had a broad sense of humor. Even in her flawed moment, she laughed at how silly she felt but kept right on trying.

We all laughed at her.

"My wife can't dance to save her life, so don't bother," Luca pointed out in a nasty tone.

"Ah, don't be like that," Tru quickly responded.

"She's doing fine," I spoke up.

Luca had a terrible habit of always pointing out her flaws, and I couldn't understand why. Her imperfections were what made her beautiful to me. Luca was a perfectionist, but he didn't have to be when it came to her. How much more perfect did she need to be for him to appreciate her?

I looked up and saw Ximena walking toward us from the Masons' house. The sun had gone down, but the bonfire had produced the perfect source of light.

"Ximena, are the kids sleeping?" Tru asked.

"Yes, I have the baby monitor, so I can hear them if they wake up," she said as she held up the monitor. "They're heavy sleepers, so I don't think they will, but just in case."

"Are you hungry? Eat something," Tru replied, walking to the buffet table with her.

I stopped dancing and sat at the table, watching Tahira and Noble continue to dance.

"She's so gorgeous," Luca said.

I couldn't have agreed with him more . . . until I realized he wasn't talking about his wife. He was talking about Ximena. I didn't understand how he could look at another woman. Why couldn't he see that his wife was so much more beautiful than Ximena? Nothing against Ximena because she *was* pretty, but she wasn't Tahira.

One day, if I ever got married, I would be in it 'til death do us part. I valued marriage, and that was why I wasn't in a rush to be married. I wouldn't want to be married until I found the perfect one. My father's wandering eyes and wayward dick was what started to tear our family apart, and I saw how broken my mother was. I would never put a woman through that kind of pain. If married men wanted to behave like single men, they should've never gotten married.

I gave Luca a stern look.

"What? Let's not pretend as if she's not hot," he said, noticing the way I was staring at him. "I know you think I'm a crazy old man. I've been married four times, and I still don't see anything wrong with having a little fun from time to time."

"Fun from time to time?"

"Don't judge me," he said.

"Not judging," I replied.

Luca looked at other women, but I didn't know if he slept around. He had now confirmed it, and I wondered if Tahira knew about it. If she did, why was she still with him?

"Why don't you come hang out with me sometime? Noble and I haven't been to the strip club in a while. Noble doesn't go to the champagne room, but I do. He's no fun. I need to go with someone who isn't married. Do you like strip joints?" Luca asked.

"No, I've never been," I admitted.

He shook his head. "What? You're not too young to know what it's like. I've been going to strip clubs since I was 17. I need to be the one to pop your cherry. You and I would have a blast. Hey, what happened to Kinsley?"

"She . . ." I started to say and then paused. I couldn't believe she acted surprised when I told her to leave. She pissed me off. I wasn't mad at Alistair because he was himself. I expected nothing less from him. A woman who couldn't pass the Alistair Test was no woman for me. "Kinsley went home."

Luca frowned. "What? Why?"

I shrugged to play it cool. "She doesn't like being around people. It's like she's socially challenged."

He chuckled. "I can tell, but we're a social bunch. We're more than neighbors and hanging out with us is something she'll get used to."

"Nah, we're not serious; nothing like that. You won't see her around here anymore."

"It's over already?"

"Pretty much."

I kept thinking about the way she disrespected me in front of my friends, and that pissed me off. Not to mention, Alistair was always in competition with me. I was sure he couldn't wait to throw in my face that Kinsley was feeling him. I didn't know if she liked him the way she liked me, but she shouldn't have gone there.

Luca got silent and went back to sending someone a text.

The band played a slower Caribbean song, so Noble and Tahira slow danced. Tahira rested her head on his shoulder. She stared in our direction and smiled. When she looked at me, I felt embarrassed because she caught my gaze, but I didn't look away. Could she tell what I was thinking? People say that eyes are the "window to the soul," but I didn't know what was really on her mind. Our prolonged stare at each other was continuous without looking away.

Her slow dance with Noble was interrupted by Tru, who wanted to dance with her husband one more time before the night was over.

Tahira moved to the side to allow the couple to dance. She motioned for me to join her to dance.

I put my hand on my chest and asked, "Me?"

"Yeah you, Alohnzo."

Before I could respond, Luca said, "Go dance with my wife. Alohnzo will dance with you, sweetheart. I have to go inside to drain the main vein." He got up from the chair, patted me on the back the way an Italian mob boss would pat his right-hand man, and headed toward his house.

As I got up and walked toward her, she smiled at me. I smiled back. She wrapped her arms around my neck, and I held her close. This was the closest I had ever been to Tahira. The flickering from the bonfire reflected our image on the sand as she danced in my arms. I enjoyed the sweet smell of her perfume. The Caribbean beat flowed through me, allowing the magic of our chemistry to expand between us. She moved quietly in my arms with her head rested against my chest.

Then she stood on the tips of her toes and whispered in my ear, "Thank you for dancing with me. He never ever wants to dance."

Suddenly, I felt her lips kiss my ear. A sudden chill moved along my body as if a breeze had swept over the beach. I froze with both fear and excitement. I didn't know what to do. At that moment, my senses had been seduced, and I couldn't think straight.

"No problem," I heard myself say.

I looked around as we danced in a circle. Tru was slow grinding with Noble and Ximena was on her way back to the Masons'.

"Alohnzo," she whispered, prolonging each letter as if to savor them.

"Yeah?" My heart was fluttering from the sound of her voice. Never had my name ever sounded so good.

"I see the way you look at me when you're up on your balcony." She lifted her head to look up into my eyes.

I stared down at her and said, "I apologize."

"No, please don't apologize."

"No, I'm sorry. I don't want to be disrespectful."

"I don't think you're disrespectful. Now, Kinsley, *she's* disrespectful."

"That's the reason why she will never be my girlfriend. She's not the kind of woman I see myself with."

"I didn't think she was . . ." She paused for a moment before she said, "Luca isn't the most faithful man. I'm sure you know that. I'm sure you all know that."

I was surprised she brought that up to me. I didn't know everything there was to know about their relationship other than what they displayed when I was around. Tonight, I got to see them in a different light. She was unhappy, and Luca didn't care.

"You know about his extramarital affairs?"

"Of course, I do. I'm not stupid," she replied. "I've never cheated on my husband, but for some reason, he loves cheating on me."

An awkward silence fell between us, and our attraction for each other only mounted higher as we continued to slow dance. I wanted to be the one to make her happy. It wasn't the right way to think because she was married. I had to have strong willpower to control what I wanted to say next. I didn't really want to suppress what I was feeling, but I had to remember where we were and whom we were with.

"Tahira, you can call me or come over anytime for any reason." I felt the need to say that because her sad energy felt as if she needed to hear that.

She replied, "Thanks . . . I . . ." She paused and looked around.

I was giving her an open invitation to talk to me, but she bit her lower lip, refusing to say anything else.

I didn't pressure her to tell me what she was going to say.

Her head was back on my chest, and we continued to dance until the song was over. In those few short minutes, I wished that we met under different circumstances. The sound of the waves along with the music didn't help the fantasy that played out in my head. When I closed my eyes and held her close, I imagined that Luca was nonexistent, and we were on a faraway island. My daydream was cool, but I didn't want to visit my fantasy world with her in my mind. I wanted to live in it, feel it—and taste her.

Chapter 9

Kinsley

"Stay the night with me," Alistair said with a serious expression, as we lay on his couch.

I stared into his dark, penetrating eyes. His dimples made me feel so weak in the knees. His approach was smooth, and he seemed to be genuine. I liked that about him, but I was still trying to wrap my mind around all that had happened between us. We had sex, and it was terrific. I should've felt guilty and slutty, but I didn't because I was a grown-ass woman, and Alohnzo made it clear that he and I would never be more than fuck buddies. Even though Alistair's offer to stay was appealing, I couldn't bring myself to stay the night with him. Not while my feelings for Alohnzo were still there.

"I would love to, but my car is still in Alohnzo's driveway. I really should get home before he realizes I'm over here." I got up and started gathering my scattered clothes from the living room floor.

"I don't know why you care what he thinks. He told you to leave, remember?" Alistair got up and found his boxers by the coffee table.

I slipped on my bra first and said, "I know he did, but still, it's like I don't want things to be weird for us at work."

"Things *are* going to be weird at work, regardless."

"Alistair, please," I said, shooting him a look that said not to go there.

He watched me get dressed with his arms folded across his chest. "Will you let me take you out to lunch or dinner sometime?"

"Thanks, but . . . no, thank you," I quickly responded.

Now was not the time for Alistair to get clingy. We had sex, and that was it. It didn't mean that we could see each other regularly. That would be too weird.

"Oh, so now you're going to treat me the way Alohnzo treats you?"

I frowned. "Don't do that. Don't flip this around. You don't feel bad about what we just did?"

"Hell no."

"How many of Alohnzo's ex-girlfriends have you smashed?"

He chuckled. "You're not his *ex*, Kinsley."

I noticed he didn't answer my question. I wouldn't be surprised if he slept with a lot of the same women.

"Look, Alistair, I don't want anyone to know what we did tonight. Everyone will think I'm a thot, which is something that they probably think anyway. . . ." My voice trailed off at the end.

"Who's 'everyone'? The neighbors? You care about what *they* say?"

"I do," I replied defensively.

"Why? You said yourself that they don't like you and—"

"Shut up. Look, don't say anything to Alohnzo about this. This has to be our secret."

He looked at me with a confused expression. "So, it's like that?"

I shrugged. "It is what it is." Grabbing my purse, I rushed out of his house.

As I walked down the steps, I could hear the party still going on out back on the beach. Alohnzo said more than likely they would be partying late. I checked my phone to see if he had checked on me to see if I made it home safe. No missed calls. Zero text messages. He hadn't even bothered.

I got into my car and started it up with tears in my eyes. I backed out of Alohnzo's driveway and drove down the street. I shouldn't have been crying, but my tears decided to defy me and roll down my face anyway. Suddenly, I felt ashamed. I felt like I had cheated on Alohnzo, even though he wasn't my boyfriend. I was mad at myself for being so fucking weak.

I stopped crying and came up with the best solution to my problem. I wasn't going to see Alistair ever again. I was going to win Alohnzo over and show him that I could be everything he wanted me to be. He could never know what happened with Alistair.

Chapter 10

Noble

I kissed Tru's lips as we danced, and my hands were rubbing all over her plump behind. Thin women were enjoyable, but there was nothing like a woman with curves, especially *my* woman. My wife's ass filled my hands as I palmed it firmly. I grunted a little as I did it.

She threw her head back and laughed. "Okay, Noble, you better watch yourself. You might get what you want in front of the neighbors."

"You already know I'm down for that." I threw my lips to her neck and kissed her.

"Cut it out, boy," she said.

Out of the corner of my eye, I saw Tahira caress his back as Alohnzo danced. Alohnzo's hands were very close to her ass. Their body language toward each other was one that made me raise my eyebrow. As soon as she saw Luca returning, she quickly let go of him and walked toward her husband.

As if in a daze, Alohnzo watched her. He snapped out of whatever land he was in and walked to the table to get a beer and downed it quickly.

"You want some more wine?" I asked Tru. I wanted an excuse to go talk to Alohnzo.

"Yes, baby, but just a little. It's almost time to end the party."

She danced with herself as I walked over to Alohnzo. I took Tru's glass and filled it halfway with some red wine.

"What was that about?" I questioned Alohnzo.

Being a businessman, he had a great poker face. "What was what about?"

Alohnzo may have had a straight face, but I picked up a long time ago that everything about Tahira made him want to become uninhibited.

"You can't hide this shit anymore from me, Alohnzo." I cracked a side grin.

"Hide what from you, Noble? Why are you smiling at me like that?"

"You and Tahira . . . You've been exchanging goo-goo eyes with her all night, and that dance . . . Let's just say it looked like you two are getting closer finally to do what both of you really want to do."

Alohnzo replied at once, "It's not what you think it is, Noble."

"Sure, it is, and I know something is going to happen to you if you keep it up." I leaned closer to him as I said it.

Alohnzo shook his head. "I don't know what you're talking about. I respect Luca and Tahira. She and I have nothing going on."

"Yet, right?"

"Come on, Noble. I think you're reading into something that's not there."

I looked back at Luca and Tahira. They were so good at pretending to be the perfect couple that sometimes I forgot that he was dogging her. I had been out with Luca on many occasions, and I met the women he was sleeping with. I used the words "sleeping with" because it was a continuous thing.

The reason he couldn't cast Tahira in his new film was that he promised the role to one of his mistresses. She threatened that if Tahira were in the movie, she would run to the tabloids about their affair. Luca told me everything, and I promised him I would never say a word. I didn't even say anything to Tru.

Alohnzo needed to be careful if he had feelings for Tahira. Luca had that old Italian blood running through his veins. I wouldn't want Alohnzo's body to be buried alive in some Nevada desert like "Nicky" Santoro in the movie *Casino*.

"You may not be doing anything yet like I said, but you should—"

"Babe, you're taking too long with my wine," Tru said as she approached us.

I handed her the glass. "Here you go, baby. I'm sorry about that."

"Come on. It's time for you to make the bonfire toast so that we can call it a night," she said. "It's getting late."

"We'll talk about this later," I said to Alohnzo.

Alohnzo shook his head and mumbled, "There's nothing to talk about, Noble."

"Humph, yeah, okay." I was going to leave it alone . . . for now.

Chapter 11

Tru

Everyone gathered around the bonfire with their glasses filled with champagne that I reserved for the toast as the band packed up their instruments and the caterers cleaned up the buffet table. Alistair was walking up to rejoin us just in time.

"Hey, grab a glass. We're about to toast. This is how we end our bonfire."

"Okay," he said, picking up a glass, standing next to Alohnzo.

Noble said, "I want to thank you all for making our third annual bonfire mind-blowing, as always. My beautiful wife did a stunning job as the host, and I thank each of you for being here. Here's to Sand Cove."

"Sand Cove!" we said in unison. We raised our glasses and drank.

Noble and I kissed.

Tahira tried to kiss Luca, but he turned away as if she disgusted him. She dropped her head as she sipped from her glass.

Watching them pissed me off because their relationship had become bullshit. I was wondering when she would get tired of faking it. Noble didn't have to tell me any of Luca's dirt. His cheating was getting out of control. Tahira cried to me so many times about it. Luca was a fool for thinking that she had no idea what he was doing. She was a beautiful woman, no doubt about that, but if she kept allowing Luca to do her wrong, I was afraid that she would go crazy.

Alistair said, "Thank you, everyone, for the warm welcome again. I came back to let you know I had a good time. See you all around."

"No problem," I replied. "It's so nice to have you."

"Good night," he said.

We all responded, "Good night," except for Alohnzo.

He didn't even look at Alistair as he left. He was staring out at the ocean as he drank.

"All right, babe, we gotta get things cleaned up," I announced.

"I'll help," Tahira volunteered, going over to the table to collect used plates and cups.

"Me too," Alohnzo added.

"Good. Thank you. You know you guys don't have to, but I appreciate it." I sauntered over to Tahira after grabbing a trash bag from the little crate that was sitting next to the table and said, "So, I see dancing with Alohnzo has you floating."

She giggled a little and replied, "He's a good dancer."

"Is it safe to say that you have a crush on him?"

Tahira placed the plates in the trash as if she were about to lie but then changed her mind. "Tru, damn, why do you have to notice every bloody thing?"

"Well, he *is* fine, so I can't say I blame you."

Tahira straightened up and replied quickly in a whisper, "It's more than a crush, but I'm married, so that's all it can be."

"As far as your husband goes, well, you already know how I feel about him. He is doing his thing, so why can't you?"

"Two wrongs don't make a right, and you know I can't go there. I'm flirting a little. If Luca is still my husband, flirting will be the only thing I do. Alohnzo makes me feel so comfortable, and I can be myself. Felt good to relax for once."

"Tahira, your husband is cheating on you!"

"Shhhh," she hushed me because my voice had risen without me realizing it. The wine plus the champagne had me quite intoxicated.

"I'll be inside," Luca said.

I didn't expect him to help. He never did. Luca wasn't the type to help with cleaning up. He usually hired cleaning crews for that, but my hubby and Alohnzo didn't mind getting their hands a little dirty. Alohnzo was picking up trash, and Noble was putting the bonfire out.

"Good night, Luca," I said.

"'Night, Tru, and everyone."

"Later, bro," Noble said as he put out the bonfire.

"Noble, get with me tomorrow!" Luca bellowed in a direct tone.

Noble replied, "Yeah, I got you."

"Good night, Luca," Alohnzo said.

Luca waved.

Alohnzo said, "Hey, Tru, I need another trash bag to collect the rest of these beer bottles."

"Thank you, Alohnzo." I handed him the bag.

Alohnzo glanced at Tahira with a hint of desire as he folded up chairs, and it made me snicker.

As soon as he was away, I said to Tahira, "I see he feels the same about you."

She looked at me with wide, curious eyes, but then she shook her head. "No, I won't go there until I'm divorced."

I searched Tahira's eyes because I never heard her say the word "divorce" before.

"Are you thinking about getting a divorce? Oh, I hope you leave Luca and soon. You and Alohnzo would actually make a cute little couple." I nudged her arm playfully.

"Let's just say hypothetically, Alohnzo and I hook up, do you think he will treat me the way he treats Kinsley?"

I looked at her as if she were crazy. "Absolutely not! He treats you better than that as his friend. Plus, you're not a ho. I will say, I've never seen him look at Kinsley the way he looks at you."

"Do you think Luca noticed?" She panicked. "I don't want him to blame me when he's the one doing wrong."

"Luca was too busy texting whomever that was. I bet he's in the house right now sweet-talking her."

Tahira's face turned serious, and tears welled up in her eyes. I realized that what I said came off a bit insensitive. No matter how much pain he inflicted, he was still her husband.

"I'm sorry, Tahira. I—"

"It's okay, Tru. I plan to serve him with divorce papers soon. I'm not happy," she started to sob.

"I know you're not happy. Please don't cry."

Tahira wiped away a tear that had managed to slide down her face. She really loved Luca, and his infidelity was taking a toll on her.

"I got your back," I said. "If you need me, I'm here to support you in any way that I can. You need to be happy. The three years I've known you, I've never seen you this sad."

"Things will be a little weird around here without me."

"What? Why would you say that? You wouldn't have to leave. If anything, Luca will have to go. He can leave, and you need to stay."

Tahira drew in a deep breath and exhaled. "Our pre-nuptial agreement is straightforward. Since we don't have any children, I wouldn't get much of anything. This is his house."

"That's bullshit! Why would you sign anything like that?"

"I was trying to prove to him that I wasn't marrying him for his money, which I wasn't. I married him because I was in love with him."

I nodded. "I understand, but I'm sure there's some sort of cheating clause, isn't there?"

She shrugged while removing the tablecloth and folding it.

Alohnzo came over and helped us break down the table, so we stopped talking about Luca.

"You have any plans for the weekend?" I asked him.

"I'm going down to the hanger to fly one of my planes," he said. "You guys have plans?"

"Noble and I may take the twins somewhere fun. Not sure yet," I replied.

Tahira didn't respond; she seemed preoccupied with her own thoughts as she set the tablecloth in my crate.

"You have plans, Tahira?" he asked, giving her that sexy look again.

"Oh, um, no . . . I don't have plans. Luca will be down at the set, wrapping up shooting, so I'll be home most likely."

Alohnzo nodded his head, staring into her eyes. Tahira instantly started blushing as she dropped her eyes from his. I cleared my throat, and Alohnzo seemed to snap out of his daze.

"Well, looks like we got everything. You need anything else?" he asked.

"No, the caterers will take the tables inside. Thank you so much."

"No problem. You ladies have a good night."

"G'night," Tahira and I said in unison.

It was cute how they tried to pretend as if they weren't looking at each other as he walked to his home.

"All right, Tru. I'm going inside," she said.

"You swimming tonight?"

"Nah, I'm exhausted. Everything was beautiful. Have a good night." She yawned.

"You do the same."

We hugged each other before she walked away.

Noble called from where he was standing by the extinguished bonfire. "You ready to go inside?"

"Yeah." I walked to him, and I couldn't help but think about Tahira and Luca's cheating ass.

I didn't wish divorce on anyone, but Luca was never going to change. She was his fourth wife, and he was still doing the same things he had done previously from what I gathered.

Noble put his arm around me as we walked down the beach toward home.

"Did you see Tahira and Alohnzo looking at each other all night?" he asked, interrupting my thoughts.

I didn't think he was paying attention, but I guess it was apparent.

"Of course, I did. Do you think Luca noticed?"

"Probably not. The only person Luca ever pays attention to is himself and whoever is on his phone," he said.

"True."

"What you think about her and Alohnzo?" he asked. "I know you grilled her about it because that's how you roll."

"You say that like I'm all up in her business."

"You *are* all up in her business. Isn't that what best friends do? What did she say?"

I laughed a little and shook my head. He knew me too well. "She knows Luca is cheating on her. She isn't the type to just go and cheat on Luca because he's cheating on her. I think that if Tahira divorces Luca and hooks up with Alohnzo, she wouldn't be wrong. Luca is a dirtbag," I said.

"So, you think she has a justifiable reason to leave Luca?"

"Yeah, don't you? You know he's cheating on her. Matter of fact, I'm sure you know more than I do."

"Can she prove it, though? She hasn't caught him."

"So, you think a woman's intuition isn't enough to go off? You're telling me that the only way a woman can accuse a man of cheating is if she can prove it?"

"That's exactly what I'm saying. If she can't prove it, then it will just be an accusation."

"Whatever, Noble. She's unhappy. I know you and Luca are close, but please don't tell me you are on his side."

"I'm not on anyone's side. Luca is my friend, and he's a man. He's made a few mistakes, but that doesn't mean that he doesn't love her. Alohnzo should be off-limits, no matter what. He shouldn't be a possibility because Luca and Alohnzo are friends. Don't you think hooking up will cause issues between them?"

"Luca and Alohnzo aren't best friends, Noble. Luca is fucking up. Why would he be upset with Alohnzo? Luca is not valuing or honoring his own wife."

"They are neighbors. Look, babe, don't get all upset with me. I know you are ride or die for Tahira. I would just hate for things to get crazy around here. I like that we all get along. Sand Cove wouldn't be what it is without everyone. Now, we gotta see what kind of dynamic Alohnzo's brother is going to bring. He's a young bachelor, you know. We were lucky enough that Alohnzo isn't the type to throw wild parties. Alistair may be completely different." Noble reached for my hand and squeezed it. "Promise me that you'll stay out of Tahira's business. I don't want Luca to think that you are encouraging her to leave him. You know what I mean?"

I rolled my eyes. Noble never wanted me in anyone else's business, and I got what he was saying because we all weren't just neighbors; we had become the best of friends.

"I hear you, baby. I'll stay out of it, I promise."

"Good." Noble rubbed my shoulder and said, "Now, what was that you were saying earlier about as soon as the bonfire is over?"

I giggled. "Oh, you know what I was saying. I'll race you to the house." I took off running, kicking up sand behind me as I moved quickly.

He chased after me as we laughed.

As my head touched my back, Noble's thrusts were powerful. With each long stroke, I climbed higher to ecstasy. Sweat was forming all over our bodies. There was nothing better than hot, sweaty sex with my husband. Slapping my bottom hard twice, he knew what I liked.

I cooed, "Yesssssss, Noble."

"You like that rough shit, huh?"

"Yes, baby, I do!"

He went deeper and deeper, faster and faster. He wasn't done yet, and my knees were trembling. Gripping my hips tightly, he pounded hard. Once Noble was about to have an orgasm, he was going to give me the very best. He made love rough, and I enjoyed every moment of it.

Collapsing on top of me, he was trying to catch his breath. "You're so sexy, babe."

"Thank you, baby. You know you are too."

He hopped up, rubbed his tight, washboard stomach, and went into the bathroom to start the water for a shower. I was right behind him so we could get in together. While he lathered up with his body wash, I lathered with mine.

"Wash my back, please," I said, turning around and facing the wall.

"I got you. . . ." He took my bath sponge and washed my back. "You still want to do something fun with the kids tomorrow?"

"Yes, we hardly get to do anything with them, so since we have some free time, let's do it. I know they will like that."

"Plus, it will give Ximena the day off," he said.

"Yeah, she's worked so hard. She deserves it."

I closed my eyes and enjoyed the way the sponge felt as it moved across my back.

"Noble?"

"Hmmm?"

"I love you."

"I love you too."

I faced him and wrapped my arms around his neck. We held each other as the hot water washed over us.

Chapter 12

Alohnzo

I woke up with the worst headache I had in a long time. I knew better than to drink too many beers when I hadn't had a beer in a long time. I lay in bed and looked up at the ceiling. I thought about going next door to ask Tahira if she wanted to grab coffee or breakfast since she didn't have any plans, but I didn't want to start anything that would cause any drama with her husband.

I couldn't stop thinking about the way her hands felt as she caressed my back while dancing. A heated, mounting tension kept growing in me. If she hadn't turned away abruptly, I might've continued to be in a daydream. I wanted to ask her if she felt what I felt, or if I simply imagined things because I wanted her so badly.

Suddenly, I heard a car honking outside.

Honk. Honk.

I sat up, eased out of bed shirtless and barefoot wearing only black boxer briefs. I walked over to the window that overlooked my driveway and stared out. Tahira was in my driveway, getting out of her white convertible Maserati, a birthday present from Luca earlier this year. She was wearing distressed jean shorts and a black-and-white striped, long-sleeved shirt. Black Prada sunglasses covered her eyes, and she had on a pair of black peep-toe Louboutin pumps.

She looked up and waved at me to come down.

I frowned a little, wondering if we had the same thoughts this morning and that was the reason why she was here. I grabbed my cell phone and looked at the time. It was a little after 8:30 a.m. I walked over to the bathroom to brush my teeth quickly and wash my face. Then I threw on the cargo shorts I had on the night before. I didn't bother with throwing on a shirt. I was a little anxious to see what was on her mind. I made my way down the stairs, out of my front door, and to my driveway. The crisp morning air hit my chest, and it felt good to breathe in fresh air into my lungs.

Putting my hands in my pockets, I said, "Hey, beautiful. What's up?"

She cleared her throat as if the sight of me without a shirt distracted her. "Can I talk to you? I mean, do you mind if I vent a little?"

"Do you want to come inside to talk?"

She removed her glasses so I could see her puffy red eyes. She looked as if she had been crying all night. "No. I won't take long. Plus, I have to get to my yoga class. Though, I'm not sure if I'm going to yoga now. . . . I went through Luca's phone while he was sleeping. . . . It's very unusual for me to go through his personal things, but he stayed on the phone into the wee hours of the morning. He didn't bother sleeping in our bed either. He slept on the couch. I need some quick advice from a male's perspective on what to do next."

"What did you find?"

"He's fucking the lead actress, the one who has my role. They're planning on meeting up once the film is wrapped up tonight to celebrate, just the two of them." She paused before she said, "This is someone who smiles in my face every time I'm on the set. I should've known something was up when he said the set was closed, and no one could come up there anymore. I think I should just go get my divorce papers and have him served."

Divorce papers? She was serious, and she wanted me to tell her it was okay to do so. This was a sticky situation, and I could've been selfish and yelled out, "Yes! Get a divorce!" but it wasn't that simple. One thing I learned about my parents' marriage was that one minute they wanted a divorce, and then next minute, they were in love. It would've been crazy for me to get excited so soon.

"Does he know that you went through his phone?"

"No. I wanted to throw the phone at him and scream, but all I could do was cry. I had the proof in my hands, and I didn't say anything. Ever since he started filming this movie, I've noticed trivial things between him and her. But I couldn't prove it until now, you know?" Her British accent was thicker when she was upset.

She sounded so sexy.

I wanted to wrap my arms around her and hold her close to me, but I wasn't the kind of man to take advantage of a woman when she was vulnerable. If it were meant for Tahira and me to be more than friends, it would happen eventually.

"Do you want to talk to him about it to make sure you didn't misread between the lines?"

"Oh, trust me, I didn't. They've exchanged naked pics back and forth. I think I should finally talk to him. I'm going down to the set right now. I've been trying to deal with Luca, but this can't wait any longer. He's getting so bloody sloppy and disrespectful. He's leaving me no other choice."

She pulled her sunglasses back over her eyes, so I could no longer see them, but she was still looking at me. I couldn't tell how she was looking at me. I only knew that I was staring at her as if she were the most beautiful thing in the world. Even when she was distraught and sad, she was so fucking sexy. Luca was an idiot, and he was pissing me off. How could he cheat on her? If she were mine, I would never let her go. I would love to have Tahira.

"I'm here for you," I said. "You can always talk to me about anything. I don't think you should act on anger, either. Go do your yoga, and then have lunch. Make sure you breathe before going over to the set. I would say let's go get something to eat together, but I think it would be better for you to have a moment to yourself, you know."

She thought about it as she paused before she replied, "Yeah . . . All right, Alohnzo. I'm going to yoga, and then I'll get something to eat. I just keep hearing my mum's voice telling me to go ahead, divorce him, and get it over with quickly. All he's going to do is deny it."

For a split second, I thought of telling her the same thing. Luca had fucked up too many times. He was lucky she wasn't packing up all her shit and leaving right now. She still wanted to talk to him so that he would have an opportunity to explain himself.

"Do you think talking is going to be worth it?" she asked.

"In my opinion, you should talk about all of your concerns. You're married. Maybe counseling will even work. I think you should find the underlying cause of why he's cheating. If he doesn't communicate with you the way you feel he should or if he doesn't address your concerns, then you will know what to do from there."

There I was, giving her the perfect advice—even though I really wanted to tell her to leave and never go back. She should've been filing for divorce immediately, but this wasn't a woman angry at a boyfriend for cheating. This was her husband. They took vows for better or for worse. She was going to have to try everything first before calling it quits.

She was standing there as if she didn't want to hear what I was saying.

"What do you really want to do? What is your heart telling you to do?"

She hesitated before she replied, "I just want to be happy, Alohnzo. I don't want to be with someone incapable of loving me, and I mean loving all of me with all my flaws. I'm tired of being belittled and treated as if I'm not good enough. The moment he stuck his dick in another woman, our bond was broken. I don't want to be with him anymore, so I don't know what good talking will do."

"I hear you. At least if you talk, he won't be blindsided by divorce papers."

"Well, he blindsided me with all of this. I didn't know I was marrying a man who had commitment issues, but I should've known. It was right there in my face clear as day. He wasted my time. I want to kill him, Alohnzo."

"I know what you mean."

She snatched off her glasses and said, "No, you're not listening to me! I want to fucking kill him for doing this to me!" She broke down and cried uncontrollably.

I quickly pulled her to me and hugged her. My heart started hurting for her, and I wasn't the type to feel sympathetic, and I never showed empathy to anyone. It was like she was exposing a soft side of me that I didn't know was there. I held her tightly until she stopped crying.

Tahira took a deep breath and said, "I'm sorry. I'm just in a lot of pain."

"I know. I can feel it. Hey, if you don't want to talk to him today, and it's too soon, wait. You want him to come clean and be honest with you, but you should do that when you're ready. If you feel like you're done, have him sign some divorce papers, even though he doesn't sign anything willingly unless it's a check."

"You know him too well. Alohnzo, I'm afraid. I'm afraid that talking to him will only confirm that he is just as unhappy with me as I am with him. Sometimes, the truth hurts."

"Nothing is wrong with feeling the way that you do. Tahira, you're an amazing woman. Although I've never been in this situation, I hope I've been able to help somewhat."

She nodded her head and wiped her tears from under her glasses. "Well, I'm sorry to come over here like this, but thank you so much for letting me vent. I would've gone to Tru, but it's so hard to talk to her when Noble is so close to Luca. There have been a few times when Noble has repeated something I've said to Tru in confidence."

"It's no problem. You can talk to me anytime about anything."

Tahira started to get into her car, but then she stopped. "Alohnzo . . ."

"Yeah?"

"I know you run every morning on the beach before work. Do you think I can join you tomorrow morning?"

"Of course. I'd like that."

"I always see you out there, and I tell myself that I need to be out running too."

I smiled at her. "It's a good workout. You headed to yoga now?"

"No, I won't make it in time. I think I'll go to the day spa for an hour. I need to relax a little before I go down to the backlots to talk to him."

"All right." I stared into her eyes. "You got this. Before you go, I just want to tell you that you look gorgeous today."

Her cheeks turned a little red, and her skin started looking a little flushed. She was blushing. "That's a kind thing for you to say."

"It's the truth. Have a good day."

"You too." She hopped into her car.

I watched and waved before walking into my house. I jogged up the stairs and hoped things went well for

Tahira. Divorcing someone was never easy, and I didn't want her to experience any more hell than what she was already going through.

I grabbed my cell and saw that I had a missed call from Kinsley. What the hell did she want? I groaned. I didn't want to talk to her because she probably wanted to talk about last night. I couldn't believe she stormed off like a spoiled kid throwing a tantrum instead of sitting down and talking to me about what she was feeling. If she would've told me that she was sorry for flirting with my brother to make me jealous, I would've listened.

I didn't expect Kinsley to leave the bonfire that way, but she made her decision, so what else was there to talk about? I took a shower for about fifteen minutes before I got dressed. I wanted to spend my day flying one of my private planes without interruptions, so I decided to give Kinsley a call so that she wouldn't feel the need to keep calling.

She picked up after a few rings. "Hello, Mr. Alohnzo Kelly. How are you this morning?" She professionally greeted me as if we were at work.

I smirked and shook my head. I couldn't figure out if she were playing games with me, but I wasn't going to feed into it. "I'm good. I missed your call, so I'm returning it."

"Well, I called because I have something that I want to tell you, and I don't want you to get upset. I'd rather tell you in person, so I was wondering if you had some free time right now to talk."

I rubbed the back of my neck, feeling irritated that quickly. I didn't know why Kinsley made me feel like this so often. My headache had gone away, but why did I feel like Kinsley was about to create a new one?

"I'm on my way out to the hanger, but . . . around what time are you thinking?"

"Oh . . . are you going to fly alone?"

"I always fly alone," I responded quickly.

She knew that. I flew alone because it was my hobby. I was a licensed pilot, and I had two single-engine pistons, a floatplane, and a turboprop. My next buy was going to be a private jet. Men had gadgets as toys, and planes were mine.

"Oh . . . okay," she replied, sounding very much disappointed. "If you don't mind, I'd like to talk as soon as possible. I'm not too far from you. It won't take very long. I promise."

"All right. How long will it take you to get here?"

"Eight minutes."

"See you when you get here."

I ended the call and left my bedroom to go downstairs to the kitchen. I was hungry. I turned on my Keurig machine to make a cup of dark chocolate coffee, which was my favorite. It was already sweetened perfectly. I grabbed my favorite Darth Vader black mug and inserted a K-Cup, and while my coffee brewed, I made an English muffin with cinnamon butter.

My cell rang. I looked down to see that it was my mother calling. Shit, not now. Not when Kinsley was on her way. My mother, Mabel, hated Kinsley, and that was something she always made very clear. I hadn't talked to her in a few weeks. As much as I dreaded having any conversation with her because she hardly ever had anything pleasant to speak of, I figured I could answer and rush her off the phone before Kinsley arrived.

"Hey, Mama," I said, trying to sound happy to hear from her.

"Alohnzo, my baby boy, how are you?" Her voice was full of cheer to my surprise. That meant that she was in a good mood, but it didn't mean that she wasn't up to something.

She was the most intrusive woman I had ever known. She always felt as Alistair's and my business was her business. As her favorite child, she loved bugging me. For that, she was my gift and curse. I didn't know if she bothered Alistair this much.

"I'm all right. How are you?"

"I'm okay, son. . . . Your father told me that he made a surprise visit to your office a few days ago."

I sighed heavily. Pop came to the office a few days ago to tell me that I wasn't doing things the way that he wanted me to. Instead of congratulating me on the success and the new clients I brought to the company, he had to point out what I was doing wrong. I didn't run the business the way he had, and that was a problem. I didn't see why he couldn't accept that technology was changing everything, and *his* style needed to be upgraded. I was the top and best advisor he had.

"Yeah, he came from the eighth floor down to my office on the fourth to scold me like I'm a child."

My pops was born and raised on the South Side of Chicago, but he was CEO and founder of Amos Kelly Advisors of Los Angeles. He wanted nothing more than his sons to go into the family business and continue to do business even when he's no longer here.

Nothing felt better than being able to stand on my own the way a real man was supposed to, but pops complained about everything. He felt the receptionist didn't greet people quickly enough, and she had too many calls on hold. Then, he complained that the break room had too many luxuries. I gave them a forty-two-inch screen TV with cable inside the brand-new cafeteria. Hot food was prepared. They had new coffee machines, vending machines, and microwaves with plush, comfortable seating and clean tables. I did it all without his permission, and I think the only reason why he didn't like it was because he didn't think of it.

Pops, like my mother, was too prying. He saw Kinsley wink at me, and he wanted to know if I was screwing her. I said no, and he asked me why not. I didn't get why he cared so much. It was as if he were trying to live vicariously through me.

"Your father merely wants to see this company continue to go in the right direction. I want to make sure you're doing okay."

"Everything is fine," I assured her.

"Your father also said that you and Kinsley seem to have more than a working relationship these days. He's under the impression that you two might be seeing each other outside of work. Is it true? Please, tell me that's not true. . . . Oh God, please . . ."

There it was. . . . The *real* reason why she was calling. She hated Kinsley, and it started when Kinsley was my dad's personal assistant. Kinsley said pop moved her to my department to save her job. He thought she would be perfect as a financial administrator, and she was.

"Mama, Kinsley and I are friends," I explained as I chose my words carefully.

Whom I was sleeping with was my business, and I shouldn't have had to explain anything to her.

"I don't think it's a good idea for you to be involved with that slut. You should learn something from your father if you never learned anything else from his *mistakes*."

She constantly brought up that my father cheated on her. Though he never divulged who he had an affair with, we assumed it was the countless assistants and employees that were fired.

The difference between my father and me was that I wasn't a married man cheating on my wife of over fifty years. Pop cheated with his secretaries, his receptionists, and interns for twenty years. He said he learned his lesson and that was the reason why he didn't go after

Kinsley. Pop claimed Mama hated Kinsley because she was young and pretty, and she didn't trust her one bit.

I didn't know why Mama didn't leave him. She refused to go. She nagged him and threatened him with a divorce once a week but was still there. Divorcing him would leave her with an enormous chunk of his money so he always smoothed things out with her so she wouldn't leave him broke. After his last affair two years ago, she demanded that he have a predominantly male staff. She didn't trust anyone, not even the women who were older, married, and had been there for over a couple of decades.

"You have nothing to worry about, Mama." I was going to have to cut this conversation short so that she wouldn't be able to tell that I was lying. She was good at that. "I'm in the middle of breakfast. I'll give you a call a little later. Is that all right?"

She seemed to be satisfied with my answer as she said, "All right. Enjoy your breakfast. Bye now."

"Bye." I ended the call, took a deep breath, and exhaled.

That was close. I knew how to get her off the phone quickly. I pulled my mug from the Keurig and took a bite of my toasted English muffin.

Then the doorbell rang. I walked with my mug to the front and opened the door.

"Hey, you," she said.

"Hey," I replied. I closed the door behind her, and she followed me into the living room. "Have a seat," I offered, gesturing toward my soft white couch.

She sat, and I sat across from her in a chair that matched the sofa. The silence between us was a bit awkward. I was waiting for her to speak since she was the one that wanted to talk.

"I want to apologize for leaving the way that I did last night. I guess I can say that my jealousy got the best of me." She played with her hands.

I sipped my hot coffee and asked, "Why would you feel jealous?"

"I'm not used to sharing you. All your attention was on your neighbors."

"I don't get you. You and I were going good, I thought. You've spent the night over here a few nights. In a short time, we've spent a lot of time together. I wanted you to mingle and mix with people I associate myself with. I don't know why that made you feel so uncomfortable."

"I don't have any friends, and I guess it was just hard for me to let strangers in my little bubble."

"I see. . . ."

"I have to talk to you about something else. I don't want you to get upset."

I hoped she wasn't about to tell me anything about Alistair. I could care less about how much he was hitting on her, but at the same time, I wanted to hear her out.

"Get everything off your chest, Kinsley, so that way, we can move on from whatever seems to be bothering you."

She stared at me for a moment, debating whether she should say what she really wanted to say. Before I could tell her to spit it out, she continued. "The way that you look at Tahira is . . . it's . . . You've never looked at me that way."

I didn't think she wanted to talk about Tahira. I thought she was here to talk about why she was flirting with my brother. I didn't respond right away. I guess I didn't think anyone saw me looking at Tahira when I thought I was so discreet about it.

I answered, "I apologize if you read into something that isn't there. She's a married woman. You and I, on the other hand, we're friends, but we know that it's a little deeper than that. What I was hoping is that you would talk about Alistair."

"What about Alistair?" she asked defensively with her eyes shifting to my black living room rug.

Her guilty expression told me that something happened between them. He was MIA from the party for a little while.

"I want you to tell me yourself," I said.

"What did he tell you?" she asked quietly.

"I'd rather *you* tell me," I said, not knowing anything.

"Well, he did invite me over when he saw me leaving because he didn't think it was right that I should leave."

"What did you do, Kinsley?" I asked, feeling myself getting upset.

"I guess I should come clean in case he got things mixed up." Her eyes met mine again. "I flirted with Alistair purposely to make you jealous, hoping that you'd get upset. Are you mad?"

"No, I'm not mad. All you did was *flirt?*"

"Yes . . . We had a drink, but flirting was all we did. I hope he didn't try to say anything else happened because it didn't. I wouldn't do that to you."

I stared at her. She was lying, and I didn't need Alistair to confirm it. Her guilty face was enough evidence for me. "You and I *aren't* in a relationship, Kinsley. You are a single woman and if you want to see Alistair, be my guest."

Tears filled her eyes, but she was fighting them hard as she replied, "I don't want your brother. I want to know if we can be more than friends. Alohnzo, I don't want to waste any more time pretending like I don't have feelings for you when I do. It's more than feelings. I'm in love with you. Will you give me another chance? Please."

I could've lied and told her I would love to be with her, but that wasn't the truth. I didn't want her the way she wanted me. Now that I figured out that she had slept with my brother—or whatever they did—I couldn't go there with her again. The sex was good, but that was all it was for me. She was emotionally attached when she didn't need to be. She didn't need to feel guilty about whatever she did with Alistair because I didn't care. However, a woman who wanted to be with me would never disrespect herself or me by sleeping with my brother. She didn't love me *that* much.

"Kinsley, I'm your boss, so it's best that we forget about what we did. It is what it is, and you are free to do what you want."

"What if I quit? Will you be with me then? Alohnzo, don't do this to me."

"I'm not going to let you quit your job, Kinsley." I studied her as she fiddled with her nervous hands. "That's crazy. Look, we're cool. You don't have to act awkward at work either. We had fun, but it's over now."

Her hazel eyes glared at me as if she couldn't believe what I was saying. "Because I want to be more than friends, now you want to say it's over?" she said quickly. "Let me ask you this; did you have plans to dump me anyway before last night?"

"This is something you and I talked about from the start. I'm not ready to be in a relationship."

"Okay, look, I'm okay with not having the title. Let's just keep doing what we were doing. I really enjoy being with you."

I stood up. "We can't have sex anymore, either."

"Why not? Are you acting like this because of what Alistair said?"

I crossed my arms and raised my eyebrows. I was going to let whatever was eating at her make her confess. "I don't want to talk about it. I want you to tell me the truth, Kinsley. Don't lie to me because I already know everything."

"Okay." She took a deep breath and exhaled. "Look, I was drunk. I didn't mean to sleep with him. I was just trying to make you jealous, and it went too far. Alistair is very persuasive."

I nodded. "I know. I want you to listen to me and try to understand where I'm coming from. I don't share women with my brother. Alistair knows this. He has tested every woman I've touched. It bothers me that he does this shit, and I didn't have time to warn you. He doesn't waste any time, and that doesn't surprise me, but I'm disappointed that *you* went there with him. I'm sorry, Kinsley, but we're done."

"*Seriously?*" she asked.

"Seriously. I hope we can remain cordial after this."

I was a man who enjoyed having sex with beautiful women, but I wasn't a womanizer like my brother. I was exclusive when I wanted to be, but with this news, I would never be able to have sex with her again.

"I don't think it's fair for you to do this. I made a mistake. I want you to forgive me."

"Forgiving you is one thing I can do," I asserted, "but I won't bend on what I just said. We cannot have sex."

"I'm not sure I can handle this, Alohnzo. I'm in love with you. What am I supposed to do with my feelings?" she cried.

She sat there on my couch, crying and pleading with me to give her another chance. I couldn't do it. I had no compassion for anyone who did what she did to me. A few of my ex-girlfriends wound up in Alistair's bed, and I never talked to them again. I needed Kinsley to respect my feelings. I had no grounds to fire her, but if she pushed me and didn't get that I was serious . . . I would.

"I wish you nothing but the best. I hope my brother was able to give you what you wanted."

"Oh my God, Alohnzo. Did you not hear what I said? I *don't care* about Alistair. At all. I was drunk," she said, looking as if she were very confused by my response.

"I heard what you said loud and clear."

"Even the part about me being in love with you?"

I nodded.

"And you have nothing to say about it?"

"I'm not sure what you want me to say. I am your boss, and you're my employee. Maybe we shouldn't have ever crossed that line. I don't want to sit here and go back and forth with you anymore. I have things to do today."

She stood up to leave with tears spilling down her face. "Okay. I guess I'll see you at work tomorrow."

She walked to the door, put her hand on the handle, and turned around before she walked out. It seemed as if she wanted to say something else to me . . . or she was hoping I would say something else. I waited, but she didn't say anything before she left.

Kinsley and I were officially over, and it felt right. Now, I was going to have too much free time on my hands. More time to sit on the deck and watch Tahira play on the beach. That wasn't necessarily a good thing. I grabbed my keys from the holder on the table in the hallway and headed for the garage. I hoped she would call me later, but then I stopped myself from thinking about her.

She was still Luca's wife.

Chapter 13

Tahira

I tried to enjoy my massage, but the pit of my stomach was on fire and turning in knots about confronting my husband. Before I took a drive to the backlots, I decided to try to eat something. I went to the Naked Lounge and ordered an Asian chicken salad and organic pomegranate lemonade. I sat in the restaurant to eat, but I wound up picking at my food.

Usually, by now, I would've already texted Luca with my warm greetings and asking how everything was going on the set. The fact that he hadn't texted to ask me why hadn't I thought about him bothered me. We would've talked at least two or three times by now. I ate a few bites while I debated whether it would be okay to go down there without at least texting him to let him know I would be coming up there.

The thought of catching him in the act had my heart beating so fast. His leading actress was on set today, and they had plans to hang out afterward. I think that's why I was so nervous. Anger should've been enough to push me to go, but I never wanted to catch Luca with any woman. On the other hand, this would precisely be the right amount of ammunition I needed to end our marriage with a bang.

I sent him a text that said: How's your day going, honey?

I took another bite and chewed. I waited. I stared at the phone looking to see if the little "thinking" box would pop up to let me know he was texting me back. I also looked to see if the read confirmation would let me know he saw it. Nothing happened. After fifteen minutes, I forced myself to finish the salad; then I left the restaurant. I drove around, trying to avoid going to the lots. The longer I waited to see if he would message me, the angrier I became. I cried out of frustration as I parked my car in the parking lot of a Home Depot. I sat there and didn't know how long I was there, but I kept checking my phone to see any sign that he got my message.

Nothing!

By the time I mustered up the courage to drive to the backlots, it was five o'clock in the evening. Security recognized me and allowed me to drive through the gates. I parked in the visitor parking, got out, and stared at my reflection through the tinted windows of the car to make sure I looked okay before walking through the entrance to Luca's trailer. Luca always spent time in his trailer drinking every day after shooting.

Though the sun was going down, I still had my sunglasses on. I held my head high as my Louboutin heels sounded like loud thuds against the pavement with each step I took. I was so nervous because I knew exactly why my husband didn't pay attention to his phone. Someone else had his full attention, and nothing else mattered to him, not even me. Suspicion was one thing but being able to see him with my own eyes was another. I was hoping like bloody hell that he was going to prove me wrong. I wanted those text messages I read between the two of them to be a figment of my imagination. Maybe I was going insane.

The closer I got to his trailer, the more my stomach ached. I didn't have to go inside the trailer to know what was going on because I could hear them.

Luca's assistant, Jillian, was standing in front of the door looking like a bodyguard with her cell in her hand. When she looked up, she stared at me with wide eyes as if she were a deer about to be rammed by a semi. The look on her face alone confirmed that Luca was being very inappropriate, but I could tell this was nothing new. She watched out for him on many occasions. She was just surprised that I was there. Before she could say a word, loud male grunts and female moans seeped out the way a teakettle whistled while boiling.

I stopped in front of her. I looked around to see if I was the only one that could hear my husband fucking another woman. Three or four people walked by, going about their business as if they couldn't hear a damn thing. Just when I thought I heard things, a few women walked past me but looked at me with the same expression Jillian had. They slowed down and even waited to see what I was going to do. Luca's infidelities had been on full display, and I looked like a fool.

Tears instantly slid down both cheeks. Shaking off the uneasy feeling and wiping them away, I took a step to put my hand on his trailer door. It was time for my husband to know that I knew all about what he was doing behind my back.

"Mrs. Moretti." Jillian stepped in my way to stop me before I could open the door.

I put my hand up. "Jillian, your best bet would be to step away from me."

"I can't let you go in there, Mrs. Moretti."

"How long have you known, Jill?" I asked, trying to mask my pain as I bit my lower lip.

She swallowed the hard lump that had formed in her throat and replied, "I think you should go home."

I pushed her out of my way, causing her to stumble back on her heels. I warned her, "Don't you step in front of me again or I'll hand your ass a whooping that you don't want. Now, back the fuck off!"

She gritted her teeth but stepped aside.

My shaking hand opened the door and walked up the stepladder. My husband and his mistress didn't hear me come in because they were too wrapped up in their lust-filled bliss. Their sounds of satisfaction became louder, and it caused me to get choked up. They were in the back of the trailer with the bedroom door closed.

She sounded like a drowning cat as she whined, "Ah, Luccccaaaaa! Ah! Yes! Ahhhhh! Yeeeeeah! Fuck me harder!"

He sounded like a caveman as he grunted, "Ooooh! Ahhh! Ahhh! Ooooh!"

The tightness in my throat grew, but I kept right on walking with wobbly legs and tears pouring down my face all the while. When I opened the door to the bedroom, I caught my husband, mid orgasm, as he fucked one of the actresses from behind. I froze because this was not the actress that was texting him. This was not the leading blonde. I was confused. I thought they had plans unless he already fucked her and sent her on her way. Greedy bastard!

He was having sex with someone I thought was cool. We worked on his last film together, and we played best friends on screen. Her name was Naomi, and she was slim, dark-skinned, and drop-dead gorgeous. She was barely 20 years old. He had her bent over the bed, and she couldn't see me, but I could see her through the mirror on the wall. With all of that hollering she was doing, neither one of them heard me come in. I thought about turning around and leaving. As I took a step back, the floor made a sound. Luca turned around, and his mouth fell wide open as soon as he saw me.

Pushing her away, he tried to scramble for his pants. He stuttered, "Ta-Ta-Tahira, what are you doing here?"

"Oh my God!" Naomi screamed frantically as she reached for her clothes to cover herself.

I struck him in his back with my fists repeatedly as I shouted, "Fuck you! You lying sack of shit! How could you do this to me?"

He ducked, trying to escape my hard blows, but it was no use. "Stop! Baby, it's not what it looks like. Tahira, stop right now!" He belted out the typical cheater's line when caught, and he said it with authority.

I stopped hitting him as my chest heaved up and down. "You can't think of anything *better* to say?" I asked out of breath.

He stared me square in the eyes. "What else do you want me to say?"

I couldn't do this. This wasn't love. Luca didn't love me.

As I backed away, he said, "You got it all wrong, baby. Let me talk to you for a minute."

"I can't do this anymore. I'm done."

"Tahira . . . Tahira . . ."

I turned to walk out.

He continued to call me, "Tahira. Tahira! You'll regret leaving me!"

I kicked off my heels and held them so I could run as fast as my feet could carry me. I didn't look back either. There was no way I was going to stay with him. He had a problem. Everyone knew that my husband was cheating on me, and I felt so embarrassed and so ashamed. I didn't know if Luca was running after me because I didn't look back once. All I could hear was my own breathing and beating heart.

I opened the door of my car, tossed my heels inside, got in, started it up, and backed out. My tires screeched when I rounded the corner. I didn't bother waving at the gatekeeper either. I drove all the way home with tears blurring my vision. I had to wipe them to help me see.

As soon as I got into the house, I ran upstairs to the bedroom, packed my clothes, but then I stopped because I realized that I didn't have anywhere to go other than a hotel. What hotel would I go to? Every hotel in the city knew that I was Luca's wife. Where could I go without being recognized? I put on a pair of flip-flops and stopped to think.

"Where are you going, Tahira?" I asked myself aloud and flopped down on the bed.

I didn't want to stay with Tru and Noble because they would tell Luca where I was. I needed someone that wasn't going to rat me out, and I needed to get out of there fast before Luca got here. I picked up my phone and scrolled, but nothing came to mind. I took my suitcase and hurried to my car. I was going to have to drive around until I thought of something. I could leave town. That way, he wouldn't find me.

I tossed my suitcase in the front seat and started up my car. Backing out of the driveway, I stopped and stared at Alohnzo's house. I had to think quickly. Alohnzo said to call him if I ever needed anything. Well, I needed him right now.

He answered after a few rings. "Hello."

"Hey, Alohnzo," I said.

"Tahira?"

"Yeah, it's me . . . Do you mind if I stay with you for a few days? I'll explain everything. I'm pulling up into your driveway right now. Can you open the garage so that I can pull in? I don't want Luca to know. If not, I'll stay in a hotel."

"Are you okay? Did he hurt you?"

"No . . ." I felt myself choking up again thinking about Luca, but I fought it. "I'll tell you everything, but I need to know if I can stay for the night. I'll figure out what to do by morning."

"I'm not home right now, but I'm on my way there. There is a key under the elephant by the door. Go in and make yourself at home. I'll be there shortly. I'll disarm the alarm from my phone."

"Okay, thank you so much. I don't want Luca to know that I'm at your house. Please, don't tell him. If he calls you, tell him that you haven't seen me, okay? Can you do that for me?"

"No problem. I'll be right there."

I looked behind me to see if Luca's car was coming before I got out of the car to run up his porch. I went right to the elephant and retrieved his spare key from underneath it. I opened the door, and the alarm went off. Before I could panic, I heard it shut off. I put his key back, rushed to the garage, then pressed the button so the door would lift. I ran to my car, got in, and parked to the far right. Quickly, I shut off the car, got out, and hurried to close the garage.

I was sweating and out of breath. I tried so hard not to cry, but it was no use. I was hurting as the images of Luca and Naomi burned behind my eyelids. I took my suitcase out of the car and walked inside.

I refused to turn on any lights as I walked over to the living room. All I could think about was Luca's naked body sweating up against that bitch's backside like a porno movie. I couldn't believe him. How many other women had he had in his trailer? Hell, *I* fucked him in his trailer from time to time in that very same position. I wondered if he brought any of his skanks to our home, in our bed. I was starting to feel faint. I needed to sit down, but I also wanted a drink. I went to the kitchen and opened the cabinets. I searched the food pantry.

As I looked, I took note of how neat he lived for a bachelor. He told me once that he didn't use a maid because he liked to clean his own house. I would've liked to clean my own house too, but Luca wouldn't allow his wife to do any manual labor.

After not finding any liquor in his kitchen, I went into the dining room. There he had a small wet bar.

"Yes!" I said as I scanned his bottles.

I wasn't going to open any of his bottles of champagne that he loved so much. There was a half-empty bottle of Crown Royal Vanilla, so I poured a little into a glass.

I sat down on his couch with my drink and tried to breathe so my heaving chest would calm down. In the dark, I took a sip and saw that my phone was lighting up as it rang on silent in my lap. Luca was calling, trying to get me to answer. I sent him to voicemail and decided to shut off the phone completely. It was only going to frustrate me every time he called. As far as I was concerned, our marriage was over.

Feeling like screaming at the top of my lungs, I was beyond angry. My anger was what I needed to keep me from going back to him. There was no way I could ever show my face on that lot again. I was humiliated. I did more than cry. My sobbing came from my drained soul. Pain flowed from me, though I struggled to keep my tears silent. My breathing was ragged, gasping to find a small bit of strength not to cry, but it wasn't working. The fire of embarrassment and anger burned under my skin, buried emptiness filled my heart, and all my pain brewed over.

I heard the front door open, and I tried to stop crying, but I was broken.

His posture was upright and poised, as always, while he set a small brown leather bag by the front door.

"Tahira, are you okay?" He examined me with a look of worry nestled in his eyes.

"No, Alohnzo. I'm *not* okay," I admitted, bringing the cup to my lips to down the drink.

"What happened?" He sat next to me and stared at the empty glass in my hand. "Do you need another drink?"

"Not right now, but probably in a little while. Luca . . ." my voice trailed off as another knot reformed in the pit of my stomach. The last thing I wanted was to tell him about my discovery, but I wanted to tell someone. "I caught Luca having sex in his trailer, but it wasn't with the woman from his text messages. He was fucking someone I had grown close to during the production of my last film."

His eyebrows furrowed deeply into his forehead, creating lines as he frowned. "You're kidding me, right?"

"No, I'm not joking. Bloody hell, Alohnzo, I'm so embarrassed. I walked on that lot, feeling like something wasn't right, and it wasn't," I cried. "Everyone could hear him fucking her! People were walking around acting like it was an ordinary thing. I have never been more humiliated in my whole life."

He pulled me close into his strong arms. His cologne was so fresh, so manly, and so inviting. I closed my eyes and inhaled him. A ripple of tingles shot up my spine. It felt good to be in his arms this way. My marriage was crumbling, and here I was in Alohnzo's arms. I wanted so badly to wrap my arms around him, but internally, I was struggling with if being here with him was the right thing. Gripping the glass that was still in my right hand, I settled for a one-handed hug.

"Everything is going to be all right, Tahira. If you need more than one night, let me know. I can understand if you need total space. I have two guest rooms for you to pick from."

I paused and eased out of his arms. "I appreciate this. I really do."

"If Luca calls, I'll tell him I haven't seen you."

"Thank you. . . . God, I want to kill him. I want him to know just how badly he hurt me, but he isn't worth it. I can't be one of those women you see on that show, *Snapped*."

He looked confused for a moment as he replied, "We definitely don't want that."

"*That's* how much I hate him."

"You don't hate him. You love him, and you're in pain."

There was an awkward moment of silence because I didn't know what to say. The more I stared at Alohnzo, the more I wanted to tell him how much I wanted *him,* and I wanted him to tell me if he wanted me the same way. But, the kind of man he was wouldn't allow himself to take advantage of me at a time when so many emotions were propelling through me. I wanted him to kiss me and tell me that I didn't need Luca anymore because he could be more than the man I needed.

"This is my fault," I said. "Maybe I wasn't a good enough wife to him. Maybe I didn't please him. All he ever did was complain about everything I did. Nothing was ever good enough."

"Don't do that, Tahira. Don't blame yourself. Luca is a grown man, and he knows *exactly* what he's doing. I'm sure he didn't think you would ever catch him, but he knows how this goes. You're not the first wife to divorce him because he cheated."

"I've known all this time that he wasn't faithful to me. I always knew there was someone else, and yet, I stayed. I wasted my precious little time."

He blew air from his lips, shook his head, and said under his breath, "Damn it, Luca." He stared at me. "I was hoping you would tell me that he wasn't cheating on you."

"Really?"

"Yeah. I didn't want him to hurt you like this. . . . I can't imagine what you felt going to his trailer and seeing him inside of another woman. The hurt, betrayal, and your frustration—I can see it all in your eyes. He hurt you to your core. I wish I could take the pain away, Tahira, but I don't know how to do that."

"You being here for me and letting me stay is more than I can ask for. Luca did exactly what he wanted to do. I'm going to call my lawyer so she can get the divorce papers ready. I'm leaving him, Alohnzo. Nobody can make me change my mind. This is long overdue."

"I support you in whatever decision you make." He took the empty glass out of my hand and said, "Let me get you another drink. You want to drink some Rosé with me?"

"Yes."

He put out his hand to help me up from the couch. The unexpected electric shock of sexuality surged through my body with just the touch of his hand. The palpable heat ignited ever so suddenly, and we found ourselves right back, inexplicably attracted to each other. This irrepressible tugging, a curious magnetic pull, was drawing me to him with such ferocious intensity, but I fought it.

"Hey, what happened between you and Kinsley?" That was the only thing I could say to change the air between us.

I needed to ask about her because it would be awkward to see her around his house. I didn't want to have to see her prancing around after having a wild night of sex with him. It was best I asked to prepare myself. I didn't want her to be here. I wanted Alohnzo. Well, that was what I pictured in my mind anyway.

"She won't be back," he said, going to his refrigerator to retrieve a cold bottle of champagne.

"Was that your decision or hers?"

"Mine. I've decided to keep things professional."

"Oh, okay. I don't think she likes me very much anyway."

"It was that obvious?" he asked as he rubbed the back of his neck.

I nodded. "Yeah, it was that obvious. If looks could kill, I would've been dead a few times. . . . So, no more sleepovers?"

"No more. We are done. She wants a commitment, and I don't."

"How come you don't want to commit?" I asked, wondering if he had an issue committing to women in general or if that only applied to Kinsley.

"I'm her boss. She said that she would quit so that we could be together, but I can't let her do that. I should've never crossed that line, to begin with."

"I hear you. You don't have a problem committing to a woman, do you?"

He popped the cork and picked out two crystal flutes from his cabinet. "Not at all. When I find the right woman, I will commit."

We stared at each other. That seductive sensation sensually swept itself across us the way it did when our gaze met at the bonfire. The unexpected display of awe from fireworks was exploding, and I was filled with a growing desire to taste his lips.

"Are you hungry?" he asked.

"A little bit."

His masculine, modern kitchen was decorated with pristine white cabinetry that receded into the wall while the black chandelier was hanging above the sleek, white dining table. I loved how his house was decorated exactly the way he wanted.

He pulled out a white chair for me, and I sat.

"I planned to cook seared lamb chops, braised cut carrots, and asparagus on a bed of whipped mashed potatoes, so I'll now make that for two."

"I love lamb." I was suddenly hungrier than I initially thought.

"Good. Relax while I get dinner started." He handed me a champagne flute.

"I always told Luca that I didn't want maids or chefs. I love to cook. My mom is a great cook. But, he insisted on having a personal chef and maids. Sometimes, we have different ones every week."

"I don't need a staff as long as I can do for myself. Both Alistair and I were taught to cook. Our father does all the cooking."

Looking at Alohnzo made me feel happy. I wasn't sure if it was the liquor that had me feeling all warm and fuzzy inside, but my emotions were at an all-time high, and the way we stared at each other, our impenetrable desire oozed from our pores. The thought of our bare skin taking up the other's space consumed me.

"Thank you again for letting me stay here," I said, watching him maneuver smoothly around his kitchen. I eased off the stool and went to the sink to wash my hands. "I want to cook with you. What do you need me to do?"

"You can peel the potatoes."

"Okay," I smiled.

"I told you that you could pick any guest room you like."

I picked up the peeler and started peeling the potatoes. "What if I said I want to stay in *your* room?"

He gave me a serious expression as he studied me. I was hoping to make him blush, but he didn't. He didn't blink as he asked, "How comfortable would you truly feel, knowing that Luca is next door?"

Oh God. He was right. I was supposed to be the one to think that way. Was I a terrible person to not care about Luca anymore? Was I in that much pain? I wasn't divorced, and I was imagining what sex with Alohnzo would be like. Since he put it that way, sleeping in his bed didn't sound like something I should've been thinking about.

Luca, my dear, cheating, unfaithful, lying husband. I wondered if he was panicking or if he even went home to look for me. Would he beg me to come back once he found me? He didn't seem to love me enough to keep his penis from dipping into other vaginas and assholes.

"I know I shouldn't be comfortable, but I think I would be very comfortable," I replied confidently before taking another sip of champagne. "Would you stop me?"

He stared at me to see if it was the liquor talking. Blaming it on the alcohol would be easy. Reading my eyes, he could see that I was sincere.

"No, I wouldn't stop you. You could sleep in my bed, and I would sleep next to you," he answered. "And that's all we would do. I'm not saying it would be easy to lie next to you and not touch you, but I would try my hardest because you're in a very vulnerable state."

I gulped the rest of my drink and lowered my eyes from his. Why couldn't he just have his way with me? I was more than willing.

"What?"

"When you swim at night, I watch you from my patio."

"You watch me?" she asked with a smile.

"Sounds crazy, right?"

"No . . . How can you see me? It's so dark out there at night. All I can see is the light from your balcony and you sitting there, but I can't tell anything else."

"When the moon is out, I can see you. On the moonless nights, I can't see you too good, but my mind—" My cell interrupted me as it rang from the coffee table. I reached over to grab it. Luca was calling. "It's him."

She rolled her eyes. "Ignore him."

I couldn't ignore him because that meant he would be knocking on the door soon, so I put my finger to my lips to quiet her before I answered, "Hello?"

"Sorry to bother you at this hour, Alohnzo, but have you seen or heard anything from Tahira?"

"No, I haven't. Is everything all right?" I asked so he wouldn't become suspicious.

"Yeah," he lied. "Everything is fine. She hasn't made it home yet. I went over to Tru and Noble's, and they haven't heard from her or seen her either. I'm starting to get worried. It's ten o'clock. She's usually home by now." I could hear the panic in his voice.

I looked at Tahira to see her facial expression. She was acting as if she didn't care that he was on the phone. She had a slight grin on her face, unbothered. Her expression was much different than the one she had when I came home.

"How long has she been missing?" I pretended not to know. "She didn't tell you where she was going?"

"No, um, we got into a little argument earlier, and she left upset. Maybe she's staying at a hotel somewhere. . . . I don't know. I've called every hotel in the city. This is not like her to take off without saying anything."

Chapter 14

Alohnzo

She didn't think I was going to respond to her that way, and I didn't think she would admit that she would feel comfortable sleeping in my bed with her husband next door. Everything about the night from Tahira's unexpected call to her needing a place to stay to her cooking dinner with me had come as a complete surprise. I was trying my hardest to be the voice of reason because it seemed to me like she was ready to act impulsively. Every part of me wanted to do what we both wanted to do, but I wouldn't take advantage of her like that.

Even though I liked how forward she was being, I had to hide the way I really felt about her. Did I care about Luca's feelings? Not really. I didn't feel bad for that cheating motherfucker. Did I think Tahira was using me to get back at him? Absolutely. I didn't want to take part in her revenge plot. She might not have thought this was what she was doing, but once it was all said and done, she would feel guilty. I saw it happen too many times.

The bottle of champagne was empty, and we had opened another. We laughed and cracked jokes for a little over an hour after we ate dinner. She helped me clean up the kitchen; then we drank some more in the living room. There were no more talks of Luca, no more discussions of Kinsley.

"I have a confession," I said.

Tahira stared at me seductively, as she had been doing since dinner, but I was doing my best to keep my composure. As much as I wanted her, I had to keep her whole ordeal in mind.

As soon as I sat on the couch next to her, she placed her hand on mine, and she brought the back of my hand up to her lips for a kiss. Her kiss lingered on my hand for a second or two. That was when she inched toward me to kiss my lips. This was something I wanted more than anything, but it wasn't the right time. This passion lived within my body, and it was living in my gut as my body was trying to understand something before my brain was ready to do so.

I backed away before our lips could connect. "We shouldn't do this."

"I want to—"

"No, you're still his wife."

"So, what?" She scooted closer to me.

She was coming so fast. Once her lips touched mine, there was no turning back. Her lips were so soft, and she was a good kisser.

"I've wanted to do this for so long," she purred up against my lips before she sucked my bottom lip.

"Is that so?"

"That's so."

I let her take another kiss from me. This time, our tongues hooked on to each other's like there was a magnet drawing them together. She tasted like the Rosé we had been drinking. The hardness inside of my jeans got harder when she unzipped them. She reached into my boxers and took me out without fumbling. She stroked me, up and down, nice and slow.

I needed to stop her, but I couldn't prevent my back from arching every time her hand worked its way up to the top. Sexy moans escaped her as she continued to jack

"That's so strange. Usually, Tru knows everything. I hope she's all right. If I hear from her, you'll be the first person I call."

"Thank you, Alohnzo. Sorry to have bothered you. Have a good evening."

"No problem, Luca. Have a good night."

I ended the call and eyed Tahira. I was waiting to see if she would change her mind and say she was ready to go home. Her husband was looking for her and sounded very worried. She looked comfortable, leaning on the couch with her feet resting on the ottoman.

"Are you ready to go home?" I asked.

"No. The only place I want to be is with you."

"Okay." I set the phone back down on the coffee table.

She laughed as if I told a joke out of nowhere. "You're a good liar, Alohnzo. You should've gone into law instead of financial planning."

I laughed with her. "Same thing my mother said, but I only lie when I need to. I don't want you to think I go around lying to people. I'm one of the most honest people you'll ever meet."

The TV was on, but we weren't watching it, so I turned it off. The important thing here was that Tahira didn't seem sad anymore. I was glad that I was the one she called. I was more than happy to let her stay, and I was going to keep my word. I turned the lights down and turned on the Napoleon gas fireplace. Flickering from the piloted flames set a romantic mood in the room. That wasn't my intention, but the moment our eyes reconnected, our sexual energy returned.

Our sexual attraction felt chemical, like a drug. Being with Tahira was like a glorious high unparalleled to anything else in the world. She was intoxicating. She was addictive. We had been drinking some, but we felt blissfully drunk, entirely inebriated by each other, and I wanted to drown in every fiber of her.

As soon as I put a condom on, I stroked in and out while covering her body completely so that I could still kiss her full lips.

"Alohnzo . . ." she whispered in that beautiful British accent against my lips while she thrust her hips toward me.

I went deeper with each stroke, causing her to lose her breath. Unable to contain her loud moan, she screamed up to the heavens, "Oh God!"

We lost track of time and were focused on the way we made each other feel. When I couldn't hold my next orgasm in any longer, I came, and my sweat-drenched body lay sluggishly next to hers. Now that we had sex, I wasn't sure how this was going to go, but I wasn't going to worry about it because we were adults. Whatever consequences we were about to face, we would deal with them.

When I covered her mouth with my lips again, she accepted me. My kisses refueled both of us. Our kissing quickly turned into more touching, and more touching turned into us devouring the other's body until sunlight broke through the darkness.

What we shared was intimate, and it was more profound than casual sex. This meant something. Before we realized it, we had been lying in each other's arms for hours.

"Let's share one of our most embarrassing moments," she suggested.

"Most embarrassing?"

"Yeah . . . I'll go first. I was in the seventh grade, and I had chili cheese fries at lunch. Right after lunch, I had PE. While we were doing crunches, I farted so bloody loud that the whole class stopped, including the teacher. I was so embarrassed that I blamed it on the guy sitting beside me."

I chuckled. "That's funny."

me off. She didn't stop until my back curved and hot juices flowed into her hand. Never had a woman been able to work me with her hands and so quickly. It usually took a lot more to get me to explode.

I exhaled and said, "Damn."

She lay her back on the couch, staring into my eyes looking like a tigress.

Luca was an idiot. He didn't know what kind of woman he had. My eyes were wide with surprise as my body shuddered at how comfortable she was. I sat there with my pants unzipped, waiting to see if she would regret it.

"Did you like that?" she asked as she grabbed one of the napkins on the coffee table.

"I did," I replied out of breath. It was hard to catch my breath, let alone talk. "Did you really make me come like that? That fast? You're making me look bad here."

"You don't look bad. It was the pent-up passion that made you let go like that."

She didn't look as if she were about to break down or cry out of guilt. She looked at me as if to say that this was only the beginning of what she wanted to do to me.

Without thinking any more about Luca—in fact, I put him entirely out of my mind—I lifted her from the couch. Wrapping around my waist, she kissed my lips hungrily. I carried her up to my bedroom, to my king-sized bed facing the view of the beach. Then I turned on the soft lighting above my bed before I eased her on top of the goose down duvet. Quickly, I took a condom out of my top drawer before I undressed her completely. Spreading her legs, I teased her clit with my index finger. She moaned as her hands found their way to her breasts, pulling each nipple feverishly.

"I want to feel you inside of me," she said in between breaths.

me off. She didn't stop until my back curved and hot juices flowed into her hand. Never had a woman been able to work me with her hands and so quickly. It usually took a lot more to get me to explode.

I exhaled and said, "Damn."

She lay her back on the couch, staring into my eyes looking like a tigress.

Luca was an idiot. He didn't know what kind of woman he had. My eyes were wide with surprise as my body shuddered at how comfortable she was. I sat there with my pants unzipped, waiting to see if she would regret it.

"Did you like that?" she asked as she grabbed one of the napkins on the coffee table.

"I did," I replied out of breath. It was hard to catch my breath, let alone talk. "Did you really make me come like that? That fast? You're making me look bad here."

"You don't look bad. It was the pent-up passion that made you let go like that."

She didn't look as if she were about to break down or cry out of guilt. She looked at me as if to say that this was only the beginning of what she wanted to do to me.

Without thinking any more about Luca—in fact, I put him entirely out of my mind—I lifted her from the couch. Wrapping around my waist, she kissed my lips hungrily. I carried her up to my bedroom, to my king-sized bed facing the view of the beach. Then I turned on the soft lighting above my bed before I eased her on top of the goose down duvet. Quickly, I took a condom out of my top drawer before I undressed her completely. Spreading her legs, I teased her clit with my index finger. She moaned as her hands found their way to her breasts, pulling each nipple feverishly.

"I want to feel you inside of me," she said in between breaths.

As soon as I put a condom on, I stroked in and out while covering her body completely so that I could still kiss her full lips.

"Alohnzo . . ." she whispered in that beautiful British accent against my lips while she thrust her hips toward me.

I went deeper with each stroke, causing her to lose her breath. Unable to contain her loud moan, she screamed up to the heavens, "Oh God!"

We lost track of time and were focused on the way we made each other feel. When I couldn't hold my next orgasm in any longer, I came, and my sweat-drenched body lay sluggishly next to hers. Now that we had sex, I wasn't sure how this was going to go, but I wasn't going to worry about it because we were adults. Whatever consequences we were about to face, we would deal with them.

When I covered her mouth with my lips again, she accepted me. My kisses refueled both of us. Our kissing quickly turned into more touching, and more touching turned into us devouring the other's body until sunlight broke through the darkness.

What we shared was intimate, and it was more profound than casual sex. This meant something. Before we realized it, we had been lying in each other's arms for hours.

"Let's share one of our most embarrassing moments," she suggested.

"Most embarrassing?"

"Yeah . . . I'll go first. I was in the seventh grade, and I had chili cheese fries at lunch. Right after lunch, I had PE. While we were doing crunches, I farted so bloody loud that the whole class stopped, including the teacher. I was so embarrassed that I blamed it on the guy sitting beside me."

I chuckled. "That's funny."

"I know, right? . . . Your turn."

"Let's see . . . Most embarrassing . . ."

"Don't tell me that you're just so cool that you've never had an embarrassing moment."

"No, I've had plenty. I'm just trying to figure out which one I want to tell. . . . Okay, one time, I was playing basketball at the gym with a few guys, and two women were doing some warm-ups near the bleachers. I threw a hard pass, and the ball went flying toward them, so I ran after the ball to try to catch it, but I ran so hard that I went headfirst into the bleachers."

She laughed. "Oh my God!"

"It's funny now, but it wasn't funny then. I had a big knot on my forehead."

"I'm sorry, but I can just imagine you flying into the bleachers."

I chuckled. "Yeah, crazy. One of the guys had it on video on his phone. They watched it on replay over and over. I had to make him delete it so that it wouldn't end up on Facebook."

She laughed.

I caressed her arm, and she rubbed my chest. There was no need to rationalize why I felt the way I did. What I felt was the instincts of my heart tugging at me. Love had manifested, and I wasn't going to shut it out.

Chapter 15

Luca

I understood why Tahira was upset with me, but she had lost her mind. She was trying to make me worry to death over her on purpose. She wanted me to have a heart attack. Yeah, that was it. I was sure that would've put a smile on her face. She must really hate me for walking in on something that she misunderstood. It wasn't what she thought it was. I would never do anything to hurt my wife intentionally because I loved her with all my heart.

I asked the Masons, Alohnzo, and Alistair if they saw her, and they all said no. After hours of trying to find my wife, I gave up and wound up going to see Naomi. I hadn't talked to her since I was with her in my trailer. Tahira walking in was unexpected because she never showed up on set without letting me know that she was on her way first.

I yelled and screamed at everyone on the set because if someone tipped her off, I was going to fire them at once. I drilled my assistant, Jillian, but she swore to me that she hadn't said a word. She said she even tried to stop her from walking in. Maybe it was a woman's intuition that brought her down to the set. When I checked my phone, I realized she had texted to let me know she was on her way to see me. I didn't hear my phone go off.

I was about to lose my wife. I fucked up.

"Relax, baby, let me help you take your mind off your troubles," Naomi cooed as she guided me to her couch.

I sat down and blew air from my lips. She unbuckled my pants and unzipped them. She helped me pull my pants down and then my underwear. Naomi wrapped her lips around me, and she sucked hard. My mind couldn't focus with the way Naomi was making me feel. I shouldn't have been over there. I should've been looking for Tahira. I didn't cheat because I wasn't getting pleasure at home. I cheated because I was an old man in fear that one day my dick would stop working, so I was getting all the tail I could get right now.

Finally, I pushed Naomi off me and pulled up my underwear and pants. I zipped them up and buckled my belt.

"What's the matter? Did I do something?" she asked.

"I'll see you another time," I replied. "I have too much on my mind. I gotta find my wife."

"What?" Naomi answered, staring at me oddly. "You know that you don't have to go find her, right? If she wanted to go home, she would be there by now. She's probably already with another man. Did you think about *that*?"

"Watch what you say. Tahira isn't like that. I need to get home. My wife is missing, for God's sake, so show some respect."

Crossing her arms over her chest, she looked at me as if I had lost my mind. "I don't understand you, Luca. You knew your wife was missing before you showed up here, and yet, you still showed up. I try to help you relax, and you push me away. I thought you were unhappy with her anyway."

"I never told you that I was unhappy with my wife! I need to leave before you piss me off. Get some sleep and clear your fucked-up head. I'll call you tomorrow."

I walked out of Naomi's house and closed the door behind me. Now wasn't the time for her to start acting as if she were bothered by the fact that I was married when she never had a problem with it before. I wasn't going to let Tahira leave me. I was going to do everything in my power to make sure we worked this out. Naomi needed to stay in her place.

I pulled my cell out of my pocket as I walked toward my car. I tried to call Tahira, but I kept going straight to voicemail.

"Where are you?"

My driver got out of the car and opened the back door for me to get in.

What if she hopped on a plane and went back to London? Silently, I rode all the way home, thinking of a way to fix this. How was I going to fix this? Nothing came to mind. I was drawing a blank. I never pissed Tahira off this badly before. Since she never ran away previously, I didn't know where she could be. If the Masons and Alohnzo hadn't seen her, then it was possible that she could've got on a flight.

As soon as I was home, I went straight to our bedroom. The lingering smell of her perfume made my stomach churn, and my heart drummed faster. I hoped she was back.

"Tahira? Are you here?" I called down the hall.

When I didn't get an answer, my heart plummeted to my feet.

"You really fucked this up," I said.

I didn't bother with turning on the light because I didn't want to have to look at myself in the mirror. I sat on the edge of the bed and sighed. It was 3:00 a.m., and my wife was not home. The only light in my bedroom was coming from Alohnzo's motion detection lights outside. I stood up and walked over to the window to look out. I never noticed how bright his lights were before, but then again, they only came on when someone was walking around.

I looked down to see if anyone was out there, but I couldn't see anything. I grabbed the binoculars that I used to watch birds, and I could see that a white cat had triggered the lights. Stray cats were rare around here. We didn't have cats, and neither did Alohnzo or the Masons. I wondered if the cat belonged to Alistair since I have never seen it before.

When the light went off, I looked up to see that a dim light was on in Alohnzo's window. His shades weren't drawn, and I could see inside of his bedroom. Two people were having sex, and I started to put down my binoculars because I didn't want to be that peeping neighbor. That was . . . until I recognized the woman. I knew that face too well, only I hadn't seen it twisted in ecstasy in a very long time. Confusion shot through me, and my heart felt like it was about to explode. I now knew where my wife had run off to. Alohnzo lied to me.

So, this is how she wants to get back at me?

When she said she loved me, I took her at her word. She said I was her soul mate, and over the years, she became a part of me. The thought of her with another man hurt me, but seeing her with my friend, my neighbor, Alohnzo, of all people, it would've been kinder to kill me. The woman I met years ago at a casting call, the one with the beautiful smile and her heart was filled with only love for me—was fucking Alohnzo.

Staring at the pleasure he was giving her, my heart
was pounding. This was all my fault. I had no one else
to blame. I slashed at her with betrayal, and she parried
me with her vengeance. My chest was tightening, and
my heart felt like it was about to beat out of my chest. I
clutched it because I felt like I couldn't breathe.

Chapter 16

Tru

I woke up to the TV blasting in our bedroom. Noble never could watch a movie without surround sound, and it got on my nerves. I had such a long day that I fell asleep with my clothes on. I eased out of bed and realized that is was three in the morning. I felt dirty and decided to take a bath. Tahira was heavy on my mind, and our damn TV was blasting. I couldn't have the tranquility I desired. After I was done taking my bath, I lowered the sound with the remote control and shook my head as I stared down at Noble's sleeping face.

His eyes popped open and looked up at me as if I were a human alarm clock or something. He was such a light sleeper when people made a movement but slept like a rock through a loud television.

"Hey, sleepyhead," I said. "You fell asleep watching a movie."

"Yeah . . . What's wrong?" He paid close attention to the worry I was wearing all over my face.

"I still can't reach Tahira."

Noble scowled and looked at the time on the clock. "Babe, it's three in the damn morning. Come back to bed."

"Baby, I'm sorry, but Tahira is my best friend, and I'm mad that she hasn't called me to tell me where she is."

"Don't sweat it," he said nonchalantly. "I'm sure she went somewhere to blow off some steam. She'll call you soon."

"I'll wait. . . . Hey, I should go ask Ximena if she can make sure to take the kids to the park this afternoon to run around for a bit. I know they get exercise at school, but I don't like that she takes them out back to the beach all the time. Little Noble and Noelle run circles around that poor girl. I would hate it if something bad happened back there. That's why we need to have a pool built."

"Baby, I'm sure she's sleeping at this hour. You can tell her in a few hours, so, come on to bed," he whined.

"Okay, but first, let me slip into my nightie."

"You don't need that on. Come to bed naked like you used to," he demanded. "Bring your sexy ass here."

I headed to the closet to get my nightgown. As much as Noble wanted me to come to bed naked, I was going to sleep in my gown. I wasn't in the mood to have sex.

"This shit with Luca and Tahira has your mind all fucked up," he said.

"Yeah. I want to know why she hasn't called me."

"I told you she probably thinks that you're going to tell Luca."

"I would never betray her like that, Noble! I mean, come on; she knows that I would never do that to her, but I get it."

I slipped into my gown and came out of the closet. Then I turned off all the lights before climbing into bed and snuggling with my husband. We had a good Saturday morning and afternoon earlier. We took the kids to the zoo. We had good family bonding time. As soon as I got the news about Tahira and Luca, I couldn't imagine what Tahira was going through.

"I'm so glad that you're good to me," I said against Noble's chest.

"Of course, baby. I would never cheat on you. You hear me?" His hands rubbed my back.

I smiled. "And I will never cheat on you."

We snuggled and closed our eyes. I could go to sleep now hoping that she was okay. Once I saw her face-to-face, I would feel even better.

Suddenly, Noble's cell phone rang.

"Who the fuck?" Noble scowled and reached over to get it. "Hello?" he answered in his deep tone that he used when he was feeling irritated. "What? Luca, calm down. . . . It's three in the goddamn morning! What? Okay . . . fuck . . . okay . . . I'll be right there." He hung up the phone and got out of bed. "Fuck!"

"Noble, what's going on?"

"Luca says he feels like he's having a heart attack or something."

"And you're going over there at this hour? What if he's faking again?"

"If I don't get over there, he's going to try to drive himself to the hospital."

"You know he's dramatic. What if he's just doing this because Tahira is missing?"

"I'm sure he's being extra, but I'm going to go over there to check. Go back to bed. If he's faking, I'll be right back."

I pulled the covers up to my chest and sighed. "All right. Call me if you end up taking him to the hospital."

"I will."

Noble dressed in joggers and rushed out of the house. I had a feeling that Luca wasn't having a heart attack and couldn't handle Tahira leaving him. Served his ass right. I didn't feel the least bit sorry for his no-good dog ass. I closed my eyes as I made peace in my mind with Tahira's decision to not call me for the time being.

Chapter 17

Alohnzo

The seagulls flew above my head as I ran on the beach as soon as the sun came up. With my earphones on, I let the running mix from Spotify decide my pace. I ran, sneakers kissing the sand, to the other side of the beach before returning. I didn't like running until I became an adult. I discovered that these feet were made to travel at speed and were as light as the paws of a lion. The morning sun was shining brightly, but the wind was brisk as it whipped against my face.

On the way running toward my house, I looked up and saw her staring down at me from my bedroom window. I was shocked that she would be standing in visible sight, especially when she was trying to hide from everyone else.

I thought about taking Tahira to my hanger, but I didn't know how I was going to get her out of the house without being seen. I never brought women to see my planes, but I wanted Tahira to get away from Sand Cove for the day. I hoped she wasn't afraid of heights.

The newness of Tahira and I was going to wear off soon, and the reality of everything was going to settle in. I hoped that time wouldn't be now because I really wanted her to take her mind off her problems.

I went inside, grabbed a bottle of water, and went up to my bedroom.

Tahira was standing near the window, looking as if she were posing for a magazine. She smiled at me warmly. "Good morning, handsome."

"Good morning, beautiful. . . . Aren't you afraid of our neighbors seeing you in the window?"

She shrugged, stepping away from it. "I didn't think of that. I was just trying to see how sexy you looked running on shore."

"Ah, is that right?" I smiled. "Did I look sexy?"

"Very." She bit her lower lip.

"You want to go somewhere with me?" I grabbed a clean towel from my linen closet and wiped the pouring sweat from my face.

"Sure. Where are we going?"

"I'm going to take you with me to fly in one of my planes."

"Really? So, you really are a pilot?"

"Yeah, I've been flying small planes all my life practically. Are you afraid of heights?"

"No, not at all, I love flying. I've been on plenty of private jets but never sitting next to a pilot. This will be my first time."

"Sweet."

"How do you propose we get out of here without being seen?" she asked.

"I'm working on a plan in my head as we speak."

When I went into the bathroom to run some water for a shower, surprisingly, she got naked and joined me. Tahira moved her body close to mine. The water poured down and dripped at our sides. The sensation of the steamy water was calming. My mind swirled like we were standing under an everlasting waterfall.

I guided her to rest her back against the wall. She lifted her leg and wrapped it around my waist. I held her up by both of her legs so that her wetness could greet me. She breathed acutely while I moved inside of her. I couldn't believe we were having bare, unprotected sex without pausing or wondering if what we were doing was right or wrong. We didn't seem to care about anything or anyone anymore.

She bit her lip to suppress her moans. I didn't want to mute her sounds. I loved the way she sounded. I thrust harder to get her to moan louder. The feeling arose from deep within my gut as I felt myself about to explode too. I pulled out quickly, and while I came into my hand, she kissed my lips.

Once we parted, we stared at each other for a moment.

I started explaining, "I know that was crazy. I should've put on a condom. I made sure to pull out. I'm sorry."

"You're fine," she said as she put her hands around my neck. "Did you see me stopping you? I'm on birth control. Remember, Luca doesn't want any children."

I took hold of her waist and planted the deepest kiss on her lips. We kissed that way for a while before we decided to wash up and get out of the shower. We dried off, dressed, and made our way to the garage.

"You'll have to duck down," I told her. "That was all I could think of."

"Okay," she giggled.

She slid down in the front seat of my car. As I backed out of the driveway, I noticed that Kinsley's Mercedes was parked in Alistair's driveway. I smirked.

She made a big deal out of not wanting him, but she's at his house this morning.

Tahira sat up and put on her seat belt once we got a little way down the street. "The coast is clear."

I laughed and admired how beautiful she looked with the sun beaming on her face. Being with Tahira like this was like a soft dream that I had many times. Her excitement was not easily hidden on her face. She pushed her pain to the farthest place in her mind so that it wouldn't be clear. The crease of her lovely brow and the down-curve of her full lips made her look sexy when she wasn't trying to be. Her eyes were a deep pool of gold, an ocean of hope. All the beauty of the universe could not compete with her. She wasn't going to let Luca break her. She may have been in pain, but she would never let him hurt her again.

"Do you want to get married and have children one day?" she asked.

It was a random question, but I understood why she was asking. She didn't want me to waste her time.

"One day. How about you? Do you want any children one day?"

"Yes, I do, very much so. I long to have kids."

"One day, you'll be able to have whatever you want."

Her cheeks were suddenly kissed pink, blooming like a spring rose. "Alohnzo, you always know what to say."

She was so damned cute. This feeling stretched throughout my whole body. It was overwhelming yet made me feel complete. This feeling had no bound or length or depth because it was absolute. It felt as though I were in a dangerous fire, but I was safe at the same time. My heart was dancing around in my chest, and a hole I was never aware was there, had been filled.

I let her pick a plane to fly, and she chose the Beechcraft 58 Baron. It was an excellent choice. It had a Jaguar interior and six cream leather executive club seats. As soon as we were up in the air, nothing could wipe the smile off both of our faces.

"Do you take a lot of women on flights with you?" she asked.

"Not at all. I usually fly alone."

"Wow. I feel special."

"As you should."

She went back to smiling as she looked down at the land below us. The morning sky was a deep steel blue swirled with charcoal that flowed into the heart of the city. A shade of salmon pink hovered over the mountains. The rest of the flight, she merely admired everything silently. I let her enjoy her silence.

I landed back at my small airport; then I took her by the hand and escorted her off the plane.

"Thank you, Alohnzo. That was so much fun. I needed to get away from Sand Cove for a little while."

"No problem."

"You're an excellent pilot. I still can't believe that I'm the first woman that you've ever taken to fly with you." That beautiful smile I was becoming fond of wouldn't go away.

"It's the truth. Whenever you want to come with me, just let me know."

She thought for a moment as she studied my eyes. "This part scares me the most because I know that my issues are far from over with Luca. My life is a mess right now, but I don't want you to give up on me."

"I won't give up on you. You're strong, and you can get through this."

I wrapped my arms around her waist and brought her body close to mine. She kissed me slowly and softly.

"Alohnzo, you comfort me in ways words can never express." Her hand rested below my ear, and her thumb caressed my cheek as our breathing intertwined.

I ran my fingers down her spine, pulling her closer until there was no space left between us. I could feel the beating of her heart against my chest.

Chapter 18

Kinsley

With Alistair's persuasion mixed in with my anger at Alohnzo for making it clear that he wanted to keep our relationship strictly professional, I spent the night with Alistair. I purposely left my car parked in his driveway so that Alohnzo could see that he pushed me to his brother. It was immature on my part, but I didn't care. I wanted Alohnzo to know that I was worth more than a good fuck.

I also wanted Alohnzo to call me and question me in a jealous rage about being over at Alistair's. When I got out of Alistair's bed, I went to my phone on the nightstand to check to see if he had texted or called. I found a long-stemmed red rose resting next to my phone, and I picked it up, which stopped me from looking in my phone.

Alistair was sweet. I wasn't expecting him to be romantic. As cute as the gesture was, I didn't know how to feel about it, other than I wished it were Alohnzo giving me a rose.

Alistair came out of the master bathroom with a towel wrapped around his waist.

"Is this for me?" I asked with a smile.

"Yes, of course. Who else would it be for?"

I smelled it. "Thank you."

"You're welcome. I want you to shower, get dressed, and then meet me downstairs. I'm going to cook break-fast for us."

I nodded because he and Alohnzo were different but alike. "You cook too."

"He cooked for you?" he asked, reading my expression.

I nodded.

He came to me and placed a kiss on my lips. I accepted the quick smooch.

"I make a mean omelet," he said before he went to his walk-in closet to get dressed.

I placed the rose back on the nightstand, eased out of his bed, and walked over to my overnight bag that was resting on a chaise in the corner of his room. I took out my toothbrush and body wash before I headed to the bathroom. Then I closed the door and set my things on the counter. As soon as I turned on the water, I set the temperature to hot. I loved taking hot showers. As I showered, I thought about how I should've checked my phone to see if Alohnzo called or messaged. I got out, dried off, and walked out of the bathroom. I took my clothes out of my overnight bag and put them on.

Before I joined Alistair downstairs, I couldn't help but look out of the window at Alohnzo's house. I wondered if he had seen my car yet. He probably didn't even notice, and that irritated me. I went and snatched my phone from the nightstand and checked. I didn't have any missed calls or texts. My face felt so hot; I was feeling flushed. I couldn't believe that my little plan didn't work.

The sound of Alistair whistling downstairs reminded me of the nights I spent at Alohnzo's house. *Alohnzo,* I thought. A sudden chill swept over me thinking about him. Sex with Alistair was good, but sex with Alohnzo was more than remarkable. Even hours after he touched my body, I could still feel him entering me repeatedly. I wondered if the other women let him do the nasty, sexy things he did to me. With him, I did anything he wanted me to do so that he would never forget me.

I left the room and walked down the stairs, pushing Alohnzo to the furthest place in my mind for the moment. I was going to work on another plan later.

Alistair moved around his kitchen as if he were a professional chef. A heavenly smell filled my nose, but I couldn't figure out what he was making. It smelled like maple, vanilla, or something. My stomach grumbled.

"Okay, Alistair . . . It smells too good in here. What are you cooking?"

"Have a seat," he said, pointing to the bar stool at the island in the center of his kitchen. "You're about to find out in a few minutes."

I sat down, and he poured me a glass of orange juice mixed with some champagne. I loved mimosas.

"Thank you," I said lifting the glass to my lips.

"No problem. Can you guess what I'm making?"

"No, I'm a terrible guesser. I don't cook, so I really can't tell by looking at the ingredients on the counter. I see a bowl of mixed eggs, flour, and sugar . . ."

He smiled. "Because you told me that Alohnzo cooked for you, I gotta show my skills and make something I know he isn't good at. I'm making crepes with fresh strawberries and whipped cream. I also have some apple sausage and cheese omelets."

"That sounds delicious."

"I think you'll love it." He winked at me.

Nothing was wrong with a man who knew how to treat a woman. I was going to enjoy this until I could figure out what I was going to do to win Alohnzo's heart.

"What do you usually do on Sundays?" he asked.

"I do laundry and play with Baskin Robbins."

I heard a meow, but I thought it was in my head until I felt something furry rub against my leg. I jumped a little and looked down to see a cute white cat with a black spot of fur above one eye.

"You have a cat?" I asked, bending down to pick it up.

"Yeah, that's Snow White. She got out last night, and I thought I lost her, but when I opened the door this morning, she was right on the porch."

I petted her head, and she purred. "She's beautiful. I didn't know you had a cat."

"I've had her for a year now. She's a good companion."

"I'm more of a dog lover, but she's sweet."

"If she were bitchy, I would've gotten rid of her a long time ago. She wanders around and does her own thing for the most part. . . . She likes you."

I smiled and rubbed her before I set her down. "I'm glad she does. So, tell me, what else is up Alistair's sleeve?"

"Stick around and you'll see."

Chapter 19

Tahira

Flying over Los Angeles was beautiful, and spending time with Alohnzo was better than I could've ever imagined. His laugh, his smile, and those piercing dark eyes made me feel crazy emotions. I wanted to be with him more than ever now, but the reality of it was that I was going to have to face Luca soon. With Luca, nothing was easy. I was going to have to fight him tooth and nail on everything, and I wasn't looking forward to it. However, I couldn't procrastinate any longer.

After Alohnzo was done showing off the rest of his planes, we went to a park. For hours, we lay on a blanket, where we looked up at the sky and talked. Before the sun set, we headed back to Sand Cove. When he drove his car on our street, I made sure to duck down so no one would see me. We wouldn't be able to do this forever, but for now, it was what we had to do.

He pulled into the garage and got out. "I'm going to check the mail. I'll be back."

"Okay," I said while sitting up from my hidden position.

I heard Tru's voice calling from the sidewalk. "Hey, Alohnzo."

My heart started racing in a panic as I ducked down. *Oh shit.*

Alohnzo quickly closed the garage from his keychain, and I got out of the car so that I could hear them. Shit, I hoped she didn't see my car parked next to his.

"Hello, Tru. What's up?"

"Have you heard from Tahira? She hasn't called me. Luca is worried. He thought he was having a heart attack last night and went to the hospital, but it was a false alarm. The doctors sent him home a little while ago. He thinks she may have gone back to London. Please, tell me that you've heard from her."

"No, I haven't heard from her. I was hoping that she would be home by now. Luca also called me last night, looking for her."

Her voice became louder, so I assumed she walked up the driveway. "Isn't that Kinsley's car parked in Alistair's driveway?"

Alohnzo didn't hesitate before he replied, "I think so."

"Wow," she paused, but then she said, "If you see Tahira, will you tell her to call me?"

"I will."

I walked into the house through the door and stayed in the kitchen, making sure to avoid all the windows.

A few seconds later, Alohnzo walked through the front door.

I met him in the hallway. "I have to hide my car. If anyone sees my car in your garage . . ."

"I think she saw it already," he replied. "She was walking up before I could close the garage."

"You know what? I'll tell her that I'm staying with you. It sounds like Luca is worrying himself to death not knowing where I am."

"You sure?" he asked, looking a little worried.

"I shouldn't have put you in this situation, to begin with. This was too risky. If I don't tell her, she'll come back."

"I support whatever decision you make."

"All right. I'm going next door to talk to Luca first to get it over with. Then, I'll go to Tru's. I'll be right back after that, if that's okay."

"That's fine," he said. "Call me if you need me."

"Okay. I'll be right back."

I entered the home I shared with Luca using my key. A female's operatic voice carried from the den and greeted me at the front door. Renata Tebaldi was singing Giacomo Puccini's *Sono Andati*. It was so typical for Luca to be so bloody dramatic when *he* was the reason why I left. What a proper song. In this opera, the character Mimi was separated from her true love, Rodolfo, and her health had declined due to her poverty. In this scene, the two of them were reunited, and they reminisced about the good times they had until she drifted in and out of consciousness. While Rodolfo held her in his arms, he realized that Mimi was no longer breathing. In his grief, he lay over her lifeless body while calling out her name.

This scene always brought tears to my eyes, but this song was not symbolic of our relationship. We wouldn't be reunited, and I wasn't on my deathbed. Maybe he was hoping I would break down, cry, and come home. Perhaps he was hoping I would change my mind. I was over this relationship. I wanted to get back to being happy. If I stayed with him, I would continue to be miserable.

I walked into the den and found him in what he liked to call his grand chair, facing the opening of the room, listening to the heartrending piece of famous classical music with a glass of scotch in his right hand. His green eyes met mine. Yet, he didn't look surprised to see me. It was as if he were expecting me.

He stood up and staggered toward me. Luca put his arms around me as he breathed his scotch breath over my face as he said, "Welcome home, sweetheart." He was trying to kiss me, as if that would make our problems disappear.

I put my hands up and pushed his chest, but he was strong.

"Stop it," I said, managing to get out of his grip. "I came here to talk. I'm not staying."

"I couldn't sleep a wink," he replied. "I thought I was having a heart attack because I couldn't find you. I'm so sorry, babe. I love you, Tahira."

I kept backing up until he stopped coming toward me. The song ended, but it came back on. He had it on loop, and who knows for how long.

"This song makes me think of you. I know how much you loved this at the opera. Every time I hear it . . ." He stopped to think before he continued, "I messed up, and I'm willing to do whatever it takes to make it work. You're my wife, Tahira, and I'm your husband."

I bit my top lip. I was trembling because I was so furious with him. I couldn't believe anything he said. "You don't love me, Luca."

"Yes, I do love you."

"You have a funny way of showing it."

"I know, but it's okay. I'll do better. . . . Where were you?" he asked, changing the subject. "I called every hotel in the city looking for you. I thought you went back to London."

I thought about keeping the location away from him, but in case Tru saw me, I was going to have to come clean. "I was at Alohnzo's. He let me sleep in his guest room. I told him not to say anything because I needed time to think."

Luca chuckled as if what I said was humorous. "I knew that rat was lying when I called." He took a sip of his drink and hummed in thought.

"He only lied because I told him to, so don't be mad at him. I even told him not to tell Tru and Noble. I'll be filing divorce papers tomorrow, so I'll be staying with Alohnzo for the next couple of days—"

He cut me off and replied with a sneer, "Of course, you'll be staying with *him*." He drank a little more and unsteadily stood to his feet. I thought I was going to have to use my little body to hold him up, but he stood, unwavering. "You think I don't know what's going on here?"

"What's going on here is that you're a liar and a cheater, Luca. There's no saving this marriage. While I'm at Alohnzo's, I don't want you coming over there causing any problems. He doesn't deserve to be put in the middle of this."

He laughed as if I said something funny again. "You think I'm going to let you move in with him? I will make your life a living hell, and you'll never be able to spend another penny of my goddamn money! As a matter of fact, I cut you off already! Don't bother trying to buy anything with your debit or credit cards. I've removed you from all of my accounts!"

"Ooooooh, you wanker. My life has been a living hell with you! Guess what? I got news for you. You don't own me. You've done nothing but make me miserable. We're done."

"I don't own you, but everything on your body I paid for."

"If I could cut off every part of my body you paid for, I would."

"I bet. You want to divorce me? With my lovely little prenuptial agreement in place, you'll have nothing. Without me, you'll be nothing but a broke and homeless nobody."

"You think I give a bloody rat's ass about your prenup? Oh, I'll get something because I deserve it! Why can't you see that all I wanted was for you to respect me as your wife! I should've gone back to London a long time ago, but Sand Cove is my home, and I'm glad I have friends here who care about me."

He cracked up and laughed again, holding his stomach with one hand.

"What's so funny?" I snapped.

"You think *my* friends are *your* friends?" He stopped laughing and looked truly evil, as his cold eyes stared me down. "They don't care about you. They only tolerate you because you're my wife!"

"Liar! Tru, Noble, and Alohnzo are my friends."

"You think because you fucked Alohnzo, you little cunt bitch, that he's your friend? You have the nerve to walk up in here smelling like him! Admit it. He's the real reason why you want to leave me, isn't it? You've wanted to get your hands on Alohnzo this entire time, and now you finally have your chance."

I fired back, "Leave Alohnzo out of this. You cheated on me, *remember?* Let's stick to what's *really* going on here."

"Will you admit it? You act like Alohnzo has shades or drapes on his windows. I saw you, the two of you. . . ." He paused to take another gulp of his drink. "On his bed. Rolling around. Last night. This morning. You know, baby, you sure know how to be spiteful, don't you?"

I kept my calm composure. I was speechless for a moment, but then I shook it off because I didn't feel sorry for my actions. Alohnzo made me feel alive and like a woman, not some object. Now, Luca knew what it felt like to see me with another man. He deserved any bit of pain he was feeling. Karma was a bitch.

"Don't you have anything to say?" he barked.

He was trying to get to me, but it wasn't working.

"It's over between us, Luca. Our bond and our marriage were broken the moment you stuck your dick in places it didn't belong. What I do from here on out is none of your business."

"Will you at least admit that you're in love with him? That wasn't just sex with him. I've seen plenty of pornos to know what fake orgasms look like. You weren't faking it, honey."

I looked up at the ceiling. He was impossible. "Quit being an ass, Luca. What I did with Alohnzo has nothing to do with you. Expect a call from my lawyer. We're getting a divorce."

He growled, coming too close to me, "This is over when *I* say it's over, sweetheart. You will *never* be able to divorce me!"

"Watch closely because that's *exactly* what I'm going to do!"

"Get out! I'm changing the locks today. Oh, and you can kiss your acting career goodbye. You can forget about getting a dime out of me too! You'll be blackballed, and you'll never be able to work in my town again!"

My upper lip curled. Now, he was trying to make me angry.

"Go to fucking hell, Luca! It's okay for you to screw everything walking, but the moment *I* do it, you can't handle it." I took the key off my ring and tossed it on the floor. "No need to change the locks. You can take your key."

"Don't you think about taking anything out of this house, either! Everything in here is mine! You'll be nothing but a broke bitch!"

"Think again, Luca! I'm going to get what's mine!"

I turned and walked out of the house. Once outside, my chest was heavy. The moment I took a deep breath, I felt a little lighter, but my stomach was burning, and the love I had for him was completely gone now. What was I going to do without money and nowhere to work? Tears escaped my eyes, but I wiped them away as I headed toward the Masons' home.

Chapter 20

Tru

The moment Tahira walked into my house, I was happy to see her, yet I was mad at her. Why didn't she tell me she was at Alohnzo's this whole time? When I saw her car parked in Alohnzo's garage, I felt hurt that she didn't trust me enough to keep her secret. I didn't know how to question Alohnzo about it, so I asked about Kinsley's car instead.

"Tahira, what's going on?"

"Hey, Tru . . . I'll explain everything."

She followed me to the kitchen where I was about to prepare lunch.

She sat on a bar stool and said, "I know you're upset with me, but I didn't want Luca to know where I was."

"You really think I would've told Luca where you were?"

"No, I know you wouldn't tell him, but you would tell your husband. Noble is too loyal to Luca to keep that secret to himself."

She was right. My husband would go running anytime Luca would call him. He was a good friend like that.

"I get it, but I was hoping you would've at least called to let me know you were safe."

"I'm sorry about that. You're one of my dearest friends, Tru. I promise that I will never do that again."

"Good," I replied, feeling better. "You talk to Luca yet?"

"I went to talk to him before I came here."

"How did that go?"

"Fuck him! I'm getting a divorce!"

"I understand better than anybody. . . . Hey, um, I saw your car in Alohnzo's garage."

"I know. I should've told you."

"It's okay. I understand why you would go to him, but you couldn't think of anywhere else to park?" I chuckled, thinking of how silly that was. If she truly wanted to hide, she should've parked elsewhere.

"I was in such a hurry to get away from Luca, Tru. I didn't think it all the way out."

"I see. . . . Do you want anything to drink? Juice, water, or wine?"

"I'll take some ice water with a lemon wedge if you have it."

I went to the refrigerator and got a bottle of water. I cut a lemon and put it in the glass with the water. I set it in front of her and said, "Tahira, you're a grown-ass woman, and I know you're going to do whatever you want to do. I really hope you're not fooling with Alohnzo to piss Luca off."

"So, what if I pissed Luca off? He deserves it, but truthfully, I've had feelings for Alohnzo for a while, and now, I'm in love with him."

"The thing is you don't have to tell me that. You hid it well until the night of the bonfire. I can see love all over you. I just don't want you to confuse lust with love. I don't want to see Alohnzo get hurt if you decide to go back to Luca."

"I'm not going back to Luca. I'm filing the papers tomorrow morning."

"Divorce is a process, and if Luca decides to be an ass, he can drag it out."

"Oh, I know, but I'm ready for that. I know Luca well enough to know he is going to try to ruin my life. He's already cut off my debit and credit cards and threatened to blackball me. I don't know what to do." Her eyes were teary, and she paused to take a deep breath.

"If you need anything, I'm here for you. No matter what it is, I got your back. Be sure to ask your lawyer about an infidelity clause in your prenup."

"I will. Thank you, Tru."

I nodded. I was done talking about Luca. She wasn't glowing for nothing, and I needed details.

"So . . . You know I have to ask about the sex with Alohnzo."

Tahira sipped some water before she replied, "You're so nosy."

"You know me. Spill it, Tahira."

"Well, since you must know . . . the sex was . . . How can I describe it? We didn't plan it. We were driving each other crazy, sitting and talking. He did naughty things until my mind and body exploded." She grinned. "Alohnzo *definitely* is everything I thought he'd be."

"Well, damn. I can see a change in you already. You look radiant. How long are you planning on staying over at his place?"

"Now that I don't have any money, I'm not sure. I have to find another acting gig before the wanker blackballs me."

"I hope he isn't going to be that childish to do something like that."

"Oh, trust me, he is. He already said he's going to."

"Well, I'm your best friend. If you need to stay here, you can. Alohnzo isn't the only friend that you have, you know."

"I know that, Tru." Tahira stood up and hugged me. "Thank you so much for being in my corner, always. Where are Noble and the kids?"

"He and Ximena took the kids out for ice cream."

Tahira raised one eyebrow at me with a confused look on her face.

"Why are you looking at me like that?" I asked as I went to the sink to rinse off the lobster tails.

"Let me get this straight. You actually *let* Ximena ride alone with your husband?"

"Yeah. They were getting in my way, and the kids were running around. I needed them out of my kitchen."

"Tru, I can't believe you."

"What? I trust my husband, Tahira. If you don't have trust in a marriage, what do you have?"

"You're right. Not every man is like Luca. I'm sorry for thinking like that," she apologized. "With what happened to me, I guess I'm a little paranoid."

"It's fine, girl. Most people think like you, but I know Noble, and he would never do that to me."

She nodded. "You're right. Noble is a great guy. Hey, I'm going to get out of here and get some sleep. I'll see you later."

"I don't think you'll be getting much sleep," I laughed. "I'm sure you and Alohnzo can't keep your hands off each other."

She giggled. "Bye, Tru."

Tahira walked out of my kitchen, and I hummed while I finished prepping our dinner. I was going to take full advantage of the time with everyone out of the house. I thought it too soon because I heard the garage door opening. Within minutes, I heard tiny feet running down the hall toward the kitchen.

"Mommy!" Little Noble exclaimed. "I had rainbow sherbet, and it was good!"

"You did? That sounds good."

Noelle said, "Hi, Mommy!"

"Hi, baby!" I bent down and placed a kiss on each of their foreheads.

Noble came in and put his hand on my waist. "It smells so good in here. You need some help?"

"No, but you can sit on that stool and watch if you like. I need you out my way."

Ximena walked in and said to the kids, "Let's go wash our hands."

"Can you make sure they play upstairs? I really want to get dinner done," I said to her.

"No problem, Señora Mason." She grabbed the kids' hands and took them up the stairs.

Noble said, "I just saw Tahira leaving here. Where has she been?"

"She's been at Alohnzo's."

He blinked hard. "Alohnzo's? This whole time?"

"Yup, she's staying in one of his guest rooms. She went to Luca's before she stopped by here."

"Did she say how that went?"

"Not so good. Luca is Luca."

"Say no more. . . . How long will she be staying at Alohnzo's?"

"A few days until she finds an apartment."

"You think they . . . you know?" he asked, hinting at the two of them having sex.

I nodded my head. "They did."

"Damn . . . I hope Luca doesn't find out or else . . ."

I scowled, "Or else what? Is Alohnzo supposed to be afraid of Luca's dramatic ass?"

"Why shouldn't he be? He's fucking his neighbor's wife. They're still married, Tru. Alohnzo shouldn't use this as his moment to fulfill his fantasy. This isn't some movie. This is real life, and the reality is that Luca is going to fuck his ass up."

"Don't talk like that."

"You're taking this too lightly. You don't know how evil Luca's mind is. I don't wish death on anybody, but

Alohnzo and Tahira are playing a dangerous game! I don't want to be around when the shit hits the fan."

Noble was pacing, and it made me wonder if he knew just how evil Luca could be. I mean, we all saw Luca throw tantrums, but I never thought he could be dangerous.

"Have you ever seen Luca kill anyone?"

Noble paused before he spoke, "I don't have to see him actually do it to know he is capable of anything when he's pissed off! You don't know what I know!"

"What *do* you know? Tell me, Noble, because if he has the potential to kill our neighbor and my best friend, then I need to do whatever I can to make sure that doesn't happen."

"You're not getting involved. Just know that Luca is capable of a lot of things."

I rolled my eyes at how silly he sounded. "Hush. Go watch TV or play a game on your phone. Let me finish cooking. Is a football game on or something?"

"I don't think so, but I get the hint. I'll let you get back to cooking."

Noble left the kitchen, and I shook my head. I stared out the kitchen window at the beach. The air was muggy, and a large, looming dark cloud was starting to cover Sand Cove.

Chapter 21

Alohnzo

By the time Tahira came back from talking to Luca and Tru, I had lit candles in the living room and set up a fruit platter on the coffee table in front of the couch. She looked troubled, but once she saw my romantic spread, a smile wiped away whatever was on her mind.

"Alohnzo, what is this?"

"A little snack before I take you to dinner. I figured you would want to unwind and relax after talking to Luca. How'd it go?"

"Well, he kicked me out and told me not to get anything else out of his house. I don't want to talk about him anymore. The thought of him makes me too exhausted."

I took her hand and guided her to sit on the rug with me. "You don't have to talk about him. I want you to relax."

She stared into my eyes as she said, "Thank you for everything. I know this isn't the best situation, and I'm sorry if I'm imposing."

"No, you're not imposing at all. Don't worry about anything. I'm here for you."

Her hand reached for mine, and they interlocked. We kissed passionately and then, tenderly. Her lips were pressed against mine with passion, love, and affection.

"You're so beautiful," I whispered against her lips.

She wrinkled her nose in protest.

"You are," I said.

"Thank you. I haven't been called beautiful in a long time."

She turned and placed herself between my legs. She rested her back and head against my chest. I kissed the top of her head as I wrapped my arms around her.

"I'm nervous," she admitted.

I was feeling nervous too because things were moving quickly between us. Now that Luca knew where she was, I felt a little on edge.

"I understand how you feel because I feel the same way. So, what happens now?"

She shrugged. "I'm going to see my divorce lawyer tomorrow morning, and I'm just going to take it day by day. Luca has . . ."

I picked up on the quiver in her voice and asked, "Has he ever been violent in the past?"

"No, no . . . It's just that he cut off my credit cards. I have nothing. He has a lot of power in Los Angeles. How am I ever going to become the star I want to be?"

"Hey," I said to calm her, "I will do whatever I can to make sure you're okay. You're too talented and beautiful to let that get to you."

She sighed and paused for a few seconds before she said, "I appreciate you so much, Alohnzo."

"Don't worry. You're safe with me." I hugged her tighter.

She melted in my arms. I meant what I said. I loved her, and I would keep her safe.

Chapter 22

Noble

After Tru cooked and served dinner, Ximena put the kids to bed. I usually cleaned the dishes whenever Tru prepared the meal. Some nights, she helped me, but she was sleepy, so I told her I was okay with cleaning up alone.

I rolled up my sleeves and got to work. I rinsed the dishes off, placed them in the dishwasher, added a detergent pod, and pressed start. The pots and pans were the only things that I never put in the dishwasher. I liked washing those out by hand.

My phone alerted me that I had a notification from a sports app that kept up with my bets. I dried off my hands, looked around, and picked up the phone. Tru had no idea that I had developed a gambling habit. I won some, and I lost some. The ones I lost cost me a lot of money, but I was good at covering it up. Luckily, Tru didn't worry about our finances.

Football season was here, which was the season I bet the most. Staring at my notification, I realized I lost my first bet of the season. Damn! The New York Giants would beat the Denver Broncos. I was out of $10,000 on that bet—and that was a *small* bet compared to the others. I looked to place my next bet.

Ximena walked in, interrupting my train of thought. "Need some help?"

"I pretty much did everything. I just have a few more pots to do," I replied, putting the phone down.

A warm smile appeared on her face. She looked at the schedule Tru printed and placed on the fridge door. Tru always posted it on Sunday nights for the week so that Ximena would know our calendar and appointments for the kids. She moved one of the magnets, and the paper fell to the floor. I turned around to see her bending over to pick it up. Before picking it up, she looked over her shoulder at me to make sure I was looking at her ass. I quickly turned around to the sink and continued washing a skillet.

Ximena put the list back on the refrigerator. I slightly turned to the side to see if she was leaving the kitchen, but she was on her way over to me at the sink. She was staring at me as if she were waiting for me to say something. I didn't make eye contact to see her exact expression, but I felt uncomfortable. I never felt nervous around her before, but she never looked at me the way she was either.

"I'll wipe off the counters," she said.

She grabbed a sponge near the sink, wet it at the faucet, and cleaned the counters, all while looking at me. I stopped washing and stared at her to see what she was looking at.

"Is everything all right, Ximena?"

She finished the countertops, and her body brushed my arm as she returned the sponge to the sink. "Yes. Have a good night, Noble."

As she walked out of the kitchen, I thought, *Since when did she start calling me Noble?* I had always been Señor Mason. Earlier when we went to take the kids to get ice cream, I noticed she was a little friendlier than usual. I didn't want to read between the lines, but I think Ximena was flirting with me.

I shook it off and didn't read too much into it. I finished the pots and pans, placing them in the dishrack. Before I headed upstairs to bed, I checked to see what team I wanted to bet on next. I put my money on the Cowboys to win their next game, and I doubled the bet to recoup the money I lost.

Chapter 23

Kinsley

I hated Mondays. It was the one day of the week that I could seriously do without. When I got to my office at work, a bouquet of purple liatris, orange roses, and yellow tulips was sitting on my desk. I looked around to see if someone had placed it on my desk by mistake. I picked up the card to see who it was from, but the card was blank.

Alistair.

He started with that red rose yesterday morning and that yummy breakfast, and now, he was sending flowers to work. We had an astounding time together yesterday, which was something I didn't expect. He was incredibly thoughtful, and this was perfect. I couldn't wait for Alohnzo to see what his brother had delivered on the way to his office.

I looked at the door to his office across the hall, and the lights were off, which meant he hadn't made it to work yet. He was usually here at least an hour before I arrived. This was unusual for him to be late.

Right before I could get settled at my desk, Alohnzo and Alistair's mother, Mabel, was sauntering up the hallway, wearing a black pencil skirt, a white blouse, and a dark pink blazer. Her pink pumps matched her blazer. She was dressed as if she worked here when she had never worked a day in her life.

I held my breath and hoped she wouldn't look at me. She paused outside of Alohnzo's door once she saw that he wasn't in his office. She turned around, and her eyes landed on me. I instantly felt the ice coming from them. This woman was a pain in my ass even when I was her husband, Amos's, assistant. When I transferred to Alohnzo's department, I was more than happy to be gone because I didn't have to see her. The way she stood there, looking at me, forced me to look up at her.

"Yes, Mabel?"

"Do you know when Alohnzo will be here?"

"No, I sure don't. I'm not his personal assistant or secretary. You can ask Farrah. She handles his appointments."

She walked into my office as if I had told her to come in. I should've closed my door when I saw her coming up the hall.

Giving her a hard look, I asked, "How can I help you, Mabel?"

"I've heard some things about you and my son, Alohnzo. I find these rumors rather displeasing. He told me that you two have nothing going on."

"He's not lying. We don't have anything going on . . . *anymore,* that is." I tossed that last part out there because I loved ruffling her feathers.

She narrowed her eyes at the flowers on my desk. "And where did these come from?"

"Not Alohnzo, that's for sure."

"Well, a woman of your caliber, I'm sure getting something as simple as a bouquet is something new. Much better than money being left on your nightstand."

Her rude insults always had a way of digging into me. As much as I wanted to curse at her and kick her out of my office, I just stared at her with a smirk on my face. If she only knew that it was her oldest son who sent the flowers. *That* would shut her up.

"You're a courageous woman, walking into my office insulting me," I said.

"How does it feel, knowing Alohnzo doesn't want you? There's no surprise that he dropped you after getting what he wanted."

I had enough of her. I said through my teeth, "Get out."

Those cold, little beady eyes of hers were piercing through me. "Gladly." She walked out with her nose in the air and her steps fast and close together.

Bitch, I thought.

I felt my face growing hot. That witch was going to push me to do something so wicked. What did she mean a 'woman of my caliber? Ugh! I looked at the flowers and decided to calm down. There were some good people in the world, but Mabel Kelly wasn't one of them. I decided to call Alistair to thank him.

I sat in my chair and dialed his cell.

He answered, "Hello."

"Hey, Alistair. Thank you for the flowers you had delivered today."

Alistair hesitated before he said, "I didn't send you any flowers. You sure it wasn't my brother?"

My smile faded, and I was confused. I picked up the blank card again, and there wasn't a name on it at all. I felt stupid to assume they were from Alistair. Alohnzo couldn't have sent them . . . or could he? Maybe he was sorry for the way things had ended. A smile came to my face, thinking about how I was going to thank him.

"Are you there?" Alistair asked.

"Yeah," I answered quickly, snapping out of my soft daydream. "Oh God, I'm such an idiot. I'm so sorry. I thought these were from you."

"It's okay. Now, I'm going to have to think of some other way to surprise you at work," he chuckled. "Looks like I have a little competition."

I tried to laugh it off. "Well, will I be able to see you tonight for dinner?" I didn't want him to feel too sorry for calling him by mistake.

"My schedule is really hectic this evening, but I can make some time. Let's meet around eight; is that okay?"

"That's perfect. You have a good day."

"You too."

I ended the call while I thought carefully. This wasn't Alohnzo's style.

Who sent these?

My phone chimed. I had a text message from an unknown number.

Do you like the flowers? I miss you. Call me.

I didn't like it when people played games with me. I had a few guys I saw off and on, so I had no idea who this was.

I texted back: Who is this?

My cell rang instantly. It was a call from the same unknown number.

I answered, "Yes?"

"Hey, sexy. You know who this is now?" he asked.

I sighed because I knew exactly who it was. "What do you want, Amos Kelly?"

Chapter 24

Luca

Before Tahira came into my life, there had been many other women. Even in my earlier marriages, there were other women, but my other wives never retaliated by cheating on me. They hit me in the pockets instead. Tahira hit me where it hurt the most, my ego. Alohnzo was younger, more fit, and good-looking. I could see why she would think he was attractive, but I couldn't handle it. How could I lose my wife to him? If he thought he could take my wife, he had another think coming. I had been selfish, cheating on her, and I was acting possessive by not wanting her to move on, but I didn't care. Tahira was my wife.

Not his!

"Are you going to divorce her?" Naomi asked as she rolled over to rest her head on my chest.

Tahira was the first thing on my mind when I woke up, and she clearly was the first thing on Naomi's. Naomi shouldn't have been asking me anything about Tahira because, at the end of the day, Tahira was still my wife.

Naomi had spent the night with me in my bed and in my home, something I wouldn't do when Tahira lived here. The best way to stroke my hurt ego was to allow Naomi to sleep in our bed. With Tahira gallivanting around with Alohnzo, I felt undesired. Naomi's lust for me proved that I was still desirable. Sleeping with Naomi helped a little, but I was still mad as hell.

"Don't ask me that," I snapped.

"Why not?" she asked, sitting up. "You've promised me for months that you were leaving her. Now that she caught us, you're changing your mind?"

"What did I say? Don't ask me any more questions about my wife!"

She drew the sheet close to cover her naked body. "Luca, I love you. Don't I mean *anything* to you?"

My desire for Naomi was wearing thin. My thirst for her pussy had been quenched, and honestly, she wasn't that good in bed. She looked better than she screwed.

"Are you ignoring me?" she asked, looking baffled.

I was annoyed. I knew why she was asking me about Tahira, especially since I had promised her for months that I would leave my wife, but Naomi was bringing it up at the wrong damn time. I couldn't have my wife leaving me for another man while our relationship was still in limbo.

I got up from my bed and started gathering her clothes. She watched in silence as I tossed them on the bed. "You've had your night in my bed, now leave," I said.

Naomi hopped out of bed, taking the sheet with her. "I thought you wanted to have breakfast with me."

"My chef is cooking downstairs right now. You can eat before you leave, but don't make this harder than it has to be. Leave quietly and conduct yourself like a lady."

"I thought I meant more to you than just a fuck! Please, Luca, don't do this to me."

I stepped real close to her and said, "Put your clothes on."

I watched her get dressed while trying to pretend as if I hadn't hurt her feelings, but I could see it all in her eyes.

This was it between us. I wasn't going to be dealing with her anymore. I had plenty of other women to keep me company, ones that didn't want anything from me other than spending a little time with me here and there.

"You're going to eat before you leave?" I asked.

She shrugged and stormed out of my bedroom.

I went into the bathroom and sent Alohnzo a text message.

You could at least face me like a man! You're dead, motherfucker!

Threatening Alohnzo through text was the only way I could express to him what I was feeling. I didn't take him for a punk, but I didn't think he would respond and so quickly.

Alohnzo replied, Don't threaten me unless you mean it.

I replied, Oh, I mean it!

Alohnzo retorted, We'll see about that. Bet you won't say that shit to my face!

Alohnzo thought he was tough. Anger boiled within me as thick as hot lava. It churned within, hungry for destruction. The pressure of this stormy sea of rage was forcing me to say things that I tried to suppress. If Alohnzo wanted to fight with me, he was going to have to realize that he would never win.

I said, Meet me at my house. You pick the time, motherfucker!

He replied, I'll be there later. I'll text when I'm on my way.

I responded, Bring your bitch ass on!

I would hate to have to harm Alohnzo physically, but he had this coming to him. I didn't just want to kill him; I wanted to put him in a pit and add shovels of dirt slowly until his mouth was full of dust. I wanted to hear him cry as the rocks rained down on him thicker than a hailstorm.

I wouldn't care if he said he was sorry for fucking my wife. I hoped he was proud.

I ran my hand through my thinning hair and stared at myself in the mirror. Fires of fury and hatred were smoldering in my eyes as I weighed the pros and cons of the many ways I could exact my revenge. I couldn't wait to get my hands on him.

Chapter 25

Noble

Ximena's hair was flowing that morning and out of her usual ponytail. Her pastel-pink dress was clinging to her body like Saran wrap, and it wasn't proper for babysitting, stopping mid thigh, and showing too much cleavage. Seemed to me like she was trying too hard to be sexy.

"Have a good day, Noble," Ximena said.

I mumbled, "Thanks."

Tru was dressed on time, so she was right behind me as she said, "I'll be working late tonight. You can go ahead and make the kids dinner before putting them to bed. Noble will be home much earlier than I will so can you make enough for him?"

"No problem, Señora Mason."

I became nervous at the thought of being home alone with Ximena. This was going to be a huge problem because I *was* attracted to her. I, by no means, was a cheating man, but I was still a man.

"I'll be going out to the sports bar after work with Alohnzo," I said quickly from the top of my head. It was a lie, but that was all I could think of.

Tru replied, "Okay. Bye, Ximena."

We rushed out the door and got into the car. I started it up and backed out.

"What was that about?" Tru asked. "You talk to Alohnzo?"

"Yeah," I answered, not sounding very convincing.

"Why are you lying? You've been acting strange all morning. You didn't even want to have your normal quickie."

"It's nothing, baby." I didn't know how to come out and say that Ximena was doing inappropriate things.

She stared at me for a moment before she said, "Wait, are you nervous about being left alone with Ximena?"

A muscle twitched involuntarily in the corner of my left eye, and my mouth formed a rigid grimace. I was nervous to tell her, but she was my wife, and we didn't do secrets. I was going to have to put it out there before she got the wrong idea.

"Yes, she makes me nervous."

"What? Why?"

"Last night while cleaning up the kitchen, she decided to help. She dropped the paper from the refrigerator and bent down in front of me. She even looked back to see if I was looking."

"Is that all?" Tru shrugged as if it were no big deal.

"No, that's not all. Listen, she brushed her body against me and called me 'Noble.' She didn't say, 'Señor Mason.' She's making me very uncomfortable."

She threw her head back and laughed. "I think you're making a bigger deal out of this than it is." She laughed again.

Frowning because of the way she was laughing, I replied with an attitude, "I don't think I am. She's throwing herself at me, Tru. I can tell when a woman is flirting with me."

She stopped laughing and saw that I was serious. "She's *flirting* with you?" she asked, looking a little sad.

"I think she is, and it's disrespectful."

"I'm disappointed."

"Me too, babe. I don't want to have to fire her."

"We're not going to fire her. I'm not disappointed in her. I'm disappointed in you."

"You're disappointed in *me?* Why?"

"Well, I don't know how to tell you this, but she's been flirting with me too."

I scowled as I kept my eyes on the road. "Flirting like how?"

"It started with a few little compliments here and there. She comes extremely close when talking . . . and then she kissed me."

"*Kissed* you? When?"

"After the bonfire. I went downstairs to get some water, and she was in the kitchen."

"How come you didn't tell me?"

"I didn't know how, and that's why I was laughing because I can't believe this."

"And you decided to keep it to yourself?"

"I've been trying to think of a way to tell you. I've never been with a woman before, but it seems like it would be fun. What do you think?"

"Are you *serious?*"

"What? It's kind of sexy. We haven't talked about having a threesome in a long time, babe. Isn't that one of your fantasies?"

"It was, but . . ." My mind was running a thousand miles a second. Nothing like this had happened in our relationship before, and I never had to question her loyalty to me, but now I was thinking about it. "You've been thinking about having a threesome with her?"

"I do think it's very flattering that she has a crush on both of us. . . . I have been having dreams about the three of us."

I swerved over into the next lane. This was my first time hearing that Tru wanted to share me with another woman. I used to fantasize about it all the time, and she would brush it off as if it were something she could never do. Our nanny was hot, but now, I had to worry about if she would be licking my wife when I wasn't around.

A car on the side of us honked, and I got back over in my lane.

"Tru . . . Do you *hear* what you're saying?"

"Yes. I know what I'm saying. I think we should send the kids over to my mom's house for the weekend, and we should all have a few drinks . . . and let's see what happens."

As good as that sounded, it felt like a bad idea. "You really think that will be good? She lives in our home. It would be better to do this with a stranger."

"I wouldn't trust a stranger. We'll both get what we want. I mean, I can't help but feel as if this is all too perfect. I know you want her as badly as I do. I think you only feel like her flirting with you is wrong because you feel like she's doing it behind my back. I'm completely okay with it."

I felt like my wife was testing me. The thought of seeing my wife with Ximena turned me on—but then it scared me. I didn't want to fuck Ximena. When I married Tru, I vowed to be with her, and I still felt the same way. She was talking crazy.

"Nah, I don't think we should do anything like that, and I don't think you should entertain this any further."

"Why not?"

"One night of passion can turn into a disaster. I know what kind of problems this can cause. My brother and his wife were swingers, and you saw what happened to them. The bitch got crazy on them and ruined their marriage."

Tru nodded. "I hear you, but this will be different. We'll tell Ximena what we want out of this, and we'll be specific. We'll talk about what will make everyone comfortable. I want to know what it's like to be with a woman sexually."

I sighed and shook my head. "So, you got it all mapped out? It's not as simple as you think. What would you do if she wanted to have me while you're at work?"

"She wouldn't do that."

"Bullshit. She tried to rub up against me when you were upstairs. I could see if she tried to do it in your face."

"I'll talk to her about that. If things get out of hand, we know how to reel it back in. I haven't talked to her about this, so I'm not sure if we're jumping the gun. She could be flirting innocently."

I wasn't feeling it. With everything that was going on with Luca, Tahira, and Alohnzo, I didn't want anyone or anything to come between us. Ximena was attractive, but now that my wife wanted to include her in our sex life, I wanted no part of her.

"Yeah, I hope that's all she's doing. Look, I'm not feeling this at all. I used to fantasize about having threesomes, but once I got married, I let all that go. I admit that I think Ximena is a beautiful woman, but there is only one woman I want, and that's you. Promise me that you won't go behind my back and sleep with her."

"I would never do that, babe. I promise. My love for you outlasts any desires."

"Will you be able to ignore the temptation? If you can't, we might as well fire her now."

"No, we can't fire her! She's really good with the kids."

"She is good with the kids, but I'm not feeling this. The next time she flirts with you, tell her to cut it out and keep it professional. I'll do the same."

Tru nodded and placed her hand on top of mine. "You got it, baby."

She was quiet the rest of the ride to work. I hoped she was getting her mind right. The last thing I needed was to walk in on our nanny going down on my wife.

Our marriage had been inevitable from the first day we met in college. We were inseparable. She was the center of my universe, and she was mine. Our love for each other radiated from us and touched the lives of everyone we knew. It would be devastating for our relationship to be torn apart because we couldn't control our sexual desires.

Chapter 26

Alohnzo

Luca threatened me, and I took it seriously. Who did he think he was talking to? His texts seemed to buzz around me like a fly that I could never swat. Each word I read seemed to infuriate me to no end. On the way to work, I couldn't get the words *"You're dead, motherfucker"* out of my head. Luca was tripping. If he would've handled his business as Tahira's husband, he wouldn't have had to worry about me. He dogged her, and now he wanted to be mad at me.

Luca was crazy. He didn't want to fight with me. I was younger, swifter, and I was in much better shape than he was. We were too grown to fight over a woman like we were some high school boys. I was going to talk to Luca like a man.

"Good morning, Mr. Kelly," Kinsley said from her office as I opened my office door to go inside. "It's not like you to be late."

"Good morning," I replied without looking back at her.

I wasn't in the mood for Kinsley's smart mouth. I thought about calling in sick, but I had a lot of work to take care of at the office. I turned on the light and set my briefcase on my desk.

Kinsley walked in and said, "Your mother came by this morning looking for you."

"What? For what?" I asked, raising my eyebrow.

I wasn't in the mood to deal with my mother either.

She shrugged. "I don't know. Before she left, she started questioning me about my relationship with you. She also said that she knows that you lied to her when she asked you about us. Why didn't you just be honest with her?"

I stared at her with a blank expression. I understood that Kinsley didn't like my mother, but I didn't know why she wanted my mother to know so badly about what we had. It wasn't my mother's business whatsoever.

"You think I want her in my business?" I sat at my desk and smirked. "Did you tell her that you're now sleeping with her other son? Of course, you didn't."

Kinsley frowned and shifted before she said, "Why would I tell her that? I told her I wasn't seeing you anymore, though."

She was fucking with me. Had to be.

I sighed, "So, you implied that we were seeing each other by saying that. Why would you do that, Kinsley? I don't involve my mother in my personal relationships, and I told you that."

"Alohnzo, she cornered me. I didn't know what else to say. What was I supposed to do with her coming at me? Your mother has had it out for me ever since I was your father's personal assistant. Once she starts, she can't stop."

I took a good look at Kinsley. There was something else going on between her and my mother, something that stemmed long before she started working for me. I couldn't put my finger on it, but I had never known my mother to hate another woman this much unless she had a good reason. What if Kinsley had an affair with my father, but they were trying to cover it up? Something wasn't right.

"Has my mother ever told you why she doesn't like you?" I badgered.

"No." Her eyes shifted to the left and then the ground before she looked at me.

Something in my gut told me she was lying to me. My mother didn't harass women for fun.

"You *sure* you haven't fucked my father?"

"No, Alohnzo," she replied. "You mother is crazy; that's all."

"Has my father hit on you?" I asked. "I think you should come out and say it. I can always ask him."

She looked shocked and appalled as she put her hand on her chest. "You *really* think that I fucked your father, don't you?"

"You're fucking Alistair, so . . ."

She narrowed her eyes. "So, you must think I'm a ho."

"Look, there's no need to get offended. We're adults here, and I'm not judging you, but there has to be a reason why my mother hates you."

"Well, she hates me without reason, and, to set the record straight, I'm not fucking Alistair—yet. We're dating."

She was delusional if she thought Alistair could be in a relationship with anyone. "Yeah, right."

"We are. He sent me flowers this morning. They're right on my desk."

I could see the flowers on her desk from where I was sitting, but I didn't see how she could be dating Alistair already. She must've thought I was stupid.

"Well, I wish you the best in your new relationship," I played along with her.

Kinsley turned and walked out of my office, closing the door behind her. I turned and looked out of my office window. The view of downtown Los Angeles was breathtaking from up here. Even though Kinsley tried hard to hide what she had going on with my father, I saw right through her.

My assistant called, and I answered, "Hello, Farrah."

"Hey, your 10:30 a.m. canceled and said she would reschedule another day."

"All right. Thanks for letting me know."

"No problem."

I hung up the phone and took a deep breath. Now that my meeting was canceled, I had time to meet with Luca if I wanted to. I took a deep breath and got upset all over again thinking about his texts.

Chapter 27

Tahira

I met with the divorce lawyer at her office once Alohnzo left for work. Edna was an older Caucasian woman in her late forties with brown hair that was cut into a pixie.

"Hello, Mrs. Moretti. Have a seat," she greeted.

"Please, call me Tahira."

"Okay, Tahira. You ready to divorce your husband?"

I sat in a chair in front of her desk and responded, "Yes, and I want to do this in the quickest way possible."

"I see. I know we spoke several months ago about it, but then I didn't hear from you. Something made you change your mind to stay in your marriage, but now you're back, and you're ready now?"

"I'm definitely ready now." I hesitated before because I didn't have proof of his indiscretions until recently. "I walked in on him sleeping with an actress in his trailer Saturday."

"You caught him cheating?"

"Yes, I walked in, and he was having sex with another woman. Isn't there some kind of cheating clause in my prenuptial?"

She leaned forward against the desk. "How much do you know about your prenuptial agreement?"

"I know that I won't get anything financially. It was designed for me to leave without any of his money or the house, but my good friend said that I should ask you about a cheating clause."

"So, here's the thing about your prenuptial; there is no infidelity clause. The only way you will get any money is if he dies while you're still married. . . . I'm sorry, but you won't receive much of anything once you're divorced. He designed this for you to walk away with exactly what you came with."

"When I met him, I had nothing." Tears welled up and slid down my cheeks. I was hoping that I would be able to keep the house at least. I sniffled and wiped them with the back of my hand.

She handed me a tissue. "Listen, I've seen these types of cases many times, and it burns me that women sign these agreements, thinking they're going to be with a rich man forever, or that they won't need anything afterward. He introduced you to a lifestyle that you've grown accustomed to, so, of course, it will be tough to adjust. You may have to rethink divorcing him if maintaining your lifestyle is important to you."

"It's not superimportant. . . . I just want to be able to keep the house. I love Sand Cove. Will I at least get alimony?"

"If the judge sees that you need it, you'll be granted alimony." She wandered off in thought. "I'm calling his lawyer right now to see if we can negotiate something before going to court." Picking up her office phone from her desk, she dialed out.

"Yes, hello, Mr. Simon. This is Edna Morgan, Tahira Moretti's divorce lawyer. . . . Yes, I'm well. Is there any way that we can set a date to discuss the prenuptial agreement and what terms we can come to for alimony payments? Okay, talk it over with your client. I'll be here all day." She ended the call and said to me, "Mr. Simon is planning to see Mr. Moretti sometime today. He'll get back to me, and I'll let you know how things go."

I nodded. "Okay."

"As soon as I hear from him, I'll give you a call."

"Thank you." I shook her hand and stood up to leave.

I left my lawyer's office feeling defeated. Yeah, I would be divorced, but Luca wasn't going to want to negotiate anything, and as he threatened, I would be broke. He was a man of his word. If he didn't want me to have a dime, I wouldn't have a dime. I tried to drive through my tears, but they were blurring my vision. I had to pull over. What was I going to do without a job or money? My tears poured out in anger. I hated Luca!

Two hours later . . .

The paramedics, a fire truck, and the police were lined up on the street. After parking in Alohnzo's driveway, I saw that the commotion was coming from Luca's house.

"What in the bloody hell?"

The police had Luca's maids and personal chef outside, questioning them. His lawyer, Mr. Simon, was talking to one of the EMTs. I walked over.

"Here's his wife right now," Mr. Simon said to the paramedic and police officer.

"What happened?" I asked.

"Mr. Moretti seemed to have suffered a heart attack and passed away. One of the maids found him in the entryway here and called 9-1-1," Mr. Simon said.

I heard him, but I wasn't sure if I heard correctly. "You said he had a heart attack?"

"An autopsy will determine the official cause of death, of course, but from the examination that was performed, cardiac arrest is the obvious thing. Did he have heart problems?"

Luca was dead?

"He did have high blood pressure, but he was taking medication for it. He was never diagnosed with heart problems. . . . He's had a few scares before, but it wound up being in his mind," I said, still trying to wrap my mind around what they were telling me.

The front door opened. Luca's body was covered in a black body bag and was being carried out of the house on a stretcher.

My heart beat harder as everything around me seemed to freeze. Though no tears immediately appeared, one hand covered my chest, as I stood there in disbelief. Was that his body in the body bag, or was this a joke? I wouldn't put it past Luca to fake his own death.

"Mrs. Moretti, are you okay?" the officer asked.

I didn't reply. I was speechless.

Luca was such an asshole, and I had been so upset leaving the lawyer's office. I hated him so much, and now he was dead. I was once in love with this man, but then I was divorcing him, and he was going to leave me broke and homeless. The tables had turned. He had left me as a widow—a very *rich* widow.

"Mrs. Moretti?" he repeated.

"No, I feel faint. . . . I need to sit down."

I needed water. I needed air. Once I left Luca's house and walked into Alohnzo's home, I sat down. My cell phone was going off with tons of notifications. With the help of social media, Luca's death had spread that much faster. So many people were leaving their condolences and well wishes on my social media pages.

News vans, reporters, and journalists filled up our street before noon. I called my mum, but she didn't answer. I sat there, staring blankly at the wall.

Tru called, and I answered. "Hello?"

"Tahira, did Luca really have a heart attack? Like a for real one?"

"Yeah . . . It's true . . . He's gone."

"Oh my God! I saw it on Facebook, and I watched the news to confirm it. I didn't know what to believe. Are you at Luca's house?"

"No, I'm at Alohnzo's. They took his body out of the house. . . . I'm still trying to process everything. I can't believe it."

Tru groaned. "I'm so sorry, Tahira. I know you two weren't getting along. . . . How are you feeling?"

"I feel like this is my fault. What if me leaving caused this? I was so pissed at him. I wanted him to die for being so cruel to me, but he was my husband. I would've never imagined being Luca Moretti's widow."

"Don't blame yourself, Tahira. It was probably going to happen this way anyway, even if you didn't leave. . . . Hey, I gotta go, but I'll come by to check on you when I get off. Okay?"

"Okay. Thank you."

As soon as I ended the call, Alohnzo called.

"Hello?"

"Tahira, where are you?"

"I'm at your house."

"Okay . . . You okay? I'm on my way."

"I'm fine. I'll see you when you get here."

Alohnzo hung up, and I sighed. Why hadn't I shed a tear? My husband was dead, and I couldn't even bring myself to cry. I was conflicted. I felt sad . . . but then again, I felt like this was what he deserved.

After sitting in silence for a little while longer, I heard the garage door open.

"Are you okay?" Alohnzo asked, looking into my eyes.

"I don't know. . . . I've been thinking. This 'til death do us part thing is overwhelming."

He came to me, and I stood up in his arms. This felt like a bad dream I wanted to wake up from. The pain of losing Luca should've been present, but in Alohnzo's arms, it was as if Luca never existed. I felt as if a burden had been lifted because I didn't have to worry about going through an ugly divorce anymore. I should've been sad. I should've cried . . . but I did not shed another tear for that bastard.

Chapter 28

Noble

I streamed the news from my cell after Tru told me about Luca. This wasn't a joke, and Luca wasn't being dramatic this time. He was really gone, and all I felt was liberation. Yes, I was sad because I lost a friend, but another part of me felt a little relieved because I owed him a shitload of money.

The first time I needed to borrow money from Luca, I remembered feeling scared because I wasn't sure if he would lend it to me considering all that he had already done for me when we first moved to Sand Cove, but if I didn't get the money, I was going to lose everything.

It was a Friday night, and I had just gotten off work. One of his maids opened the door after a few seconds of me standing there sweating, praying that I wouldn't leave empty-handed. I didn't have a plan B, so Luca was going to have to come through for me.

"Good evening, Mr. Mason," she said, opening the door for me to walk in.

"Good evening. I need to talk to Luca."

"He's having dinner with his wife. I'll let him know you're here." She closed the door and walked down the hall toward the dining room.

My palms were sweaty as I wiped the perspiration that had appeared on my forehead. I could hear my heart beating loudly. I licked my dry lips and paced a little.

The maid walked toward me as she said, "He wants you to join him in the dining room."

"Thanks."

She walked past me and up the stairs.

Each step toward the dining room, I felt like I was going to pass out, but I had to pull myself together. He was either going to say yes or no, but I prayed he didn't say no. When I entered the dining room, the table was set up beautifully with candles and a red tablecloth. Luca was sitting at the head of the table, and Tahira was sitting on his left side.

"Noble, my man. What's on your mind?" he said as soon as I entered the dining room.

Tahira smiled up at me as she drank her red wine.

"Good evening, Tahira. Luca, can we talk somewhere privately?"

"Okay . . ." He examined me shortly before he said, "Tahira, can you excuse us?"

She frowned. "But we just sat down for dinner, and I'm starving. You can't go into your office?"

"Nope." He twirled his fork into his pasta and put the food into his mouth.

"I can come back after dinner," I said.

"No, you're here now." He looked at Tahira. "Pick up your fuckin' plate and eat it upstairs. Don't make me say it again."

She rolled her eyes, picked up her plate and wineglass, and left the dining room without another word.

"Close the door, Noble."

I went to the double doors and closed them behind Tahira. As I walked toward the table, he said, "Whatever it is that's bothering you must be serious. You've interrupted my romantic dinner with my wife."

"I know, and I'm so sorry, but, yes, this is very serious . . ." I paused to swallow the hard lump in my throat. "I need a huge favor."

He continued to eat. "What kind of favor?"

"A loan . . ."

"A loan?" He chewed and swallowed, observing me. "Why do you need a loan?"

"I lost a really big bet . . . and . . . I need enough money so that I won't have to put my house up for sale."

He wiped his mouth with his cloth napkin. "Are you fuckin' nuts? I warned you about that gambling shit, didn't I?"

"You did . . . But I was doing good. I usually win back what I lose, and I thought I could win it all back this time, but . . . Let's just say I fucked up."

"Noble . . . Tru is going to skin your ass alive."

"I know. That's why I can't tell her. I hate to ask you, but I don't know what else to do. My credit is fucked up as you know, so it's not like I can walk into a bank and get a loan. I know you helped me in the past, and I really didn't want to show up like this . . . but I don't have anyone else."

He thought for a moment as he cut into his medium-rare steak. "Anyone who borrows money from me knows that I don't fuck around." He pointed his steak knife at me. "You and I are friends, and I trust you, but if you fuck me over . . ."

"I would never fuck you over, Luca."

"You bet your life on it?"

I swallowed the lump that wouldn't go away again. "I swear to you, I'll pay you back every dime you give me."

"Listen, I will only agree to let you borrow the money if I get my money back, plus 30 percent interest."

"Thirty percent?" I asked, hoping I heard him wrong.

"You heard me. . . . Those are my terms."

His rate of return was too fucking high, but what other choice did I have? "Okay," I heard myself say.

"And, if you don't pay me . . . I'll tell Tru *everything*." The tone of his voice made me believe him.

I nodded. "It won't have to come to that."

"All right. How much do you need?" He got up from the table, walked over to a cabinet, and pulled out his checkbook.

Luca saved my ass that night. I owed him my life because, without him, my home, the business—everything would be gone. I had been a few months behind on payments, which was why he had been sweating me, but I was working on it. But since he died, my debt was erased.

I headed home, and Tru was working late at the office. When I drove down our street, a few reporters and vans were camping out as if they were waiting for something big to happen. I hated reporters. Since Luca was a celebrity, news outlets wanted to be the first to update the world on any conspiracy theories surrounding his death.

I pushed the button from my rearview mirror to open the garage and drove inside. When I walked into the house, the kids were running around upstairs. The thuds from their feet had become a soothing sound instead of an annoying one. Ximena was instructing them to do something in Spanish. That was the first time I heard her speaking Spanish to them. When I closed the door, she stopped talking at once as if she didn't want to be caught talking to them that way.

I hung my coat in the cloak closet next to the food pantry.

Ximena came down the stairs and entered the kitchen. "Oh, hello. Dinner is in the oven, Noble. The kids have eaten already."

I cringed at her calling me by my first name. It took everything in me not to go off on her. Luca's death was looming, and I was ready to snap at anything. Grabbing a beer out of the fridge, I loosened up my tie and walked over to the recliner. I sat, took a gulp, and closed my eyes. I tried my best to relax, but I kept thinking about Luca.

I swallowed more beer. Suddenly, two hands rubbed my shoulders, and I jumped up with my eyes popping open.

"I'm sorry to scare you. Are you okay?"

"Ximena, we need to talk."

"About what, Noble?" she asked, standing in front of me.

"First, do not call me Noble. Señor or Mr. Mason is fine. Sit down for a few minutes."

She hesitated, "I should be getting back upstairs to tend to the children."

"They'll be okay. It will only take a minute."

Ximena sat on the couch across from where I was seated. "Okay . . . What is it, Señor Mason?"

"My wife told me about the very awkward moment you two had the other night and—"

"I wouldn't say it was awkward. She wanted me to kiss her, so I did. I am attracted to your wife, and she's attracted to me."

"Are you a lesbian?"

She shook her head. "No. I'm bisexual. She assured me that this would be something you wouldn't have a problem with. Will it make you feel more comfortable if you were involved?"

I was confused. Tru made it seem as if Ximena kissed her out of nowhere. She didn't say that she and Ximena had already discussed this.

"I'm going to set the record straight right now. No matter what Tru told you, you'll never be able to have her or me sexually. A threesome is out. If you want to keep your job, I suggest you keep things professional with my wife from now on. If I find out that you're sleeping with my wife behind my back, I'll throw your ass out of here so fast, you won't have any time to explain."

"I don't understand." She stood up and approached me. "I see the way you look at me. I know you want me. I know your wife wants me." She straddled my lap and tried wrapping her arms around my neck.

"Stop!" I pushed her off.

She fell to the floor, looking at me with wide eyes.

"Pack up your shit and get out of my house. You're fired!" I got up from the recliner and headed up the stairs.

Tru didn't have to worry about Ximena anymore. I wasn't going to let her turn our household upside down. It was time to find a new nanny.

Chapter 29

Tru

It seemed like a dozen new cars were parked along our street. Luca was famous, but damn! This was out of control. Journalists and paparazzi were stalking his house as if the man hadn't died. They had no respect for his family's privacy.

I couldn't imagine what Tahira was going through. I hoped they would give her space to deal with all of this, but it wasn't going to be anytime soon. This was too much for me, and I wasn't even married to the poor bastard.

Alistair was standing in his yard, looking confused, so I stopped the car, and rolled down my window.

"Hey, Alistair."

"Hey, Tru. What's going on out here? Why are all these people here?"

"I take it you haven't been watching the news."

"No. I've been at the office since dawn, and I never watch the news. I'm just now getting home. I would've asked Alohnzo, but he isn't answering my calls."

I wished he had watched the news so I wouldn't have to be the bearer of sad news. "Luca died this morning of a heart attack."

"Aw, man, I'm sorry to hear that. How's Tahira doing?"

"She's taking it pretty hard, of course."

"I can only imagine. How are you doing?"

"I'm okay and you?"

"I'm fine. Well, thanks for letting me know. You have a good night."

"You do the same." I rolled up the window and drove down to my house.

I parked inside my garage, got out of the car, and walked inside.

Ximena met me at the door with tears flowing down her face. "Señora Mason, please talk to Señor Mason. He fired me! I don't want to lose my job. I made a serious mistake, and I'm sorry."

"Ximena? What are you talking about?"

With tears in her eyes, she came closer to me. "I really need you to talk to him, please. He fired me."

"What happened?"

"Why did you tell your husband about the other night?"

"Because he's my husband. What did he say to you?"

"You told him everything, didn't you?"

"Hell no, I didn't," I replied quickly but quietly. I didn't want Noble to hear us. I couldn't bring myself to tell him that I had sex with Ximena that night. He made such a big deal off one little kiss. I knew he would lose it if he knew it all. "I'll talk to him. Stay put. You're not going anywhere." I reached out and caressed the side of her face.

She nodded and wiped her tears.

I walked upstairs and checked on the kids first. They were sleeping in their beds in their rooms, so I went to my bedroom, and Noble was watching the news. The pained look on his face let me know that he was taking Luca's death out on Ximena.

I sighed. "Hey, babe."

"Hey," he replied gloomily.

"Did you fire Ximena?"

"I sure did. Is she still here?" he replied without hesitation.

"Why would you do that without consulting me? I thought you weren't tripping off that little kiss."

He sat up. "This isn't about that kiss! Did she tell you that she jumped in my lap and tried to get me to kiss her? This is *not* cool, Trudee. You might like this shit, but I don't. Since she can't keep things professional, she has to go!"

"Noble, you can't fire her for this! We agreed that we would talk about anything first before we decided to fire our nanny. She's one of the best things that could've ever happened to us. The kids love her, and she's great with them."

"We can always find another great nanny. I'm starting to feel like you want her around for your own reasons. Is there something else you want to tell me?"

I narrowed my eyes at him and crossed my arms over my chest. "No! I told you everything. Stop making this about what happened between her and me. Who's going to watch the kids while we're at work? We can't find another nanny tonight."

"I'll take the day off and call the other candidates we had to see if they're still looking for a job. It's not that hard. There are plenty of good nannies out in the world that will take their jobs seriously. We don't need a live-in either. We can find one that will come early and leave when we get home."

"I don't want another nanny! I want Ximena!" I yelled.

Noble looked at me with so much hurt in his eyes that it made me want to retract my words, but I wasn't going to. Ximena was the best damn nanny we ever had, and it wasn't because I was sexually attracted to her.

He got out of the bed saying, "I can't believe you! Do you see how serious I am? This is *not* a game. How many married men you know would turn down sleeping with their nanny while their wives aren't home? I can answer that! Not too many! I'm a rare breed, baby. Can't you give me credit for not wanting to cheat on you?"

We were shouting, and I didn't want to wake the children. I pulled him deeper into the bedroom toward the window and lowered my voice. "It's not cheating if I approve of it, Noble."

He stared at me with his mouth slightly agape before he said, "So, you're telling me that you wouldn't be mad if I screwed our nanny behind your back?"

"It wouldn't be behind my back because I already told her I was okay with it. I'm telling you that I'm fine with it."

"Why are you fine with it? That's the part I have trouble understanding. . . . Wait, did you do more than kiss her? Are you offering her to me because you already had her?"

It was time to come clean.

"I didn't think it would go that far, but," I said non-chalantly, "after we kissed, we went to her bedroom and kissed some more. Next thing I knew, she was going down on me . . . and I went down on her . . ."

Noble had tears coming to his eyes. "You cheated on me with our nanny, Trudee." His chest was heaving up and down. "I can't believe this shit. Just because you slept with another woman doesn't mean that it doesn't hurt the same. So, I guess everybody is going to sleep with everybody around here. Is this what Sand Cove is going to be about? What's next? You going to fuck Alistair or Alohnzo next? Should I start fucking Tahira too?"

"Don't be like that. I'm sorry you feel as if I betrayed you. It wasn't right but look at it this way . . . You and I can have the best of both worlds. You get to fuck another woman with my consent. How many husbands get that luxury?"

Noble invaded my personal space. Through clenched teeth, he said, "If you love me, you'll see to it that this will be her last couple of days. I'm putting out an ad for a new nanny. Let me leave before I say something I'll regret. I'll be at the Cigar Lounge." He stormed out of the bedroom and closed the door behind him.

I didn't see why he was so upset. He was acting like I said I was going to leave him for her. I could never leave him for her.

I sighed and plopped down on the bed. I was going to give him a few days to cool off. He was taking Luca's death hard, but after he cooled off, he wouldn't want Ximena to leave anymore. There was no way I was going to find another nanny.

Chapter 30

Kinsley

Amos wanted me to meet him at BOA Steakhouse in West Hollywood at eight o'clock sharp. I still had dinner plans with Alistair, but I told him I would call him back as soon as I got a chance. When I got to the steakhouse, Amos smiled.

Alistair and Alohnzo got their good looks from their father. I would never give Mabel any credit. She may have been cute when she was younger, but as an old woman, her evil ways made her ugly. Amos's hair was entirely white, and it made him look distinguished.

He placed his arm around my waist gently. "I really missed you, Kinsley."

I hugged him. "If it weren't for your wife, we wouldn't have had to call it quits, but I'm sure you know that."

He pulled out a chair for me to sit. "I'm going to make up for it. I ordered you your favorite Cosmo, and I have some appetizers on the way."

"Nice. What made you send me those flowers?"

"I had been thinking about you. Plus, I couldn't let my son take my favorite girl away."

"You don't have to worry about Alohnzo. He dumped me. Before we get dinner underway, is it safe to be here? Your wife is crazy, and I don't need her showing up at the office, talking crazy to me. Now, Alohnzo is suspicious, and since I'm seeing Alistair, I don't want him to find out.

No one else needs to know anything about what's going on between us. What if she decides to have Alohnzo fire me?"

"You're seeing Alistair?" Jealousy was in his eyes. "You figure if you can't have one, you'll have the other? Why don't you admit that you only want them because you can't have me?"

"Amos, none of this was my intention. Alistair came after me. I still have feelings for Alohnzo, but he wants nothing to do with me."

"I see. I don't want you to worry about Mabel. I'll make sure she doesn't bother you again."

"I don't understand her."

He took a deep breath and exhaled. "Don't worry about her. I'll handle everything."

A text came through my phone, and it was Alistair wondering what time we were going to meet up. *How am I going to wing this?* I was going to have to make dinner with Amos quick. I wanted to see Alistair because I felt horrible about my confusion with the flowers. If Amos would've put his name on it, I wouldn't have been confused.

I texted, I'll see you in an hour. Be ready.

I put the phone down and stared at Amos. His eyes bore into me as if he were trying to read my soul. He questioned, "You're seeing Alistair tonight?"

I thought about lying but decided against it. It wasn't as if Amos didn't have a wife waiting at home for him, so I didn't need to lie.

"Yes, but that has nothing to do with what we have going on."

He placed a thick envelope on the table with his hand resting on it. "If I give you this money, are you going to take it and run? I want to be assured that you will be available *anytime* I need you."

"Mr. Amos Kelly, when have I ever taken your money and run? I can promise you that you'll have me anytime you need me. How much is in here?" I tried to take the envelope off the table, but he kept his hand on it firmly.

"Now, I look at this as investing in our relationship. I need collateral."

I smirked. "And you think I come with a price?"

He chuckled. "I think you're priceless, but I plan to take care of my investment."

He cleared his throat as the waiter came and placed the appetizers and my Cosmo on the table.

"Are you ready to order?" the waiter asked.

"Give us a few more moments," he said.

The waiter walked away. Amos's hand remained on top of the envelope, so I removed my hand and picked up my drink.

"I know you're not a prostitute, but I think the money will make things easier for you. My wife can be a headache, and so can my sons. The money will make all of the trouble worthwhile—unless you want to decline the offer."

"Oh no, I'm okay. As long as Mabel doesn't find out."

"She won't find out, trust me. This time is different. I'll be more careful."

"How can you be so sure? Does she know where you are tonight?"

"She thinks I'm at the casino with a few friends. You keep me happy, and the money will keep flowing. You let me handle my wife." He slid the envelope across the table to me. He then handed me a check as well.

I took it from him and stared at it. It was written out for $1 million.

"Why is there cash in this envelope if you wrote me a check?"

"The cash is a $10,000 bonus for coming out tonight."

With a smile on my face, I said, "I'll do whatever you want whenever you want as long as it's within my limits." I put the check and the money into my purse.

"We can start tonight. I want you to follow me over to Beverly Wilshire Hotel, room 357."

I bit my lower lip. Alistair was waiting for me, and I couldn't stay with Amos past an hour. It was going to take me an hour to drive from Beverly Hills to Sand Cove. The last thing I wanted was for Amos to cancel the check because I couldn't keep my end of the deal.

"All right, but I can't stay long."

"You might as well call Alistair and tell him you won't be able to make it."

"All right," I mumbled.

"You seem anxious to see him."

I straightened up my posture and replied, "No, it's just that I thought he was the one that sent the flowers, and I feel like I need to make it up to him."

"I know you, Kinsley. You don't like casual sex. You play for keeps. If I weren't married—"

"But, you are, and I'm okay with that."

"What about Alohnzo?"

"What about him?" I fired back.

The waiter was on his way back, and I still didn't know what I wanted to eat. I picked up the menu and spotted lobster and steak. I hadn't had that in a while.

"Are you ready to order?"

"Yes, let me have the chicken fettuccine, and the lady will have . . ." Amos paused, looking at me.

"I'll have the lobster tail and steak, medium rare, please, and a loaded baked potato with extra sour cream."

He picked up our menus and walked away. Amos drank his brandy in silence while I sipped my drink, feeling happy that I had all this money in my purse. Now, if I could get things on track with Alistair, I would have myself a boyfriend. I was going to prove to everyone that I could have a real relationship. The "whore" image they were trying to toss me had me feeling unsettled. I wasn't sure if this would work, but it was worth a try.

Suddenly, I felt Amos's hand travel up my thigh, reminding me that tonight, I was his *investment*. Alistair was going to have to wait.

"That check can be canceled before you can get it in the bank if you don't do what I say. No more Alistair. No more Alohnzo. You hear me?" His hand dug into my thigh, and it hurt.

"Ouch, that hurts, Amos."

Amos had been rough with me once when I said I would tell his wife about us. I had to apply makeup to hide the bruise on my cheek. His powerful hand made me quickly remember who I was dealing with. Amos was going to get his way, and I needed to follow his rules.

He dug deeper. "Do you *hear* me?"

"Yes, I hear you."

"Do you understand me?"

With tears in my eyes, I replied, "I understand."

He released my thigh and drank his brandy as if nothing happened. I had gotten myself back into Amos's trap.

Chapter 31

Tahira

Talking to Luca's family all evening about what they wanted to do with his body left me exhausted. They wanted to know what was written in his will, but I had no idea because Luca kept that from me, and I assured them that there would be a reading of the will after we buried him. I ended the last call and stared at the side of Alohnzo's face as he watched HGTV. He loved that network. I lay next to him on his bed. His bed was so soft that I never wanted to leave it. Being with Alohnzo made me feel complete.

He caught me staring and asked, "How are you feeling?"

"I can't wait 'til this all passes. I gotta deal with lawyers, Luca's family, and I'm not looking forward to the will reading. I'm sure he didn't leave anyone anything."

He lifted my chin. "Hey, you shouldn't worry about that right now. You'll be fine. You have enough stress as it is."

His eyes were filled with kindness that seemed so innocent and genuine, endless as wide as the sea. He made me happy. I wrapped my arms around him and held him close.

My cell phone rang. "It's my mum." I answered, "Hello, Mum."

"Tah, I'm boarding my flight now."

"Okay. What time is your flight expected to come in?"

"I have one layover, so around noon tomorrow. If there are any delays, I'll be sure to let you know."

"Okay. I love you."

"I love you too." She kissed the phone.

I kissed the phone and ended the call. I bit on my fingernail and stared up at the ceiling. I hadn't seen my mum in a few years. I missed her so much. I hated that she had to come at a time like this, but I was glad that she wanted to be here for me.

Alohnzo cuddled up next to me. "Are you going to swim tonight?"

"It's cool outside tonight. . . . I don't know . . ."

He put wet, sensual kisses on my neck before resting his head there. I ran my fingers across his head. I couldn't help but get lost in his world. Being with Alohnzo put my problems to the very back of my mind. I never met anyone like him. If he was afraid of commitment, I had a tough time seeing that. With me, it was as if all his reservations went out of the window. He was flying free, the way he did when he flew his plane.

"I'll come out and watch if you do," he replied with a naughty grin.

I laughed, reflecting on all the times he watched me from his deck. "There's no need to watch. Skinny dip with me in your heated pool."

His eyebrows rose. "Now, *that's* an idea."

"Luca never wanted to do anything spontaneous like this."

Alohnzo took off his shirt and threw it down on the ground. "I'm not Luca."

"That's for sure." I giggled and tossed off my shirt in the same manner. Within seconds, we were naked, dashing to his heated pool.

Chapter 32

Kinsley

"Glad to see that you finally made it," Alistair said as he held his front door open for me. "I was starting to get worried."

I wasn't there on a happy note. I promised Amos that I would end things with Alistair. It was the only way to keep Amos from physically hurting me out of jealousy. After giving Amos the kinky sex he wanted, I told him I would only come to let Alistair know that I wasn't interested in him anymore. Amos had a hard time keeping up with my youthful energy anyway, so it was over faster than I thought it would be. I washed up and rushed over to Alistair's house.

"Hello," I said, stepping inside of his home with a bag of leftover food from the restaurant. "I'm sorry I'm late, and I'm sorry I didn't call you to keep you updated. I had a business meeting over dinner, and it wound up running too long. I didn't want to be rude and keep texting on my phone, you know."

He eyed me with a look of suspicion as he took my coat and hung it up for me. Since he didn't know me very well, he had to trust my words.

"It's all right. I told you that I would wait up for you."

"I'm happy you did because I wanted to see you."

"I've been thinking about you all day."

I smiled and touched the side of his face with the palm of my hand. "Same here."

"You find out who sent the flowers?"

I removed my hand and brought it down to my side. Why was he bringing up the flowers? He must've been thinking about that all day too.

"Yeah, um, in fact, it turns out that I was selected for Employee Appreciation Day," I lied smoothly. "I got too excited, thinking about how romantic you had been all weekend that I assumed it was you," I giggled.

I couldn't believe how quickly I came up with that one. I was very quick on my feet, so much that I even impressed myself.

He licked his lips before answering. "Cool. I figured you ate already, so I didn't make any dinner plans or anything for us. I went to this taqueria with a few coworkers, drank some Dos Equis, and came home. What's in the bag?"

"I brought you some tiramisu." I held up the restaurant bag that had two pieces inside along with my leftovers.

"You brought some for me? You're too sweet. Let's go to the kitchen."

I followed him as my nervousness consumed me. My hands were starting to shake, and I could feel sweat forming between my breasts. It felt hot in his house.

"The craziest thing happened earlier," he said. "Did you hear about what happened over here today?"

"Over here?" I frowned. "No, what happened?"

"You know who Luca Moretti is, right? You didn't hear about what happened to him?" He grabbed two forks out of the drawer.

I stood at his kitchen island. Of course, I knew who Luca was. He was the arrogant asshole who thought his films were the best in the world. He won one Oscar and thought he was so much better than everyone else was. The way his old ass paraded around with that bitch of his made me want to puke. The fact that Alohnzo thought she was some goddess made me even sicker.

"No, what happened to him?"

"He died this morning. The street was filled with news reporters and everything. I'm glad things have died down now, but I'm sure they'll be right back tomorrow to do some digging."

I was instantly annoyed, but I didn't want Alistair to pick up on it. "She probably killed him," I said.

"I thought maybe Alohnzo killed him to have Tahira to himself, but Tru said he died of a heart attack."

I rolled my eyes. Just the thought of Alohnzo and Tahira fooling around made my stomach hurt. "Not to change subjects or anything but the best thing about BOA is their tiramisu. I promise you, it's the best you'll ever have. That's why I brought you some. I didn't bother to ask if you like tiramisu."

"I like it. I've never been to BOA, but it's one of my father's favorite restaurants. He's constantly bragging about it. I'll have to check them out sometime. Maybe we can go together."

His father was a trip, and I had gotten myself wrapped up in his sticky web once again. I should've tossed the flowers and told him I wanted nothing to do with him, but I was afraid that he would ask Alohnzo to fire me. I had to remind myself that I was here to end things, but I wanted to eat this dessert first.

I took the dessert out of the bag and handed him one. "Here you go."

He opened the container and put his fork to the dessert. Then he took a bite and started nodding. "I think you might be right. This may be the best damn tiramisu I've ever had."

"I told you." I opened my container and started eating it. I hummed and closed my eyes. "The best."

Alistair eyed me. I wondered what he was staring at as he looked at my hair, my clothes, and the way I ate the dessert. "Who were you in a meeting with tonight?"

Alistair didn't come off as the insecure type, but he sure was trying to figure me out. If he were anything like Amos, this conversation wasn't going to end well. I wished he would leave me alone and eat his dessert.

"I had dinner with an associate."

His eyes glanced at me again. "An associate?"

"Yes."

"You sure it wasn't Alohnzo that sent you the flowers and took you out to dinner?"

I laughed casually at his crazy, jealous assumption. "I promise you it wasn't Alohnzo."

"If it wasn't Alohnzo, then who?"

There was no stopping this man. He wasn't satisfied with any of my answers because he was insecure as all men were.

"It was a simple dinner meeting with a *woman,* and that's it. Don't tell me you're the jealous type?"

"No, I'm far from the jealous type. One thing about me is that I'm observant. So, you've had your dress inside out all day?"

I looked down, and he was right. I had correctly managed to put on all of my clothing including my panties and bra and straighten out my hair. I was in such a rush, however, that I didn't notice that I had my dress inside out. Go figure.

"You mean, I've gone all day with my dress inside out, and *no one* bothered to tell me? That's rude." I laughed it off while continuing to eat my dessert.

He blinked as if he couldn't believe me. "Look, Kinsley, I don't want to start out this way. I hate liars. I don't want you to feel like you must lie to me. If you can't be honest with me, then there's no point in doing any of this. The one thing I can't stand is a liar." The sternness of his face reminded me of Pablo Escobar on that show *Narcos*.

I swallowed hard but kept up with my story. "I wouldn't lie to you."

He hummed, closed his dessert box, and said, "I think you should leave now."

I scowled. "Are you serious?"

"Very. Do me a favor. Go ahead and lose my number. I don't have time to play games with you. I thought you would at least be honest, but you've been lying to me all day. I'm not sure if this is how you usually deal with people, but I can always tell when people aren't honest with me. Frankly, at this point, I don't care who sent you flowers, and I don't care who you were fucking before you finally decided to show up."

I couldn't believe what was happening. *I* was supposed to be the one to end it, but he was stopping it before I could get a chance.

"Fine, have it your way." I grabbed my dessert and stormed toward the front door.

He handed me my coat, and I trotted out his door and down the steps. Shit, I thought I did a damn decent job at coming up with a few good lies. *Was I that obvious?* I thought I covered my tracks. *So much for that,* I thought.

Alistair and I were over, and now I could cash Amos's check. With Amos's tight grip on my life, I was going to have to do everything he wanted me to do. I swallowed the hard lump in my throat, feeling upset with myself because I had no control.

Before I could get into my car, I heard two voices laughing, coming from Alohnzo's house. I knew that laugh anywhere. I walked over to the fence that separated Alistair's house from Alohnzo's. I couldn't see anything, but I could hear their laughter. My curiosity wouldn't let me leave without understanding what was going on.

I climbed the six-foot fence and hopped over. There was a light post on the side of his house that hung over the side of his deck. I wrapped my arms and legs around it and climbed it the way I had done the ropes hanging from the ceiling at the gym. I held myself up, and I could see Alohnzo and Tahira. My mouth slightly parted open, and I felt this twinge of jealousy once I saw that they were both completely naked.

My breath caught in my throat. This bitch couldn't wait to get her hands on the man I wanted when her husband hadn't even been dead for twenty-four hours.

They kissed as though they had kissed a dozen times before.

I wanted to scream to let them know that I could see them, but then what?

Suddenly, an idea hit me. I wondered how the tabloids would feel about her romping around naked not even twenty-four hours after her husband's heart attack. Clinging to the pole, I managed to take my phone out of my purse. I zoomed in on them and took a few photos. I looked at my evidence to make sure the pictures came out clear before climbing down. Then I hopped back over the fence and got into my car parked in Alistair's driveway.

I looked at the pictures again to make sure I had what I needed. Since Tahira took Alohnzo from me, I was going to do everything in my power to make sure I ruined her life. I could sell the pictures for a high price, and in no time, they would be on the cover of tabloid magazines.

She wouldn't be the cute little actress they all had grown to love, but the coldhearted bitch she really was. Alohnzo's squeaky-clean image would also be ruined, but I didn't care. He picked her over me! I couldn't help but laugh at the thought of Mabel's face when she saw her son plastered on grocery store gossip magazines.

Chapter 33

Noble

I went to my regular spot at the Malibu Cigar Lounge on Pacific Coast Highway. This time, things were different. I was there without Luca. I liked smoking cigars from time to time, but over the year, Luca had come here without me because I promised Tru I wouldn't smoke cigars anymore. She hated the smell of them. Being here reminded me of him, so I was unsure how long I would be able to stay. Tru had me so stressed out, smoking was the only thing I could think of to calm myself down.

The place wasn't pretentious by any means. The lounge was sophisticated with a laid-back environment and an excellent view of the ocean to enjoy a great smoke of the best cigars in the world and a beautiful grade of brandy to go along with it.

I started looking at some football stats online from my phone to see if I wanted to bet on another team. I hoped I would get lucky enough to win big. With Luca dead, I didn't have to worry about paying him back, so *that* was a weight lifted from me, but then again, if I got in too deep, I had no one to save me.

I checked our account balance before placing a bet. Our savings were low. I checked our business account. I hated borrowing money from that account, but it was my last resort.

Luca never checked his bank balance or moaned about money problems. He knew how to invest and stack. Money didn't matter to him; it never did. I wanted to be just like him. Gambling had ruined me.

When I was younger, money meant food. Then, later, it was a house and a family, but after our business effectively exploded, I became wealthier than any lottery winner. Numbers with many zeros filled my bank accounts. With gambling eating away at everything I worked so hard to build, I was nearly broke. I was descending the rich list, and if I didn't find a way to get it back, I was going to have to tell Tru that I lost the money in bad investments.

Hours had gone by, and I wasn't ready to go home, but I needed to.

It was a little after one in the morning when I paid my tab and left a hefty tip. I still had to go to work in the morning, and if I didn't go home, it was going to be hard for me to get up. I gulped the last of the brandy and headed out of the lounge.

The alarm from my phone woke me up. It was 6:00 a.m. and time to get ready for work. I looked around and realized I had slept in the guest room. My head throbbed. I squinted, and my dry mouth had thick saliva. I wasn't used to drinking and smoking like that anymore, and I felt every bit of it. I moaned before getting out of the bed. I went to the kitchen and poured ice-cold water from the refrigerator into a cup. As the icy water quenched my parched throat, I closed my eyes. The aching in my skull ebbed and flowed like a cold tide, yet the hangover was still there. I understood why they called it a hangover. It felt like the blackest clouds were over my head with no intention of clearing up until late afternoon.

I finished the water and went up to the master bedroom to see if Tru was getting ready for work. I was sure she hit snooze on the alarm as she always did to get a few more minutes. Just as I thought, she was in a deep sleep with the comforter wrapped tightly around her. I got into the bed and wrapped my arms around her.

She groaned.

Kissing her neck and then her cheek repeatedly, I rubbed her breasts through her ivory satin gown and played with her nipples until they were hard.

After yawning and stretching, she moved my hands away. "I'm not in the mood this morning, especially after the way you left last night. You didn't even bother to come to bed, Noble. What time did you come in last night anyway? Where'd you sleep? The guest room?" she bombarded me with questions, and my head was throbbing.

I didn't respond as I gazed into her mahogany brown eyes.

"You're not going to tell me?" she asked.

"I slept in the guest room. I got here around 1:30 this morning. What's up? You not going to give me some this morning? I think we can squeeze in a quickie."

She rolled her eyes at me.

"You mad at me for firing Ximena?"

"Why do you smell like smoke? You better not have been smoking cigars. You know I hate that smell."

"I went to the lounge last night because I was stressed out. I'm going to wash it all off me. Can I get my morning fix after that?"

Silence met us as she continued to glare at me.

I raised my eyebrows, feeling confused. "Tru, why are you mad? I'm not mad anymore."

"I'm not mad. I'm irritated."

"Why?"

"Go get in the shower, and then we'll talk about it." She turned completely away and tossed the covers over her head.

I gently pulled the covers off her and said, "Come shower with me."

Groaning again, she sat up. "I showered last night. Something you should've done before getting into my bed. Now, I have to wash the covers."

"Blah blah blah. Come shower with me, Tru. Don't act like that."

She smiled a little. No matter how mad she was at me for firing her precious Ximena, she couldn't stay upset.

I got up from the bed and stripped out of my clothes. I was naked, waiting for her to get undressed too. While she got out of bed, I went into the bathroom to get the shower ready. When it was steamy, I got in.

"Trudee, you better be in here in the next two seconds."

The shower door opened, and she stepped in. "I swear you're the most impatient man on this earth."

My hands traveled to her ass, and I palmed it. "Quit your complaining, woman. You know you love me."

"I do love you, Noble. I don't want us to bicker and fight. I don't like going to bed upset with you. You know I like it when you palm my ass like that."

"I know what turns you on. I'm your husband, and I know you better than *anyone*."

No man and no woman could touch her and make her feel the way I did. Ximena might have aroused her, but she couldn't hold a torch to me.

"Kiss me," she demanded.

I planted one on her pillowlike lips. Her moan filled the bathroom as I backed her up against the black-tiled wall. With her wet hands around my neck, she indulged in my kisses. I lifted both her legs to wrap around my waist. The hot water gushed over us as I eased inside of her. I placed my hands on the wall to secure her, then thrust into her and rocked back and forth inside.

Whispering against her lips, I said, "I forgive you. Make sure that was the last and only time, or else next time, I won't be so forgiving."

I watched her face twist in ecstasy as she closed her eyes tightly and bit down on her lower lip. Moving slowly and deeply, I made sure she could feel me. No woman could do that. I had nine inches of thickness that could go places a dildo couldn't.

"Ooooh . . . ahh," she exhaled loudly.

"Promise me that you'll find a new nanny."

"Okay, I'll find a new . . . nanny."

"Say it like you mean it." I thrust harder.

"Yes! I mean it!"

"Do you love me?"

"Yes, I love you!"

I pleased my wife, and she pleased me until we both had an orgasm. For the first time ever, I allowed myself to be late to work.

Chapter 34

Tru

I couldn't get dressed fast enough. Noble was late to work, and he cursed until he left. He headed to work without me, which was fine because I decided to take the day off anyway. I needed it. I couldn't remember the last time I took a day to do something for myself. Being a wife, mother, and businesswoman had consumed most of my life. Every now and then, it was okay to take a break.

After putting on a pair of pink Juicy Couture sweats, I went down to the kitchen to have breakfast with my kids.

Noelle and little Noble were sitting in their booster seats at the table having breakfast with Ximena.

"You not working today?" she asked.

"No, I decided to take the day off."

"Did you get to talk to Señor Mason?"

"I did." I was hoping she wouldn't ask me any questions or details about what was said.

"And what did he say? Do I still have to leave?"

I went to the refrigerator to grab the carafe of orange juice. "He won't change his mind. This will be your last week. We're looking for a new nanny. If we find one before the week, then you will have to leave sooner."

She sobbed, putting her face into her hands. This was what I didn't want to have to deal with. I hated that I put her in this situation, so I went over and put my hand on her back.

"Please, don't cry. I'll help you find another family and give a friendly recommendation. I'll even make sure that you leave with sufficient funds so that you won't have to worry if you're not hired right away. I'll even get you a nice apartment and pay the rent until you are stable enough."

"Does this mean that you won't be seeing me anymore?" she asked.

I was afraid that she was going to want to see me again, and I intended to do so until Noble ruined my little party. What we did that night after the bonfire was so hot. It was something I had been curious about since I was a teenager. She fulfilled a fantasy, but now I feared she had sparked something in me. This wasn't out of my system. I wanted to be with her again, but Noble meant more to me.

I resisted. "Look, the best I can offer is money. We won't be able to see each other again in that way, but with some money and a new job, you'll be fine."

"I thought you liked me."

"I do, but this isn't right. I love my husband too much to make him feel inadequate."

"You weren't thinking about your husband that night."

"I really think I was caught up in the moment. It was fun while it lasted, right? I mean, come on, I want to keep my marriage intact."

She tilted her head to the side. "You know you don't want to stop seeing me."

"I don't, but it's for the best." I looked at how happy and well-mannered the kids had been since having Ximena around. I was going to miss her in many ways. "I honestly didn't think that he would've turned you down," I said. "Noble looks at other women all the time, and I heard what he said about you to our neighbors. I thought this was something that he wanted."

"He's selfish. He wants you all to himself. I feel so stupid."

"What is there to feel stupid about? Noble's ego is bruised; that's all. He feels like I cheated on him, and in a way, I did. I had to own up to that and apologize."

"He could have more pleasure too. I want to please both of you." She touched the top of my hand.

"Relax. I'm sorry things didn't work out the way we both planned. I'll make sure you're taken care of, though. Right now, I have to put out an ad."

"What if you don't find another nanny? These kids need me."

I exhaled through my nose. "You really want to stay, Ximena?"

"I want to stay. I love working for you, and your kids, I've grown to care for them."

"Will you be able to keep it professional?"

"Of course, I can. We can forget that this ever happened." She backed away from me. "Another family may not be as nice as you are."

I nodded. "Okay, let me work on Noble and see what I can do."

She smiled and wiped her tears. "Would you like some breakfast?"

"Yes, please. It smells too good for me to say no." I took my juice and sat at the table with my kids.

Noble wasn't going to change his mind. He was a stubborn man, but I had to say something to get her to calm down. In my heart, I retracted the incident, and I wished I never went there. If Noble had done this to me, I could never forgive him. I was hoping this wouldn't change our marriage. Noble mattered too much to me.

Chapter 35

Alohnzo

I had to be at work in an hour. I rolled over in bed and saw that Tahira wasn't lying next to me. Right when I thought that she might have been in the bathroom, she walked in with a tray of food. A huge grin spread across my face as I sat up.

"Breakfast in bed?"

She placed the tray on my lap. "Yes, breakfast fit for my king. I love how you have your kitchen set up. Everything is so easy to find. You're so organized."

"I try to be. This looks great. You eat already?"

She gave me a quick peck on the lips. "No. Mine is downstairs. I'm going to get it."

Before she could walk out of my room, I said, "Luca truly didn't know what he had."

She didn't appear to be sad when I mentioned his name. "I'm glad the bastard is dead."

I thought I was the only one feeling relief, but her words were ice cold. "Well . . . I wouldn't say it quite like that."

"Well, it's the truth. He made my life a living hell. . . . I'm going to grab my plate. I'll be right back."

I cut the French toast and put a piece into my mouth.

She came back with her food on a tray, got comfortable on the bed, and said, "We should hang out after you get off work. I want you to meet my mum. What do you think?"

"Sounds like a plan to me."

"Is it okay if I bring her here?"

"That's fine with me. Matter of fact, if she wants, she can stay in the guest room if she doesn't want to stay at a hotel."

"She booked a room, but I'll run it by her."

We finished breakfast; then she took the tray downstairs. I eased out of bed to take a shower. While I washed, I wondered if Tahira was in shock about Luca's death. She seemed to feel at peace with it, and it was odd, but I understood why she would feel free.

When I got out of the shower, Tahira was on the phone talking. I didn't know with whom she was talking, but she was confirming that Luca wanted to be cremated.

Tahira sighed heavily as she ended the call. "God, these people! I can't wait for all of this to be over so I can go on with my life. I bet if it were me who died, Luca wouldn't give a bloody rat's ass what happened to me."

I went to the drawer to get my underwear. "You don't know that. You were madly in love with him once."

"I was . . . once upon a time." She paused before she asked, "What time will you be off work today?"

"Five."

"Okay, I'm not sure if we'll be here when you get off. My mum has only been to the United States once, and that was on my wedding day. We'll be out most of the day, sightseeing."

"Okay, no problem." I kissed her before going into the walk-in closet to find a suit to wear.

"That was Luca's oldest daughter on the phone. She wanted to make sure that I was going to meet up with her to discuss his funeral sometime this week," she grumbled.

"How do you feel about that?"

"I don't want to deal with it. I wish that one of his daughters would take over, but as his wife, this is what I signed up for."

"I can't imagine what that feels like. I just want you to know that if you ever need some time to grieve or cry, you can take all the time you need."

"You know, I got to thinking. Why would I shed so many tears for a man who treated me like a dog? I was nothing more than an object, a decoration he had on his arm to make himself look good. He belittled me, made me feel bad about myself, and didn't respect me. I feel free now. He never loved me. Luca is better off dead."

I rubbed the back of my neck. "Look, I get it. Luca did and said some heartless things, but I don't want you to feel this way. I want you to try to remember all the good things you two shared. Can you do that for me?"

She looked at me, her black eyes drilling into mine. As her eyes became a bottomless pool of darkness, wickedness swam in them.

Chapter 36

Mabel Kelly

The first time I suspected Amos of sleeping with Kinsley was the first time I met her. My intuition told me that he found this gutter rat elsewhere. Though his mouth said she was an educated young lady who had goals of being a financial advisor one day, I knew he was lying through his teeth.

It wasn't hard to tell that he hired her based on her looks. My husband had a bad habit of fucking the help. I was devastated after I had a private investigator bring pictures and audio recordings of his conversations. Kinsley was affair number three. I had managed to get rid of every woman he touched except for her. What was it about her that he couldn't let go of?

Kinsley was an opportunist. There was nothing anyone could tell me to change my mind about that. What kind of woman slept with someone's husband—and then his two sons? A whore who was looking for a payday, that's who, and my husband and sons put themselves in a position where she could walk away with everything we worked so hard to have.

My husband prowled and pounced on young women who thought that fucking their way to the top was what would work best for them. Amos and his whores would be the death of me; I felt it in my bones. I had too much pride to lose him to the likes of Kinsley Smallwood, or any other woman, for that matter.

Kinsley had lied about her whole life. She wasn't from Baldwin Hills as she so proudly claimed. She was born and raised in Compton but then moved to Ladera Heights when she was a teenager because her mother died of a heroin overdose. Why lie about it? I investigated everything there was to know about her. Before she started working for the company as my husband's personal assistant, she had nothing. My husband paid for her education and gave her a life she could only dream of.

I wanted him to fire her since the day he hired her, but he clearly didn't do that. He just moved her to work for Alohnzo. My baby! My pride and joy! Amos was so full of himself that he didn't consider that his whore would fuck his son the way she had fucked him. She was only doing what she did best—lie on her back. He couldn't stand to lose to his son in this game he started, and I knew it would be only a matter of time before he would try to get her back under his control. I knew him better than he knew himself. She had been a weak spot for him because he cared for her for whatever reason.

I would be damned if she thought she could get rich off us, so I hired a private investigator to have her followed for some time. It was expensive, but it was worth it. Every man she ever slept with, I knew about. It crushed me to know that Alistair had been added to her list, but my sons were weak like their father. Kinsley had worked her way into my family, but I wasn't going to let her get away with it.

As soon as Amos walked into the house after leaving the sleazy hotel, I was sitting in the foyer, waiting for him.

"As much as I told you to stay away from the whore, you just couldn't, could you?" I asked, turning on the light.

He blinked at me in disbelief but then scowled. "Mabel, go to bed."

"I'm not going to bed with you! You smell like the cheap bitch. I think you should know that she's been with both of our sons, Amos. You promised to get rid of her—and what did you do? Pawn her off on Alohnzo. What kind of hold does that bitch have on you?"

"Mabel . . ." He paused but then walked up the stairs.

"Don't you dare, Amos! Don't you think you're about to lie in our bed next to me after you fucked her! I hope you know that tomorrow, I'm firing her my damned self—since you're not man enough to do it!"

"I'll sleep in the guest room," he replied, taking his suit jacket off.

As he calmly walked into the guest room and closed the door, I barged into the room, glaring at him with both hands on my hips.

I was so sick of this bitch. She was like cancer spreading and killing my entire family. I couldn't cry anymore, not when I was all cried out. My heart was already too cold.

"You listen to me, you trifling son of a bitch! This is the reason you have a secret bank account, isn't it? You'd rather squander your money on worthless whores. Every dime you gave her tonight, it better be your last or I will take *everything* you have! You hear me?"

He sat on the bed and took a deep breath. "Mabel, why do you feel the need to make threats to me?"

"You leave me no other choice."

He thought about it before he said, "Well, if you feel the need to fire her, do it."

I rolled my eyes and stormed out of the room. I was going to go down to the office first thing in the morning to fire her myself.

Chapter 37

Kinsley

I couldn't wait for the bank to open fast enough so I could deposit Amos's check. Since I was already late for work, I thought about packing up my things and getting on a flight out of the country. I didn't want to be trapped under his dumb rules, and I didn't want to be abused or mistreated any longer. Amos wanted things his way, and I had to play by his rules if I wanted to spend his money. I felt like crying because I had made a mess out of my life. I should've never stayed at Amos Kelly Advisors for ten years. I should've left a long time ago.

I really wanted to go to Jamaica for a vacation, so I was leaning on going there until I figured out where I was going to live. I went to work after I left the bank to see if I could execute a plan. I had more than enough money saved now. Amos's check for $1 million was a nice cherry on top of what I already had, but it wasn't like I would starve without it. I was paid well working for them.

I closed the door to my office as soon as I was there. I didn't want to be bothered. I should've stayed home. I logged into my computer and started looking at places I could vacation. Jamaica. Africa. Thailand. Dubai. China. Korea. India. I knew nothing about third world countries, but I wanted a fresh start. I desperately needed to make a change. I couldn't be Amos's mistress forever. No matter what he wanted, it was time for me to make my own decisions.

Suddenly, I thought about the pictures I took. I hadn't sent them off, so I looked up the contact information to TMZ through my phone. I clicked on their email link and inquired about how much they would pay for these pictures.

A series of hard knocks on my office door had me looking up from my phone. The office door flung open. When I saw who was standing there glaring at me as if I were the scum-sucking bottom-feeder, scavenging on the ocean floor, I felt my blood curdle.

"What the hell?" I fussed.

Mabel had walked in as if I had said it was okay. Amos assured me that I wouldn't have any more issues with this woman. Yet again, this crazy bitch was walking into my office as if she had the god-given right to do so.

"What are you doing here?" I barked, standing up.

She pointed at me with her stiff, crooked finger. "Didn't I tell you to stay away from my family?" She slammed down pictures on my desk of me with Amos at BOA last night and some more of me coming out of Alistair's home. "You don't listen! I thought I made myself clear! First, you wanted my husband, then Alohnzo, and now Alistair! You disgust me!"

I said with a smug grin, "You hired a private investigator. Good for you."

"How much did my husband give you this time?"

Shaking my head quickly, I replied, "Why don't you ask him instead? He's *your* husband, Mabel. He just pays me to have sex with him."

She came around to my side of the desk. I tried to back up, but this old lady was fast. With both of her hands on my shoulders, she shook me. "Give me the check!"

"It's in my account. Take your hands off me!"

I didn't want to push this elderly woman, but I had to. She was stronger than I thought. I tried to push her, but she wasn't budging.

"Looks like someone ate their Wheaties this morning," I smirked.

Her eyes were wild and filled with rage. Her fingers were digging into my skin.

"You're fired!" Mabel screamed. "Stay away from my family!"

I could see Alohnzo out of the corner of my eye coming into my office. It seemed as if everyone was coming to see what all the screaming was about. Now, everyone could see how crazy his mother was. I hoped someone called security.

"Let me go!" I screamed to see if Alohnzo would get her off me.

Alohnzo said, "Mama, stop this."

Alistair barged in next and grabbed her. "Mother, let her go!"

Mabel released me and snatched the pictures from my desk. She threw them at Alohnzo and Alistair. "Look at these! Look at them!"

"What's this?" Alistair asked with a troubled frown taking over his handsome face.

I lowered my head and held my breath to wait for his response. I knew I should've called in sick. I wished there was a back door I could run out of, but there was no way out of this. Now everyone was about to know the truth.

"Your father and little Miss Trashy, here, had dinner last night and fucked in some trash hotel right before she came to see you. He's been paying her to have sex with him for years just in case you didn't know. I should've told you two sooner, but he begged me to keep this a secret. If I would've known she would come after you two, I would've at least warned you."

"I don't understand," Alistair scowled.

"Son, wake up! She's a prostitute. Why else would your father give her all this money? You think she got a job here because she's smart? He picked her up off the street and gave her a job because he wanted his whore close to him."

"I'm not a prostitute, and that's not what happened. You're nuts."

Alistair gave the pictures back to his mother after studying them. Alohnzo refused to look at them, and he didn't look at me.

"What part is true, Kinsley?" Alistair asked.

"None of it," I lied. "I went to Amos to help me out. We do not have a sexual relationship. He gave me money because I'm in a bit of a bind. It's a loan. He was kind enough to help me out. Your mother is a nutcase. She has no right storming in here, pushing me around because she's paranoid."

"Have you talked to Pop?" Alistair asked Mabel.

"Your father will lie like he always does. Fire her, Alohnzo! Why was she coming out of your house last night, Alistair?" Mabel took another picture from the desk and shoved it into Alistair's chest. "I don't know why the men in my life are so weak! What is it about her that you all can't stay away from?"

Alistair didn't know how to respond. He was still confused by everything.

Alohnzo blew air from his lips and said lowly, "We can't talk about this here. Everyone is watching. Mother, go home. Alistair and I will meet you there."

She shook her head vigorously. "No! This is a family issue! If you all would've kept your dicks in your pants, I wouldn't have to do this. She's nothing but a gutter rat, and you let her in."

"Alohnzo, her accusations hold no weight," I said. "You and I already talked about this. Everything she says is a lie." I was going to take this lie to the grave with me.

"Truth be told, I should've never gotten involved with you. You fucked my brother to get back at me and confessed. I should've known you were lying when I asked you about my dad because all you do is lie."

I stared at him with hurt in my eyes. "So, you're going to believe her over me?"

"You're fired," Alohnzo said firmly. "You have no place here."

Tears threatened to well in my eyes. I wasn't going to give Mabel the satisfaction of seeing me cry. "This sick woman hired someone to follow me when it's her own husband who clearly has infidelity issues. I'm not the first woman, and I sure won't be the last. Instead of taking up her issues with him, she decides to come down here, harass me, and then have me fired. Ask her how many other women Amos has paid to lie with him?"

"Shut up!" Mabel shouted. "Get out now!" She tried to dive at me, but Alistair held her firmly.

"Mother, calm down. Go home, please. Everyone is staring at us. Let's not make this any worse than it already is," Alistair said.

"I'll leave but not before I say this. If you don't stop seeing my husband, whore, I'll be forced to do something I don't want to do to you! I know where you live!"

I rolled my eyes. She didn't have to threaten to come to my house. I was leaving town with my money.

Security walked into the room. Whoever called security wasted their time.

I snatched my purse and walked out of the office with my head held high. Security followed behind me as if I were going to put up a fight. It was a good thing I took those pictures of Alohnzo and Tahira. Soon, they would be all over social media. The world was about to meet the real Alohnzo Kelly, and Mabel was going to lose the rest of her mind. The Kelly family wasn't going to get the best of me. I couldn't have been happier to be leaving.

Chapter 38

Tahira

"Mum," I said as she walked toward me with her luggage.

We hugged in the middle of the airport. With a quick kiss on my cheek, she said, "Tah, you look so good. I was expecting to see you in bad shape, but you look so good."

"Thank you. So do you."

My mum's skin was the color of toffee, and her eyes were medium brown. She had understated beauty. She was so disarmingly unaware of how beautiful she was. Her skin was utterly flawless. She didn't have to use face masks or expensive products as I did. She was all about simplicity. She made everything she did look easy. When she smiled, everyone laughed because they couldn't help it. I always felt as if I had been warmed by summer rays no matter the season whenever she was around.

"How are you doing?" she asked. "This can't be easy, baby."

"I'm okay, Mum. I'm taking it one day at a time. My neighbors have been there for me. I can't wait to introduce you to them. They're magnificent people, not to mention, the beach is breathtaking."

"I can't wait to meet them and get my feet in the sand. So, tell me more about Alohnzo. I feel like you're hiding something from me . . ."

"Well, Mum, you know I can't hide anything from you. I'm in love with him."

"I can tell. I always said not to settle for less when it comes to love."

"I know, and I felt like that was what I was doing with Luca—just settling."

"You shouldn't be afraid to leave your comfort zone to be with someone who could be better for you. You need to accept the love that you deserve. I know Luca's sudden passing is unfortunate, but I also know how he treated you."

"So, you don't think it's crazy to be with Alohnzo at this time, especially with Luca just dying?"

"Luca wasn't kind and loving to you. Truthfully, your marriage was over a long time ago. It's unfortunate that he's no longer here, but you can't be upset at destiny."

I hugged her, and we got out of the airport. On the way to the house, we talked. Her life had been busy with her new hobby in ceramics and a potentially new boyfriend.

"Mum, I want you to tell me more about your boyfriend."

"Well, George is his name. He comes to the house and tinkers around with mechanical stuff. I like him. I haven't been with anyone since your daddy passed."

"I know. I'm happy you're dating again, Mum. I really am."

She giggled like a little girl being given a lollipop.

Once inside of Alohnzo's house, I gave her a tour. I showed her the guest room, where she would be sleeping since she agreed to stay here. She loved everything about the beach house. She couldn't wait to get into her bathing suit and go out for a swim.

"We'll go out there in a bit, Mum. Do you want anything to drink?"

"Yes, I'd like sparkling water, if you have it."

"Alohnzo has the raspberry flavor," I said with a smile.

I went into the refrigerator and took two bottles out. I handed her one. While we drank, we laughed about old times when I was in London. I missed being home, but only to visit. Sand Cove was the only place I wanted to be.

My phone rang. I huffed and rolled my eyes, praying it wasn't someone else calling to talk about Luca, but I relaxed to see that it was Tru.

"One second, Mum, I gotta take this call."

"No problem, I'll go get into my bathing suit." She walked upstairs to the spare bedroom.

"Hello," I answered.

"Tahira, where are you?" she asked, sounding as if she were panicking.

"At Alohnzo's. Why? What's wrong? Why do you sound like that?"

"I'm on my way over there right now."

"Okay . . . My mum is here. I want you to meet her."

"Okay," she said and then hesitated before she continued, "I'm not sure if you want me to discuss this in front of her."

"Tru, you're scaring me. What's going on?"

"Open the door." She hung up.

I unlocked the front door and peeked out of the side window to see vans pulling up.

Oh, bloody hell! The reporters are back again.

I wondered if this had anything to do with what Tru had to talk about. Tru was coming up the steps. As soon as I opened the door, reporters started swarming the yard, calling my name.

"Tahira! Tahira! Tahira, can you talk to us? What is your relationship with Alohnzo Kelly?"

I closed the door quickly as soon as Tru was inside and asked, "Why are they asking me about Alohnzo?"

Tru held her phone in front of me. It was a series of pictures of Alohnzo and me naked in his pool last night on some gossip site. "Somebody took these pictures and gave them to TMZ. You think Alistair would do this?"

I gasped, but no words would come out. I couldn't think of anything to say. I felt violated. Taking the phone from her, I read it. I didn't see how people like reading this trash. It was mostly fiction, but people didn't care. The juicier the story, the sweeter. People loved to pore over these stories of gossip and scandal, lapping up every unsavory detail. I didn't see how they enjoyed these neighborhood gossips about divorces, affairs, and wayward teenage antics. Now that it was me they were talking about, I could see how far they liked to bend the truth.

"With all these paparazzi cameras, I wouldn't be surprised if it was one of them climbing up his deck. They're saying all kinds of dreadful things about your character, Tahira. No one knew that you were already divorcing Luca except for the people of Sand Cove. Somebody had to leak this story. I'm telling you right now it wasn't us."

"This is awful. They have no idea what's really going on."

My mum came down the stairs, dressed in her beach attire, a sundress over her bathing suit and a large sunhat. "I didn't know you had a guest, Tah."

"Yes, Mum, this is my neighbor and friend, Trudee, but we call her Tru. Tru, this is my mum, Madeleine."

"Nice to meet you," my mum said. "Call me Maddy."

Tru hugged her. "Nice to meet you, Maddy. You're gorgeous. I see where Tahira gets her stunning looks."

Mum turned a little red as she slightly laughed. "Thank you, my dear."

There was a knock on the door. I held my breath and hoped it wasn't a reporter bold enough to try to get a story out of me. I looked out of the peephole. A Caucasian woman in a business suit with her hair slicked back in a bun and a tall black man were standing at the door.

I opened it reluctantly. "Can I help you?"

"Yes, are you Tahira Moretti?" she asked.

"Yes, I am, and you are?"

Before her, she held a badge. "FBI. I'm Agent Tyler, and this is my partner, Agent Stanton. We need to ask you a few questions. Do you mind if we come in?"

"What is this regarding?" I asked, feeling confused.

"The homicide of Luca Moretti. Ma'am, if you don't want these reporters in your personal business, I think we should take this inside."

I opened the door and let them in, then quickly closed it. "This is my friend, Alohnzo's, house."

"Is Alohnzo home?"

"No, he's at work. . . . Wait, did you say homicide? That's a mistake. Luca wasn't murdered. He died of a heart attack."

She gave me a hard look as she replied, "That's what someone wanted us to think. The autopsy report came back this morning."

"Oh?"

"Yes . . . Have you ever heard of a drug called digitalis?"

"No," I replied.

"Digitalis also known as Foxglove was found in his system after the autopsy. He was poisoned, Mrs. Moretti."

My heart started racing, and I couldn't think of how to respond.

"Do you mind if we speak in private?" Agent Tyler asked as she glanced around the house. "We have a few more questions to ask."

"No problem. I'll be back," I said to Tru and Mum. I led Agent Tyler and Stanton to the kitchen.

"Mrs. Moretti, where—"

"Please, call me Tahira," I corrected.

"Tahira. Where were you the morning Luca Moretti's body was found?"

"I was at my divorce lawyer's office filing my divorce papers. I recently found out that my husband was cheating on me, so I hadn't been home in a few days. My neighbor is allowing me to stay here until I get on my feet."

"Alohnzo Kelly, right?"

"Yes."

"Was Luca angry that you wanted a divorce?"

"He was pissed because he thought I would never leave. This wasn't Luca's first affair. It was just the first time I caught him."

"How did that make you feel?" she asked. "Were you upset?"

"I was more hurt than upset. He broke my heart."

"When was the last time you saw him alive?"

"Sunday night. I went by our home to let him know I was staying with Alohnzo and that I wanted a divorce. He begged me to stay with him, but I couldn't. He changed the locks on me, and I've been right here."

"Would you mind giving me access to your phone records?" Agent Stanton asked.

"No, I have no problem with that at all. Just tell me what to do."

He studied me with his hard eyes, reading me to see if I was honest. "You didn't go back to his house Monday morning?"

"No, I went to see my lawyer about getting the divorce papers filed as I said."

"What is your lawyer's name?" Agent Tyler drilled.

"Edna Morgan," I replied.

"I'll be giving Edna Morgan a call to check your alibi," Agent Tyler said.

"Go right ahead," I replied.

"How long were you at her office?" Agent Stanton asked.

"It was brief, about twenty minutes, maybe."

"After that, where did you go?" he continued.

"I drove around to clear my mind."

"Hmmm . . ." she hummed. "Does Luca have any staff?"

"Yes, um, two maids, a personal chef, and an assistant."

Agent Tyler was writing everything I said down in a notebook while Agent Stanton eyeballed me.

"Were the maids employed by an agency or hired directly by him?" she badgered.

"He used an agency, and he changed out maids weekly. His chef also changed every other month or so. His personal assistant, Jillian, has been with him since before we were married."

She nodded. "Do you know anyone that might have been mad at him or any known enemies?"

"None that I know of . . . Luca had different women during our entire marriage."

"Were any of them married?"

"I'm not sure."

"Well, we'll be doing a full investigation to find your husband's killer. Here's my card. Call me if you have anything you want to tell me." She handed me her card.

"Thank you."

I walked the agents to the front door and closed it.

Tru had been pacing the floor but stopped.

Immediately, my mum stood up. "Luca was murdered?"

I replied, "That's what the FBI is saying."

Tru said, "This has officially turned upside down. Who the hell would want to kill Luca? This is nuts! What are you going to do about these tabloids?"

"What tabloids?" Mum asked with a deep scowl.

"Someone took pictures of me with Alohnzo and turned it into the tabloids."

"The tabloids are saying she's this heartless woman, romping around with Alohnzo right after her husband died," Tru added.

"Where are the pictures? I want to see them," Mum said.

Tru looked at me, and I nodded, letting her know it was okay to show her. Tru pulled it up on her phone.

Mum took a deep breath. "Oh, dear . . . This is a bloody circus. Well, your husband was seeing other women for years. How come there aren't any tabloids about him? Two wrongs don't make a right, but now you must correct the public. I know you're not going to hide in shame. You'll have let everyone know the truth."

"I plan on doing that before the FBI thinks I killed him to run off with Alohnzo."

Tru's eyes widened. "Whoa. Wait, is that what they said?"

"No, but the way they were looking at me, it was like they think I did it."

"That's bullshit. Pardon my language, Maddy!" Tru exploded. "I gotta call Noble."

I shook my head and rubbed my temples. This was a nightmare.

Chapter 39

Alohnzo

"Mr. Kelly, there's an FBI agent here to speak with you," Farrah said through the intercom.

An FBI agent? After all the drama with Kinsley and my mother earlier, I didn't know if I could handle anything else. If this was Kinsley stirring up more trouble because she was fired, I was going to lose my mind.

"All right."

I locked my computer and went over to my mini fridge to get a bottle of water. I took a sip and Farrah escorted the agent into my office.

A woman walked in and did a quick surveillance of my office with her eyes in a few short seconds. The seriousness of her face made her look a little mean. She held a blue folder in her right hand and her badge in her left as she stood in the center of the room.

"Hello, Mr. Kelly. My name is Agent Stephanie Tyler, and I'm investigating the homicide of Luca Moretti. Do you mind if I ask you a few questions?"

"No, not at all." I signaled for her to take a seat on the sofa on the left side of the room. "Agent Tyler, did you just say homicide?"

She didn't sit. "Yes, Luca Moretti was murdered."

"Wait, no . . . The reports said that he had a heart attack."

"Mr. Moretti was poisoned, and the autopsy confirmed it. Have you ever heard of foxglove?"

"No."

"Digitalis?"

"No . . . What are they?"

"Foxglove, aka digitalis, is a cardiotonic drug. When used improperly, it can make the heart stop or cause a person to suffocate. Foxglove is a very toxic plant. It is so poisonous that ingesting only .5 grams dried or 2 grams of fresh leaf is enough to kill."

"Whoa," I replied. "I wouldn't know where to find anything like that."

"Where were you Monday morning?"

"I was here at work."

"I'm sure a time card or something will verify that."

"I don't clock in or out, but my secretary and other employees can vouch for me."

"You're the boss, I take it?"

"No, I'm the CEO's son."

"I see. . . . You live next door to Mr. and *Mrs.* Moretti, correct?"

I noticed how she emphasized the Mrs.

"Yes, I do."

"And what is your relationship with Mrs. Moretti?"

"Tahira and I are friends."

"Just friends?" She went into the folder and pulled out a few photos I had never seen before. "Is this the two of you on your deck last night?"

I didn't frown or blink, but I was shocked. I didn't know there were eyes in the sky, but I should've known the risks of having paparazzi camped outside all day and night.

"Yes."

"Who would take these pictures of the two of you and turn them over to the tabloids? It's a hell of a juicy story.

Newly widowed Tahira Moretti is seen naked in the arms of her neighbor. Everyone is dying to know how long the two of you have been in a sexual relationship."

I shrugged as if it were no big deal. No matter how bad she tried to paint the picture, I was unaffected by it. "That's just fabricated news to sell a story."

"Hmm . . . Fabricated, you say? This looks like you're more than 'friends,' Mr. Kelly. Kissing . . . Hugging . . . Groping . . . A blind man can see that you are having an affair with Luca Moretti's wife."

"Tahira and I didn't start seeing each other until she found out that her husband was cheating on her."

"When did she find that out?" she asked, but I could tell she already knew the answer to that.

"Saturday afternoon. She went down to the backlots and caught him sleeping with an actress in his trailer. So, we've only been sexually involved for two days."

"Was she angry when she told you about what happened when she went down to the backlots?"

"She was angry because she had just found out that her husband was cheating on her. She was crying because she was hurt. She told me Saturday morning that she felt like he had been cheating on her, and she happened to catch him that afternoon. I told her she could stay at my house that night because she had nowhere else to go. Her family lives in London."

"That was when you slept with her for the first time?"
"Yes."

"Taking advantage of a woman in pain. Is that your thing, Mr. Kelly?"

"Not at all. I care about Tahira."

She looked at me from head to toe as if she didn't believe me. "Where were you when she went to talk to him Sunday night?"

"I was at home, waiting for her to come back."

"Is there anyone that can verify that information, Mr. Kelly?"

"No. I live alone."

"I bet getting rid of Luca has been really convenient for both of you. You have Tahira all to yourself. This is a classic case of lovers wanting to be rid of the husband. He's not in your way now. You've had plenty of time to plot, living next door and all."

"Excuse me?" I felt my insides starting to tense up.

She pulled out a sheet of paper from the blue folder. "I was able to obtain Mr. Moretti's phone records. The last person he texted was you. Pretty interesting thread of texts. You two were threatening each other back and forth, arguing like two immature boys."

"That's because he threatened me first. He sent the first text. Can you see that?"

"I do see that. You told him you would go to his house. Did you ever show up?"

I paused because I felt like if I said anything else, she would try to pin Luca's murder on me. "I don't have anything else to say unless my lawyer is present."

"I thought you'd say that." Her cell rang, and she turned her back to me to take it. "Agent Tyler . . . Yes, all right. I'll be home soon." She ended the call and turned back to face me. "Mr. Kelly, take my card and give me a call if you hear anything that may be related to this investigation. Thank you for your cooperation."

I took her card and watched her leave. The next thing I had to do was call my lawyer.

Chapter 40

Stephanie

I was born in a suit because my father was a police offi-cer. As a child, I knew what I wanted to do with my life. I wanted to catch the bad guys just like my daddy. I stood at five foot nothing. My straight hair was pulled back into a low bun. From my belt hung a standard-issued Glock and my badge. I was a serious woman with a dangerous gun. Life had no color for me—no shades of gray, either. Life was all black or white, right or wrong, legal or illegal.

When I wasn't taking care of my daughter as a single mother, I was preparing paperwork or chasing down criminals. I wanted to make a difference in the world.

I preferred to work alone, but I had a partner who respected when I wanted my space. I never had a fragile ego or anything. I just didn't trust anyone without visible weaknesses.

The FBI had been my childhood dream, and I lived it. I couldn't keep a man, which I didn't really care about. I cycled through men faster than I could blink. My job always came first, and I couldn't stand it the other way around. My teenage daughter was my world, but even she took a backseat to my career.

"Mooooom," Chloe screeched as soon as I walked into the house. "I made Principal's Honor Roll."

"You called me while I was working like it was an emergency and made me come home because you made Principal's Honor Roll?"

"Yeah," she said as her shoulders sank a little. "I was excited."

"I thought you broke a bone or something. . . . Anyway, I'm here now. Congratulations, Chloe Bear." I hugged her.

Chloe was the typical honors kid with brown eyes behind black-rimmed glasses. She held plenty of book knowledge in that brain of hers. She was in an oversized gray sweatshirt and a pair of denim shorts. Her left arm held thin silver bracelets that matched the silver heart locket hanging from her long necklace.

I walked into the kitchen to see what I could make for dinner. I really needed to get back to work on this Luca Moretti case, but I could take a tiny break from it.

"Mom, I don't know why you're looking in the refrigerator. We don't have any food because you haven't been to the store. It's on your list of things to do, remember?"

I closed my eyes. I forgot. I got so wrapped up in the case that I forgot to go to the grocery store. "That's right. Shit."

"I have something else to tell you."

"What?" I scowled with a deep frown until I noticed she had this gigantic grin spread across her face.

"I got in, Mom! I got into Columbia University!" She took the letter out of her pocket and waved it in the air.

She only had two more months before graduating from high school, and she didn't think she would get into Columbia because they took such a long time to respond. But it was the response she was looking for.

"Aw, Chloe Bear, I'm so proud of you. You did it, honey."

She handed me the letter, and I read it for myself.

I smiled, feeling like all my fussing and cussing to keep her grades up was well worth it, but then reality set in. With her going away to college in New York, I would no longer be able to protect her like I had all her life.

"Wait. Hold for one damned minute," I said, handing her the letter.

She was already looking to post her news on social media now that I knew.

She kept her eyes on the screen as she responded, "Huh?"

"Before you share your wonderful news with the World Wide Web, I have a few questions, so can I have your undivided attention?"

"Okay . . ." She lowered the phone.

"Have you talked to your dad about this?"

"No."

"Why not? He's your father. He has a right to know that you will be spending your college days in his city."

She looked up at me with a strange expression. I knew my question was blunt, and my delivery was brash, but I wanted her to have a relationship with her father. I couldn't be the middle person anymore delegating and arranging meetings between them. I figured he was the reason why she always wanted to go to school in New York anyway.

Chloe started looking uncomfortable as she flopped down on the couch. I could see it in her eyes. She hadn't heard from her father for a long time.

"Wow, Chloe, when was the last time you talked to him?"

"This is uncomfortable, Mom. I mean, how do I tell you that I feel like contacting him is a waste of my time? You were married to him once, so you should already know how difficult it is to get him to commit to anything, especially me."

"The last time I talked to him, he made it seem like you two have a beautiful relationship, and he couldn't wait for you to move to New York. He promised me that he would look out for you."

"Please, can we not talk about my dad?" She rolled her eyes. "I feel like I've tried everything to get him to call me back. Every time I call, it's like he's busy, doesn't have time, or he's working late. Blah blah blah."

I sighed because her father worked just as much as I did. These bills weren't going to pay themselves. Danny loved her. I didn't know what was going on with him, but I would find out later.

"I know how much your father means to you, Chloe. You're the only kid he has. You are all we both have. Don't give up on him. I'm going to call him to see if he's able to take just a few minutes to hear your good news. Is that okay?"

She hated it when I tried to make Danny do anything, and she hated it even more when I made excuses for him. She thought it was his job to do things on his own without me telling him to. She was right. I shouldn't have had to contact him and ask him to call his daughter, but sometimes I had to.

"Is that a yes or a no?" I asked.

"I don't know," Chloe whined and then blew air from her lips.

I realized that this conversation wasn't going to go anywhere unless I took a gentler approach. Interrogating her wasn't going to work.

"Well, if you get a chance, call him again. You need anything from the store? Should we go get some Chinese or something? I'm starving."

"Yes, that sounds so good right now." She perked up. "Can we get some Lucky China Garden?"

"Absolutely. Go get your shoes on and let's go. I have some work to do."

She ran up the stairs to get her shoes, and within minutes, she was back down. We got in the car and drove to the Chinese food spot.

"You think we should've called in our order? I hope it doesn't take that long."

"Mom, you can enjoy a little time with your daughter."

"You're right. There is no rush. You got me until after we're done eating."

Chloe smiled. "Thank you."

"No problem. So, we haven't had 'the talk' in a long time. Since you'll be going away to college, you need any condoms? You can't rely on a man to get them all the time. I see nothing wrong with girls carrying them if they need 'em. You need 'em?"

"Oh my God, Mom. How many times do I have to tell you that I *don't* need them?" She sighed and mumbled, "Plus, I'm already on birth control."

"You're *what?*" My eyebrows furrowed into an intense frown.

"It's not a big deal, Mom. I'm 18. I went to the doctor a few months ago, and I got a transplant in my arm."

"What? The doctor didn't get my permission."

"Mom, anything I do in the doctor's office is under physician and patient confidentiality. She's not supposed to say anything."

"Does this mean you're having sex?" I panicked.

She rolled her eyes. "Not anymore, I'm not."

"Chloe, *who* were you having sex with?"

"This boy I started dating, but you don't have to worry about him anymore. We broke up."

This felt so weird. I hadn't noticed that my angel was no longer an angel.

She huffed and puffed as she said, "When are you going to see that I'm not a little girl anymore? At least, I won't get pregnant. Isn't that what this conversation is all about? You don't want me to ruin my life with having a baby before I finish college."

"Yeah, but no. I hope you still use condoms."

"I use condoms, and I know all about STDs. I'm responsible. I got this." Her eyes were on her phone.

This conversation was now officially too much, but I was glad that Chloe was a responsible young lady. I raised her well, and Danny did what he could from another state. He might not have been in her life physically, but he never missed a child support payment, birthday, or holiday.

"All right," I heard myself say. "I guess you have everything under control."

She nodded her head. "I'm going to Columbia University, and I'm not pregnant. You did your job. I love you."

"I love you too, Chloe Bear."

I wanted to ask more questions, but I wasn't sure if I could handle knowing anything else.

Chloe had a paper to write, so she took her food upstairs as soon as we returned home. I took my notes out and sat in the kitchen. Before I could dig into my food, my cell rang. It was my partner, Agent Stanton.

I answered with a mouth full, "Hey, what's up?"

"How did the questioning go with the neighbor who's banging the dead guy's wife? Sorry I couldn't go with you at the last minute."

"No worries. You had home obligations. I get it. . . . Alohnzo was evasive to me. Seemed to be hiding something. He didn't lie about his relationship with Mrs. Moretti, but he bitched up and said he wouldn't say anything else without his lawyer." I took another mouthful of food.

"Typical. Well, this guy Moretti banged more hoes than a little bit. His phone records show that he was sleeping with at least five other women. Three of the women are married, but we need to question one in particular.

Naomi. She's the one that Tahira caught him sleeping with, and she was the last one to see him alive other than his staff. One of the maids said Naomi spent the night the night before he was found unresponsive."

"Wow."

"I discovered something else," he said.

"What?"

"There's a couple that lives on the other side of the Morettis. Trudee and Noble Mason. Going through Luca's computer, we found some emails between him and Noble. Looks like Noble owed Luca some serious money. Luca threatened to tell Trudee about his gambling habit if he didn't make good on his payments."

"Oh, really?"

"Yeah. Want to go by there together tomorrow?"

"Sure. The Masons work?"

"Yup; they own some cosmetic corporation. They're home in the evenings."

"We'll stop by tomorrow evening, then," I said and wiped my mouth with a napkin.

"So far, how many suspects do we have?" he asked.

"I don't have anything solid, but Tahira and Alohnzo are at the top of the list," I replied. "As soon as you find out more about this Naomi chick, let me know."

"I will. I'll see you at the office in the morning?"

"Yup."

"Okay. See you then," he said.

I ended the call, and while I ate, I let my mind get to thinking about all the possible suspects. Sand Cove was going to be turned upside down.

Chapter 41

Stephanie

I did my normal routine of making sure Chloe had breakfast before she drove herself to school. I decided to get her a car when she got her license because I didn't like her walking to and from school alone. There were too many predators watching young girls, and they were following them home. I heard too many of these cases, and though our neighborhood was safe, I didn't want to take any chances.

I arrived at the office close to 8:30 a.m. My partner, Agent Stanton, was pinning pictures on the board. He liked to have visuals whenever we were investigating a crime. He created a link chart on a bulletin board, showing the people, locations, and he drew lines to show how they were connected. I liked to use my phone and computer to put my notes on. I looked at the board. It was a pretty creative way to pinpoint clear motives.

Agent Stanton was a black man and clean-cut as if he were still in the military. When I wanted efficiency, he was my man. He backed me up with his muscle and his perfect aim. Stanton did everything by the book. When I needed to get something done, he wasted no time. He was the perfect partner. Given a chance, I would keep him as a partner for the duration of my time with the FBI.

His conversations weren't always interesting, but he noticed things no one else did. At crime scenes, I'd flash the badge and do all the talking. He just listened, read their body language, and followed their eye movements. Then, he would ask them the perfect question at the perfect time with such an innocent tone of voice, like he genuinely just wanted to know. I could rely on Stanton to notice whatever was odd: a picture at an angle, a footprint going the wrong way, furniture and objects misplaced.

"Good morning," he said.

"Good morning."

"I tried to call Naomi with the number that was found in the famous director's phone."

"And what happened?" I asked.

"It's disconnected, and her phone was in Luca's name."

I hummed. "Do we have an address on her?"

"Nope. Not yet."

"What's her last name?"

"Green. Well, that's her actress name. When I ran her through the system, it states that her actual name isn't Naomi, but she's been booked under her real name, Yaharrah Emmanuel, in the past. We'll need to check into her background more thoroughly."

"How did the background check go with Alohnzo and Tahira?"

"Their background came back clean."

"All right. Let's go back over to Luca's house," I said. "I want to see if there is anything else there that we might've overlooked. Place Naomi higher on the list. Since she was the last one to see him breathing, we need to find her."

"I agree."

My cell vibrated against my hip. It was my ex, Danny, calling.

"I gotta step out to take this," I said.

"No problem. I'm going to see if I can find anything else about this Yaharrah Emmanuel," Agent Stanton said.

I walked out of the office and stepped outside. "Hello?" I said.

"Hey, you need to speak with me?" Danny replied.

"Yes, I do. When's the last time you talked to your daughter?"

"I've been working overtime and double time. I figure she's been too busy with school, so I haven't reached out in a while. Is everything okay?"

"Everything is fine, Danny. She has some news she wants to share with you."

"She can call me anytime."

"She says she has, and you don't return her calls."

He took a deep breath and exhaled. "I've been working so much that I hadn't realized how many months have gone by. What's the news?"

"I think it would best if she told you."

"Tell me just in case we don't get a chance to speak right away."

"She got into Columbia University in New York, so she'll be out your way in the fall."

He was so silent I thought the call dropped.

"Danny? You there?"

"I'm here. I didn't know she wanted to go to Columbia anymore. She hadn't talked about it with me."

"It's her dream. Nothing has changed. Why do you sound sad about it? Aren't you happy? Isn't this what you wanted? You told her that was where you always wanted her to go since it's your alma mater."

"I know . . . it's just . . ." he paused before he said, "I got married, Steph. That's one of the reasons why I hadn't been in touch. I didn't know how to tell her. My wife has been asking to meet her, and I've been pro-crastinating."

I looked up at the sky. Chloe was going to be crushed because she should've been the first one to know that her father was thinking about marrying someone.

"Well, congratulations, I guess. She's going to be pissed that she wasn't at your wedding."

"We eloped. You know I'm not into fancy weddings. We kept it nice and simple. I've been working so much because we're building a house." He paused and hesitated before he said, "She's pregnant."

I could see why he would be afraid to tell me that. Another bomb dropped, and I felt myself get angry. It was one thing that he got married, and it was another thing that Chloe would no longer be the only child. Eighteen years between her and a little brother or sister. How was I supposed to break this news to her?

"Danny, you need to call your daughter and tell her everything. It doesn't matter how upset she may get when she hears this. *You* need to handle your business. You're *still* her father."

I ended the call. I hoped he would call his daughter and talk to her. I wasn't going to be the one to relay that information to her. I stepped back inside the building, and Stanton didn't waste any time to give me an update.

"This Moretti conducted his life like an Italian mobster."

"Why do you say that?" I asked.

"He threatened someone's life at least twice a week. His text messages and emails show that he was involved in more than just other women's panties. And, get this . . . His neighbor, Noble Mason, went to him like he was a loan shark."

I went to his computer screen and said, "You mind if I sit here and read through these emails?"

"Not at all." He stood up and walked back over to the board.

Chapter 42

Noble

I arrived at home right before the sun could go all the way down. Our street was now more hectic because of the news that Luca was murdered. I had a challenging time getting through all the reporters and cameramen because they were acting like they didn't want to move out of the way. I had to honk my horn to get them to move.

Finally, I pulled up into the garage, and as I was getting out, a black man and a white woman were coming up my driveway.

"Can I help you?" I asked with my eyebrow raised.

"Are you Mr. Mason?" the woman asked.

"I am, and you are?"

"Noble Mason?"

"That's me. Look, I don't know anything about Luca's death, so there's no need to come over here questioning me. You should be over at Alohnzo's house. He's the one that's fucking Luca's wife."

"I'm FBI Agent Tyler, and this is Agent Stanton. Do you mind if we come inside and speak to you and your wife for a moment? Is your wife home?"

"Yes . . . Come inside."

Agent Tyler and Agent Stanton followed me through the garage and into the house. Ximena was sitting on the living room floor playing with building blocks with the kids.

"Daddy!" little Noble shrieked.

"Hey, li'l man."

"Daddy," Noelle said with a broad grin.

I hugged them both. "Where's Mommy?"

"She's upstairs," Ximena said.

"You can have a seat in the den. I'll go get her," I said to the agents. "Ximena, take the children to their rooms." I headed up the stairs.

Tru was watching TV while lying in bed. She looked up at me. "Hey, babe. Your dinner is in the oven."

"Cool. Um, FBI agents are here to speak with us. Can you come downstairs for a moment?"

She rolled her eyes and groaned, "Oh no, I bet it's the same ones that badgered Tahira yesterday."

"Put something decent on. I don't think they're leaving until they ask us whatever it is they want to ask."

I loosened up my tie as Tru got out of the bed and changed out of her pajamas. She tossed on her bra, T-shirt, and a pair of sweat shorts. We met the agents in the den, where they were scanning all our family photos.

"Hello," Tru said. "I saw you two yesterday."

"Yes, you were at Alohnzo's when we questioned Mrs. Moretti about the murder," Agent Tyler said.

"Let's all have a seat. Do we need to have our lawyers present?" Tru quizzed.

"If you feel the need, but I don't think it's necessary," Agent Tyler replied with a straight face. "As you know, we're investigating Luca Moretti's murder. He was poisoned."

She looked to see our reactions, but this was something Tru had already told me. We had never heard of the drug, so I wasn't sure how she wanted us to react.

Agent Tyler went into her folder and pulled out some photos. "Have you seen these?" She showed us pictures, one by one, of Tahira and Alohnzo naked on his deck.

Tru nodded. "Yes, on social media."

"I saw them on the news today while at work," I admitted. "You think Alohnzo killed him? He has a motive, you know."

Tru hit me on my arm. "You don't know that. He doesn't know that. Alohnzo would never kill Luca."

Agent Tyler continued, "Did you know about Tahira and Alohnzo's affair before it was leaked to TMZ?"

"Yes, but it's not what you think," Tru replied quickly.

"You don't know what we think," Agent Tyler fired back. "Where were the two of you on Monday morning?"

"We were both at work," I said.

I noticed her partner wasn't saying anything. His eyes were glued on Tru and me.

"And you are both entrepreneurs. You started your own cosmetic and fragrance corporation a few years ago, made a nice piece of change, and bought this big, fancy beach house. I must say, Sand Cove is very nice. I bet it was hard to grab a piece of this real estate without having good friends in high places . . . considering you didn't have the credit for it."

Tru fluttered her eyelashes, something she did when she was irritated.

I didn't know where this conversation was headed, but it wasn't going to be good.

"What exactly are you trying to imply, Agent Tyler? My husband and I have worked hard for everything we have. We didn't *need* a hookup to buy this home. Everything we have, we worked hard to get it, and our credit is just fine."

"You sure about that?"

Tru looked at me, and I didn't say anything just in case this agent was blowing smoke up our asses.

"Isn't it true that Luca helped you get the loan for this house?" Agent Tyler questioned.

"No," Tru answered. "He was the one that told us about Sand Cove. We moved in a few months after he did, but he didn't help us get the loan."

"Mr. Mason, is it true Luca Moretti helped you get the loan?"

"Kind of . . . Luca was good friends with the real estate and lending company, and he put in a good word for us because I had a few issues on my credit."

Tru whipped her head in my direction. She didn't know that. She had no idea that I had outstanding loans before we got married.

"What does this have to do with his death? I don't see what our house loan has to do with his death," I replied, trying to take the heat off myself.

"How long have you owed Luca money, Mr. Mason?" She handed me a copy of a few emails between Luca and me.

Nervousness swirled in my stomach. Tru leaned over to see what I was reading. There was no need to hide it now. The agents were exposing my dirty secret.

Tru immediately said, "I think you're confused, Agent. My husband and I aren't in debt, and we sure don't owe Luca any money. Right, Noble?"

I looked at the emails, blinking. She had the most intense exchange that Luca and I ever had. *How in the hell did she get these?*

"You look surprised, Mr. Mason," Agent Tyler said with a hint of evil in her smile. "I take it you don't pay much attention to your finances, Mrs. Mason. I guess you don't know that your company is on the cusp of going bankrupt."

Tru held her tongue as she kept glaring at the side of my face. I refused to look at her. I was too focused on the threatening emails Luca sent and my reaction to those threats.

"Your husband had a habit of borrowing large lump sums of money from Luca time and time again. In one of these emails, Luca is threatening your husband that if he didn't pay him back the money, there would be 'consequences.' How much money do you owe him, Mr. Mason? Do you know?"

"That's none of your business," I replied, feeling my defensive wall come up.

"I'm afraid that *is* my business. Now that he's dead, you don't owe him anything, right?"

Tru snatched the paper from my hand and read in silence. Seemed like with each line, her chest heaved up and down harder. "When did you first start borrowing money from Luca, Noble?" Tru asked.

I never wanted her to find out this way. I planned to tell her everything one day after I recouped each dime I lost, but Tru was all about financial security. She always had been. Her shopping habit alone cost me a lot, but my gambling habit had become a different kind of monster.

"I was paying him back in installments," I replied.

"What? Since when? How much do you owe him?" Tru shrieked.

I put my head down, refusing to answer the question. "Am I a suspect, Agent?"

"It's my job to find out who killed Luca Moretti. As of right now, we have to know everything about your financial situation."

Tru uttered, "Noble, you better tell me how much you owe him, and you need to tell them."

I still didn't respond.

"The thing is, Mrs. Mason, we already know how much he owes. I want to see if Noble will tell us the truth. This is all about your character. If you lie to us, we know what kind of person you are."

"I don't really know how much," I replied as I shifted in the couch.

"Since you don't know, would you like me to tell you? Maybe you lost track or count, but I highly doubt that. With your house and your company on the line, I find it hard to believe that you don't know how much money you owe someone you call your best friend."

Since this smug bitch knew how much, I dared her to say it. I was going to call her bluff. She couldn't possibly know.

"In Mr. Moretti's safe was a book he kept full of how much money he gave out to you. His interest rates were ridiculous, yet you still borrowed money from him. You first borrowed money three years ago. The amount was huge. Quite a nice friend to let you borrow that much, but you didn't stop there, did you, Noble? You were in over your head right before he was murdered. The interest had grown so much that you owed him $2 million."

I closed my eyes. That figure sounded so wrong coming out of her mouth—but it was right.

"Two million dollars?" Tru shouted. "Why would you need that much money?"

"Now isn't a proper time to talk about this," I said to her. "We'll talk about this later."

"No!" Tru shouted. "That's a whole lot of money, Noble. What is going on?"

"You don't want me to answer that," I said with a hint of shame in my voice. I lowered my eyes to my feet, refusing to look at her. I was busted.

The agent narrowed her eyes. "Your wife doesn't know that you have a gambling problem, Mr. Mason? How do you manage to keep such a secret like that?"

I shook my head slowly.

"Gambling? You never said you liked to gamble. When do you have time to live this other lifestyle like gambling in the casino?"

"It's not like that. . . . I don't need to sit in the casino . . . I have an app on my phone."

"Oh God. You have an app that lets you gamble?" Tru's eyes were nearly bucking out of her head. By now, she was sitting on the very edge of the couch.

Agent Tyler interrupted us. "Why weren't you able to pay him back before he started threatening to tell your wife?"

"I didn't have the money, okay? I thought I would be able to win it all back, but I've been losing." I paused. "Luca helped me when I had no one else to turn to. I was going to lose my business *and* my house, but he made sure that I didn't. He only threatened to tell Tru recently because I wasn't holding up to my end of the deal."

"How did you feel when he said he would 'bury you in the desert' if you didn't pay him back in full by next month?"

I felt tears building. She was forcing me to talk about something I didn't want to talk about. My shit was in my face—and it stunk.

Agent Tyler looked over at Agent Stanton. He nodded at her.

"Here's my card. I'll be checking out your alibi." The agent handed Tru the card and walked to the front door with the other agent. "You all have a good night. Beautiful family, by the way."

Tru walked them out. As soon as she got back to the den, she folded her arms across her chest as she watched me pour myself a drink. She curled her lips up into a snarl. "Let's talk about this gambling issue, Noble. Why didn't you tell me that you had all of this going on?"

"I'm a proud man, Tru, as you know, and I got in over my head. I made too many stupid bets. Luca only started acting like we had a problem because I hadn't been making payments. Business, as you know, is changing anyway, baby. With technology and businesses like Amazon, we're having a tough time keeping up. I don't know how much longer we can stay in business."

"I can't believe this!" she raged, ignoring what I said about our business. "With that high-ass interest rate, I would've never agreed to the loan!"

"What was I supposed to do, Tru? I don't have the credit to get a loan anywhere else. We were going to lose this house if I didn't borrow that money."

"Well, you better be done with gambling as of today because I can't go through this with you! I won't lose everything because of your stupidity! You have a lot of nerve talking about *my* secrets. I'm telling you right now since our money is low, we aren't firing Ximena!"

I shifted my stance and stared at her. "How you figure that?"

"Because I said so."

I huffed, "Whatever."

"Not whatever. She's not going anywhere," she spat.

"This isn't the same as cheating, Tru. You *cheated* on me!"

"Yeah, and you *lied* to me! Betrayal is betrayal. What kind of consequences do you think Luca had in mind when he sent those emails to you? You sure you didn't threaten to kill him?"

"Are you *serious?* You think I'm a *murderer?*"

She didn't respond.

"Baby, you can read the emails for yourself. They're sitting on the coffee table. I told him to back the fuck off because he was acting like I wasn't going to be a man of my word. Someone poisoned Luca, and it wasn't me. Those agents better take a closer look at Tahira and Alohnzo and leave me the fuck alone."

"Leave Tahira out of this. She wanted to divorce him—not kill him."

"You sure about that? Didn't you tell me that her lawyer said she wasn't getting a dime? You know how much Luca's life insurance policy is? She's his primary beneficiary. Let's not even talk about how much she's getting from his will. She just hit the fuckin' lotto!"

"Shut up, Noble. How do you know how much his policy is or what's in his will?"

"Because I know."

"Well, I know my friend. Neither Alohnzo nor Tahira have a reason to kill him. Leave the investigating work to the FBI. You worry about cleaning up the financial mess you got us in. . . . Do you, at least, feel *bad* about borrowing it?"

"Of course, I do. I feel even worse that I didn't have a chance to pay him back."

"How long were you planning on keeping that from me?"

I shrugged. "I don't know. . . . I honestly thought that I would be able to pay him back before you ever found out."

"Must feel pretty good now that you don't have to pay him back," she said.

"Now you sound like that damn FBI. No, Tru, I feel like shit. I mean, there's some relief, but at the same time, I should've never gotten myself in the situation to owe him anything."

Tru nodded her head. "I hear you. . . . Well, Ximena stays."

"Okay, whatever you say, Tru, baby. Are you mad at me? I thought you'd be ready to make me sleep on the couch tonight."

"No need for that. . . . There's one thing my mother always told me."

"What's that?"

"Always keep separate savings from your husband and pretend as if it's not there." She stepped closer to me and wrapped her arms around my neck. "I would tell you how much money I have, but I'm not going to do it. Just know I have enough saved to get us out of the hole you created."

She released me and returned upstairs. As much as I wanted to be upset that this was *another* secret she hid from me, I couldn't. I was going to have to trust that my wife wouldn't creep with Ximena just like she was going to have to believe that I wasn't going to gamble anymore.

Chapter 43

Alohnzo

As soon as I pulled up into my garage and closed it, I sighed. This mess about Luca being murdered had the entire world thinking that Tahira and I killed him. The shit people were saying in these tabloids was too much. These people camped out in Sand Cove with their cameras was too much. With Tahira and her mother staying with me, I felt like papparazzi was going to dig up another story.

Speaking of tabloids, my mother was having a fit. She blamed the leak on Kinsley, and she could've been right. She came up with this plausible theory that Kinsley leaked the story to spite her. I thought about it. Kinsley was at Alistair's that night. She could've easily taken the photos from his deck, though I didn't see anyone on his deck. Then again, I was too wrapped up into Tahira.

I got out of the car and walked into the house. I checked all the windows to make sure the shades were down as Tahira said she had done earlier. The papparazzi was aggressive as hell, and they would do anything for a story. I didn't need them conjuring up anything else.

"Hey," Tahira said, coming out of the kitchen.

"Hey," I replied. "How are you guys doing?"

"We're good. Mum's cooking dinner right now. I haven't had my mum's cooking in forever."

I walked toward the kitchen. "It smells good in here. What is she cooking?"

"She's making fish and chips. You will never have fish and chips that taste this way again unless she makes it. It's soooo good."

"I can't wait."

She took my hand as we walked into the kitchen.

Her mother was standing over the stove, dropping battered fish fillets into the hot cooking oil.

"Mum, Alohnzo is home."

"Hello," she said. "I would hug you, but I have batter all over my hands. How was your day?"

"I had a good day. You enjoying your stay?"

"I hate the paparazzi, and I want to see more of Los Angeles, but under the circumstances, I understand how difficult that will be. It was nerve-wracking enough with those people trying to look over the fence. We've stayed behind these shades all day."

"I hate this situation. They aren't supposed to be on my property. I may have to call the police if it gets too out of hand."

"You want a beer or wine or anything?" Tahira asked.

"A beer would be nice. Thank you."

Tahira went to the refrigerator and got herself one and one for me.

"Things have been really crazy today," Tahira said. "I just got off the phone with Tru right before you walked in. The same two agents went and questioned her and Noble today."

"What kind of questions did they ask them?"

"Well, it appears Noble borrowed $2 million from Luca, which is something I didn't know. They were asking them a bunch of questions about it."

"You serious? Wait, I wonder if that was what Noble and Luca were talking about the night of the bonfire. I walked up to them, and they stopped talking as if I interrupted them."

"They probably were. Luca didn't play about his money. I'm surprised I hadn't heard of anything before all of this."

"So, do they think Noble has motive to kill Luca because he didn't want to pay him back?"

"Seems like it . . . Luca may have been pissed because Noble hadn't paid him back, but I think those agents are wasting their time. There are plenty of other people who had it out for Luca. He treated his staff and personal assistant like shit! I know this is all part of their investigation, but they need to interview those maids and that chef. They were the only ones there that morning."

"Do you think anyone on his staff is capable of doing it?"

"They were the only ones who had enough time and access to the house. Luca was an asshole to everyone. They need to question his assistant. I saw her on Saturday at the backlots. She usually comes to the house to run errands for him. It's strange how the agent didn't mention her name at all."

"Maybe she isn't a suspect."

"Enough talk about this stuff," Tahira's mother said. "Dinner is almost ready. Give me about ten more minutes."

Tahira smiled and replied, "Okay, Mum."

"Go sit in the living room or something. I don't want you watching me. I cook better alone."

Tahira nodded while sipping her beer. I sipped mine and followed her to the living room. We sat on the couch and stared at each other for a little while.

"I can't wait for all of this to be over so that you can rest," I said.

She leaned against me and placed her head on my shoulder. "I hope they get this done fast. I don't need them dragging this out. I want to have him cremated, give his ashes to his children, and be done with it."

I placed a kiss on her forehead. "This will all be over soon enough."

Chapter 44

Stephanie

"Fuck," Stanton griped after hanging up the phone. "We are wasting our time with Noble Mason. His alibi checked out. He and his wife were in a business meeting at Constantine the morning the maid found Luca's body."

I looked up from my computer and replied, "Well, there goes that. We might as well cross him off the wall." I didn't think Noble killed Luca, but it was worth looking into. I tapped my fingers on the desk and asked, "Did we ever find out if Alohnzo went to Luca's house that day?"

"No," Stanton answered. "We were able to verify that he went to work that morning, but then he left. No one knows where he was for a few hours, and his lawyer won't let us question him without a warrant."

"This Alohnzo really works my nerves," I said.

"We also don't know where Tahira was after she left her lawyer's office. She said she cried on the side of the road due to bad news she received from the lawyer, but she cried for *two hours?*"

The phone rang on my desk. I picked it up. "Hello?"

"Hey, Agent Tyler. I got the full background check on Naomi Green, aka Yaharrah Emmanuel," Rick, the clerk assigned to assist them, said.

"Great. Lay it on me."

"She's been arrested a few times for petty theft and misdemeanors before Luca cast her in a movie three years ago. She was arrested again a few months before his death for spousal abuse. As we combed to find her spouse, we discovered he's dead. He died of a heart attack just a month ago."

That raised a serious red flag. "You're kidding me. *A month ago?*"

"Not kidding."

"Thanks, Rick."

"No problem."

I hung up and shook my head.

"What did Rick say?" Stanton asked.

"Little Miss Naomi's husband died of a heart attack just a month ago. . . . What if he *didn't* die of a heart attack but from the same drug that was found in Luca's system?"

"That would blow this case wide open."

"It would, and it would prove that the people of Sand Cove are innocent."

The phone on Stanton's desk rang. He picked up. "Hello? Really? You sure? What's your name? Okay, no problem. Thanks." Stanton slammed the phone down on his desk. "We just got an anonymous tip that said that Naomi is at some little restaurant near Echo Park right now."

"Let's go," I replied, putting on my sunglasses.

We took the busy freeway. We made it through traffic and pulled up to this Mexican taqueria. It was packed with people. We walked in and scanned the restaurant, hoping the anonymous tip we got wouldn't be a waste of time. It was a little busy because it was lunch hour. People were waiting for their orders; some were seated looking over menus. Everyone was moving so fast that I didn't know how we would find Naomi. We only knew what she looked like from her acting IMDb on the internet.

Walking toward the back of the restaurant, we spotted Naomi sitting at a table. Her legs were neatly tucked under the table, hidden from sight. Her skin was a smooth mocha, and her hair was braided. She was looking at her cell, drinking a margarita, and yet her expression was so far away. Her eyes were scanning whatever she was reading.

We walked up to her, and she looked up at us with a perplexed look.

"Naomi Green? Or should we say, Yaharrah Emmanuel?" I asked. "Do you mind if we ask you a few questions?"

"Who are you?"

I flashed my badge. "FBI."

Without warning, she flipped over the table and made a dash for it. I wasn't expecting to chase her. She was fast as she bolted out of the restaurant.

My feet slipped outward on the wet pavement because a man was hosing down the sidewalk. I did my best not to fall.

Naomi skated over the wet concrete like an ice skater without falling. It didn't slow her down. She rounded the corner, and I did too.

The frigid air shocked my throat and lungs as I inhaled deeper, faster. My heart was beating frantically. I had to give all or nothing.

I could hear Stanton panting behind me with an effort to keep up. He never could run well.

"I'll go get the car to cut her off," he huffed.

I kept running after her as she ran through a park. She vaulted a fence and fell on her face. I hopped over the fence. Before she could run, I tackled her back down.

"Yaharrah Emmanuel, you're under arrest for the murder of Luca Moretti," I breathed out slowly, feeling winded.

"Why are you doing this? I didn't kill him."

"If you didn't kill him, why'd you run?"

"I don't know."

I slapped the handcuffs on her. For now, she was under arrest, and we would find out the truth once down at the station.

Chapter 45

Alohnzo

"Mr. Amos is in the conference room with Alistair," Farrah announced as soon as I came back from lunch with Tahira.

Pop mentioned he wanted to have a meeting to talk to Alistair and me about what happened with Kinsley last week. I wasn't in the mood to discuss it because now that she was gone, I didn't see a need to talk about her anymore, but I decided to hear him out since this was the first time he wanted to talk about it.

"Thank you." I walked into the conference room.

Alistair and Pop were sitting in complete awkward silence before I walked in. Pop was sitting at the head of the table. Alistair on the right, and I sat on the left. We all looked at one another without words. We knew we were going to have to talk about this sooner than later.

Pop cleared his throat and said, "I'm glad you two could meet with me this afternoon. I'm sure we all have our matters to attend to. I want to apologize to both of you for not telling you the truth about Kinsley and me before. I'm open to any questions that you may have."

"Why didn't you fire her instead of transferring her to my department?" I asked.

"I felt bad for her. It wasn't her fault because I pursued her. She loved her job, and I wanted her to keep it. I thought I could stop my feelings for her once she stopped being my assistant, but when I found out about you, Alohnzo, my jealousy wouldn't allow me to lose. If she wouldn't have told me about you, Alistair, I wouldn't have known. I made her cut things off with you because I wanted her."

Alistair gave Pop this look that he reserved for anyone when they said something he thought was stupid. "Look, Pop, I feel you took advantage of her because you knew she would do anything you said for money. You were wrong for that."

"Like you took advantage of her because you knew she was using you to make me jealous," I scoffed.

Alistair sucked his teeth and shook his head. "Don't make this about you, Alohnzo. This is about Pop. Pop, why'd you get involved with her again after you knew she had been with Alohnzo and me?"

"I did it because I needed to win. It was wrong. I knew I could control her with money. Greed and power have made me do things over the years that made me misuse my power. If in life we are defined by the choices we make, then I'm a monster."

"Kinsley isn't what Mama thinks she is. She is bleeding for love." Alistair looked at me. "She wanted love, and she thought you could give it to her, Alohnzo. You failed her." Alistair was very defensive about her. "She had love stamped on her retinas each time she looked at you."

"Kinsley and I didn't have that kind of relationship. Once I saw how easy she moved on to you, I knew she wasn't the right one for me. Why do you care anyway? You got what you wanted out of her," I said.

"I don't care," he responded with a shrug. "I only wanted her because she was with you. It wasn't fun anymore. This whole thing with Dad made it worse. So, what's next?"

"I want us to get over this hump. No woman should ever come between us. I tried to call Kinsley to apologize and let her know that she can keep the money, but she changed her number, and she didn't answer the door when I went to her place," Pop said.

"Looks like you don't have to worry about that problem anymore. You can finally do right by Mama," I uttered.

Pop gave me a hard stare. "I love Mabel. I'm not perfect. She stuck with me all these years with all my faults."

"I hope you learned your lesson. I don't want to hear about another woman, especially not one from this company," I said.

"You have my word, son."

"I'll hold you to it."

We were back to being silent for a few moments.

"You guys have any other questions for me?" Pop asked.

I shook my head, and Alistair did the same.

"Let's hug it out, so we can go about the rest of our day."

We all stood up, and I hugged Pop first before I hugged Alistair. The wedge between us seemed to have been lifted. I could speak for myself when I say that Kinsley was no longer an issue.

The rest of the day seemed to go fast. I avoided all news and social media outlets because the stories and conspiracy theories were getting worse. Some of the stories were just horrible lies. It made the people of Sand Cove look money hungry, and they made Luca out to be some saint. Luca was far from that.

When I got home, I had to drive through the paparazzi just to get to my garage. As the garage was closing, I heard them shouting, "Alohnzo, Alohnzo!"

Tahira greeted me with a hug and kiss as soon as I walked through the door. I was starting to get used to having her around. I didn't know what her plans were, but I wasn't in a rush to see her go. I was happy the weekend was here so we could spend some time together.

"I ordered a pizza," she said. "Mum is upstairs resting, and I didn't feel up to cooking."

"That's fine. What kind did you order?"

"Combination. I know that's one of your favorites."

I nodded with a smile. I looked up to see that the news was on. Tahira was watching it. "Have you heard anything from that agent?" I asked.

"No, have you?"

"No."

"They were saying something about Luca on the news earlier, but I missed what they were saying when I ordered the pizza."

I turned up the volume when I heard Luca's name.

"There's been a new development in Luca Moretti's homicide. Actress Naomi Green was arrested in Echo Park this afternoon. Though she has not confessed to the murder, police say she's now a suspect. As reported earlier today, a drug found in Moretti's system was the leading cause of death according to pathologists," the news anchor said while live footage showed Naomi Green being escorted in handcuffs into a building. *"This is four days after the discovery of Luca Moretti's body. He was found unresponsive by his maids this past Monday morning. Naomi Green was having an affair with Luca Moretti for some time. She has made no comment, and so far, her reps have not returned our calls."*

"Is that the woman you saw in his trailer?" I asked.

"Yeah. That's her." She inhaled and exhaled deeply.

"You think she killed him?"

She looked out the window and saw the delivery driver pull up to the curb and park. "The pizza guy is here," she said. "I'll pay for it."

"It's already been paid for."

I opened the door as the pizza man was walking up the steps. He unzipped his hot bag and took the large pizza out.

"Here you go," he said.

"Thank you."

"Nice beach house. I've never been this way. The house is for sale next door. How much they want?" He pointed at Alistair's house.

"It's not for sale. My brother lives there. He moved in about a week ago."

"He should take down that sign. I know I can't afford it, but it's nice to dream."

I stepped out and looked to see a sale sign hanging in front of the house. I frowned as the delivery guy jogged down the steps to his car. As he drove away, I walked over to Alistair's house.

Walking up the steps, I paused at the top. Through the windows, I could see that there was no furniture inside. The house was empty. Alistair didn't say anything about moving. This was strange.

I walked over to my house and took the pizza to the counter.

"Yes, pizza," Tahira said. "Mum is sleeping, but we'll save her some."

"Did you see any moving trucks today?"

"No, but then again, I didn't go outside because of all the reporters that were out there. Why?"

"Alistair moved out."

"What?" She opened the pizza box. "You think he moved because of what's been going on lately?"

"I don't know." I took my cell out of my pocket and called him. My call went straight to voicemail. "Hey, Alistair, this is Alohnzo. Why didn't you tell me you moved? Call me when you get a chance, or I'll see you on Monday at work."

Tahira took a bite of pizza and stared at me. "What's the matter?"

"Nothing. We had a meeting this afternoon with our father, and he didn't say one word about moving."

"He didn't tell you he was moving in either."

"True . . . This is the typical Alistair but still feels a little strange."

"You want some pizza?"

"Yeah, but first I have to change out of these clothes. I'll be right back," I said.

Chapter 46

Kinsley

I knew the moment I started to cry that I was not okay with being fired. I cried slowly with tears dripping down my cheeks, and the soft hum of my voice echoed internally. I existed, and I was somebody, so how come I didn't feel like it? I felt worthless and so alone. I meant nothing to anyone. I was sinking deeper within myself.

For the past couple of days, I did some research on the Caribbean islands as I spent a few nights in Hotel Olas on Swans Cay. It has a beautiful view of the Caribbean Sea. During my search, I found a tiny island called Boca Del Toro with a one-bedroom house for sale. It was perfect for me. This was somewhere I could learn to love myself and reinvent who I wanted to be. It would be temporary until I found another home to call my own.

I made the arrangements to meet with the sellers. They gave me a free little boat to travel in when I was ready to go. I went back to the hotel, and I enjoyed the Caribbean for a few days before I went to my new home. I was a little afraid that I had spent all my savings on a run-down island and a house that wasn't livable. After talking myself into seeing what I bought, I grabbed my things and started my brand-new adventure.

The island couldn't have been more than a half mile wide as I walked. The sea had disappeared from my view and seemed to be lost behind me. The atmosphere was very damp and heavy. I could hear thousands of insects active among the leaves. This tiny Caribbean island was more beautiful than other Caribbean islands I'd seen. It was more beautiful than it looked online. The colors were too intense to be real. The dazzling blue of the ocean, the immaculate white beach, the vibrant green of the rain forest . . . This was my new beginning—a fresh start.

My feet planted themselves in the beautiful sand underneath the shallow water. My eyes felt like they didn't know how to blink because I was in awe of everything I was looking at. I tied the boat to the ragged dock with missing planks and walked along the shore to see that the white sand was truly beautiful.

The shimmering blue waters encircled the island and sparkled in the presence of the sunlight. A majestic waterfall that looked like a sheet of blue velour swishing down greeted me. The edges were hemmed with whipped white lines. The water plummeted like a huge waterspout. I closed my eyes. I couldn't believe it was all mine, but I also felt like my loneliness had caused me to go crazy.

"Kinsley," a deep voice called.

I looked up as a man came out of the shadows looking so handsome. As he got closer, my heart stopped. At first, his eyes were cast to the white sand, and then after finding me, he seemed to suddenly realize he was at his destination, an unspoken rendezvous. His face split into a grin, and he flashed those deep dimples I grew to love.

How did he find me? Before I could draw in the air my body needed, I melted into his arms. I could feel his firm torso, and his heart was beating hard from within his chest. His hands folded around my back and drew me closer. I felt my body shake as I cried. I released all the tension I had inside of me. This was more than a pleasant surprise.

He pulled his head back and wiped my tears with his index finger. He ate me with his eyes as he ran his hand through my hair. When he kissed me, it was sweet and gentle. I wanted to speak, but I all I could do was cry for a moment. I needed him, and I hoped he needed me.

"Alistair, how did you find me?" I asked.

"Do I really have to tell my secret?"

"I guess I shouldn't care. What are you doing in my paradise?"

"My paradise is you. You haven't left my mind once since I first met you. I'm in love with you, Kinsley."

"You say that like you mean it."

"I wouldn't have come all this way if I didn't mean it."

"Should we talk about what happened at the office with your mother and me? Your father?"

"Shhhh," he hushed. "Listen to me. I sold my house and resigned from the family business. After meeting with my father, I realized that it didn't matter what kind of mess he got you into. I don't blame you for any of it. I know how I feel about you and how I felt the moment I met you. This isn't about taking what Alohnzo didn't want either. I admire the kind of woman you are. You're a go-getter. No matter what anybody thinks about you, I got a chance to see your heart. You're funny, smart, and beautiful. If you'll have me, I'm yours. I mean, that's *if* you want me."

With tears still cascading down my face, I was speechless. No one had ever professed their love for me in that way. Alistair searched my soul and saw me. I wasn't some sex toy or object to him. That was all I ever wanted.

"Of course, I want you."

He lifted me off my feet and spun me around. After giving me one of the most passionate kisses I've ever had, he said, "Nice piece of property you have here. I was surprised that the seller would list your name and so quickly."

"Ah, so that's how you found me."

He chuckled. "Show me the house. It looks very nice from what I could see."

"I haven't been inside yet. This is my first time here."

"You've got to be kidding! You bought a house and an island without seeing it first?"

"Yeah."

"You're crazier than I thought. Lucky too."

I grabbed his hand, and he held mine in his. "We can explore it together."

He nodded with a smile. "I like that."

Chapter 47

Tahira

I had Luca's body cremated the way he wanted. In his will, he requested to have his ashes spread over the beach and water of Sand Cove because he loved it so much. His family was supportive, and they helped with anything I needed. They didn't care about what the tabloids said about Alohnzo and me. They knew about Luca's cheating. They were glad that I could move on with my life the way I wanted to.

At the will reading, Luca left me 80 percent of his estate and the house. His two children received 10 percent each. I was shocked to see how much I was given, considering how stingy Luca was with money. His life insurance policy also paid out $1 million.

The moving company was going to arrive first thing in the morning to move all of Luca's belongings to a storage facility until I was ready to deal with selling them.

Alohnzo, Tru, Noble, and I were going to have a bonfire in remembrance of Luca. My mum had already returned to London. My neighbors agreed to be a part of the bonfire celebration/memorial. For it to be the beginning of September, the weather was still warm. Fall weather hadn't made its way to us yet. We were going to release his ashes into the ocean and send out little lanterns with tea lights in them on the waves. Tru helped me to come up with that idea.

I sat on my new queen-sized bed in my house and remembered the first time I laid eyes on Luca. He was so charming that I didn't care about his age. Though I didn't miss him, I would never forget him. I took off the wedding ring and held it in the palm of my hand. Many of our memories were good, but the bad ones outweighed the good ones. The way he would smile at me when I said something humorous made the memories of our marriage happy thoughts. What I once treasured was now a memory, a shadow lingering in the depths of my mind. It was strange to lose something I once had, like a limb torn from my body without a chance to save it. Only, I wasn't upset or sad at all.

For the first time, I didn't have to hide behind a mask. I didn't have to pretend to be happy. I could be honest with myself and my neighbors, free to be me. Luca's death was the release valve I needed to move on with my life.

My cell phone rang. I answered it. "Hey."

Tru replied, "Everyone is outside waiting for you. You need any help?"

"No, I'll be out there in a few minutes."

"All right."

I stood up and put the ring on the dresser before picking up Luca's gold urn filled with his ashes. When I made it out of the house, Tru, Noble, the twins, and Alohnzo were standing along the shore wearing all white as I requested with their lanterns ready. I was wearing a white sundress. The bonfire was blazing, and the sun was starting to set.

"Hey," Alohnzo greeted me with a warm hug and a kiss on my lips.

"Hello." I looked around at everyone. "Thank you, everyone, for doing this for Luca."

"It's no problem," Tru said.

"All right, you guys, light the lanterns," I said.

Noble took a lighting stick and lit six floating lanterns, one for each person. I opened the golden urn.

"All right. Here we go. Rest peacefully in your final place, Luca," I said.

I poured his ashes slowly into the water and watched the waves wash them away.

"Release the lanterns," I instructed.

They let their lanterns go, and the soft wind carried them as they drifted above the water. The yellow ball of fire in the sky changed into different hues of oranges and tangerines. It merged with the sky the way powdered juice dissolved in a pitcher of water. Parts of the sky looked like billows of cotton candy as they blushed at the falling sun as it was halfway into the water. Silhouettes of the lanterns flew up across the sky, and their reflection in the ocean made it beautiful.

"Aaaaaaw," Tru said. "Look at the lights," she told the kids.

They stared up with wide eyes, looking so adorable in their white clothing.

"Luca will always be a part of Sand Cove," Noble said as he wiped his tears. "He may be gone, but his spirit will always be here."

He took Luca's death the hardest because they were indeed best friends. Tru put her hand on his back as she lowered her head in sadness as well.

We all watched the lanterns in silence. I thought of all the good times Luca and I had on this beach and smiled. We had some great laughs here.

"Are you still going to London?" Tru questioned.

"Yes. I leave tomorrow. I haven't been home in a while. I think it's time to visit."

"How long will you be there?"

"About a month or so."

"I love London," she said. "I wish we could go with you. We are in no shape to take a vacation right now, but give me a year, and I'll go with you."

"I would love that."

"Are you going alone?" Tru asked while looking at Alohnzo with a sly grin.

Alohnzo and I hadn't revealed that we had plans to go together, but since Tru was so nosy, he said, "Yes, Tru, I'm going too. I need a vacation."

Raising her eyebrows, she said, "Oh, really?"

I nodded. "Yeah, I'm going to show him where I grew up."

Tru shifted and cleared her throat. "Is it safe to say that you two are dating officially?"

"Tru . . ." Noble groaned, warning her to stop prying.

I laughed, and Alohnzo laughed with me.

"What? She's my best friend, Noble, and she usually tells me everything. You don't mind if I ask you, do you?"

"No, I don't mind," I replied.

Tru clapped her hands. "I'm so happy for you two."

I stood close to Alohnzo, and he wrapped his arms around my waist. I couldn't wait to spend a month with him in London. He had been there for me when I needed him. He never complained or griped. Alohnzo had been everything I imagined him to be. Whether we were going to be an official couple was up in the air. Right now, however, we were just enjoying each other.

"I wish I would've been able to give Luca back his money." Noble's eyes were filled with sorrow. "Since it's your estate now, Tahira, I can pay it back over time."

"No, it's fine. You can't beat yourself up over this for the rest of your life," I said. "You have a beautiful family and a wife that loves you to death. You don't owe me anything. Consider the debt paid."

Noble looked surprised, but he was grateful. "Thank you."

"It's no problem."

"Don't borrow any more money, and we won't have any issues," Tru said to him. "Do the rest of y'all hear me? Don't let this man borrow any money if he comes asking."

"Baby, stop. My gambling days are over," Noble asserted. He wrapped his arms around her as they gazed out at the water. Tru cuddled against him.

We all had an invisible refresh button.

Through teary eyes, we watched the sun fall behind the horizon, painting the sky a different shade of red and pink. I thanked God that this day had come and gone. All the pain I suffered . . . All the hurt I felt . . . everything. Gone. Tomorrow was a new day, and I couldn't wait to see what it had in store for me.

A raindrop fell on my forehead and then my arm.

"Is it about to rain?" Tru asked, feeling a few drops herself.

"We better get the kids inside before it picks up," Noble said. "You guys have a safe trip."

"Thank you," Alohnzo and I said in unison.

Chapter 48

Stephanie

Thick sheets of rain obscured my vision as the windshield wipers tried to clear as much water as they could. It was time to get new ones. I had to get new ones the last time it rained, but I didn't find time to get them. I was doing my best to rush home to Chloe because she had to catch a flight to New York. I wanted to see her off. Her dad sent for her, and they talked about his recent marriage and a new baby on the way. To my surprise, she was overjoyed and so happy to hear his news. She couldn't wait to get there.

My cell rang, and I answered through my Bluetooth. "Hello?"

"Yaharrah Emmanuel, aka Naomi Green, was just released from jail," Stanton announced.

"What? Why?"

"Turns out she didn't kill Luca Moretti."

"What do you mean she didn't kill him?"

"Her ex-husband really died of a heart attack. As of right now, there isn't any proof that she did it. They're doing their best. You know that anonymous tip we got?"

"Yeah," I sighed.

"Turns out it was the same number that sent Naomi a text to meet her at that restaurant."

I groaned. "You mean to tell me that his killer is still running around out there somewhere?"

"That's what I'm saying."

"Why did she run if she didn't do it?"

"She thought we were there to arrest her for an outstanding warrant."

"Did she name the person she was supposed to meet up with?"

"No, she said she didn't know who it was. The person claimed to be a good friend of Luca and said Luca wanted her to give her something special, something he was supposed to leave for her in his will."

"You're shitting me."

"No."

"Fuck!" I slammed my hand on the steering wheel. "So, are we reopening this case?"

"Waiting for the word. I'll keep you posted."

"Thanks," I replied dryly.

Stanton ended the call. I hated to be wrong, and I felt like this case was over with. Whoever the killer was had outsmarted us. Whoever the killer was thought they got away with murder.

I steadied myself as I pulled up into the driveway of my home. I hardly ever stumbled.

"A Tyler never stumbles," my father used to say.

We were a family of strong men and women. Our skin was made of iron, and our souls were made of steel. We were brave. I wondered what my father would say if he could see me. It wouldn't be possible for him to see me because he died ten years ago, but I felt him with me each day, nonetheless.

There was no use in crying or going over where we went wrong in this case. Overall, I was bothered by what Stanton just told me. I could feel anger resting on my chest, waiting to take over. It sat there like an angry ball propelling me toward an anxiety attack I didn't need. I turned the car off and got out of it.

The air smelled like the rain that was falling. There was something about being outside of my car that evaporated my anger. I wasn't sure, but my body had started to relax. For now, I would rest.

I stepped into the house, and it was silent.

"Chloe?" I called.

I didn't hear anything.

I closed the door and went up the stairs. The door to her bedroom was open, and I knew then that I had missed her. She couldn't wait for me.

I sent her a text. Sorry, Chloe Bear. I wanted to see you off. Have a great flight and make sure you call me as soon as you land. I love you.

Sitting on her bed, I waited for her to reply. I was hoping she would be home to take my mind off my latest failure. I didn't want to think that maybe I was losing my touch. I thought about retiring, but I had a few more good years left in me.

My phone dinged. I looked down to read the message.

Chloe replied, It's okay, Mom. I tried to wait for as long as I could, but I didn't want to miss my flight. I love you too.

I sighed and looked at her neat and tidy bedroom. At least she cleaned up before she left. I left her bedroom and closed the door. Without having anything to do, I decided to head to one of Luca's favorite spots, the Cigar Lounge, along the coast. We didn't check that place out. I wasn't sure what I was going to find when I got there, but I figured it would be a good place to look around.

The place was packed. I looked around at the busy booths and tables. Men, young and old, had a glass of liquor and were engrossed in conversations. A group of four young women in their early thirties was giggling as a few stern, older women nearby looked on and frowned. Some businessmen in their expensive suits were lighting up cigars. The noise and smoke level were high, but it didn't bother me.

Making my way over to the bar, I asked the bartender, "Can I get a vodka tonic with heavy ice and extra lime?"

"Sure, are you a member?" he asked.

I frowned a bit. "No. I wasn't aware that I had to be a member to be here. No one stopped me at the door."

"Anyone can be in here as long as you're 21, but members get discounted drinks."

"Ah, gotcha. I don't mind paying full price."

He made my drink and set it in front of me. "You keeping your tab open or paying?"

"I'll pay now."

"That'll be eight dollars."

I took a ten-dollar bill out of my wallet. "Keep the change."

"Thanks."

"Is the owner around?" I asked.

"I'm the owner. Who are you?"

I flashed my badge. "Agent Stephanie Tyler. I'm working the Luca Moretti case. You know him?"

"I thought they arrested that actress he was messing with," he said, looking at my badge carefully before I put it away.

"She was released. She's innocent. I need you to help me, if you can."

He looked around cautiously before he leaned over the counter. "What do you want to know?"

"Have you heard anything that could lead me in the right direction? I've questioned everyone in Sand Cove, but I didn't get very far."

He glanced across the room at the four laughing women. "Did you question his assistant? She's right over there."

I turned around without being obvious to glance at the women. "No, we didn't get around to it yet."

"Her name is Jillian. She's the one with the blond hair. She worked for him for a long time. If anyone knows Luca, she does. She managed his whole life, including the women he slept with. She might be able to help you out."

I nodded and sipped my drink. "Thank you. What's your name?"

"Everyone calls me Smith."

"Smith, thanks for the drink." I eased away from the bar and made my way over to the group of women. "I don't mean to interrupt anything, but I was wondering if I can talk to you, Jillian."

"Do I know you?" she scowled.

"No, but I wanted to ask you a few questions about your former boss, Luca Moretti."

She froze as soon as I mentioned that name. "And you are . . .?"

"I'm FBI Agent Tyler, working the case."

She gave me a good look before she said to her friends, "I'll be right back. Order me another drink, please."

They nodded slowly, eyeing me.

Jillian was much taller than I as she stood up. She had to be nearly six feet. Her heels clicked against the hardwood floor as I followed her outside of the lounge. It was no longer raining, but we stood underneath the awning.

She lit a cigarette and puffed on it. "What do you want to know, Agent?"

"It's my understanding that you were his assistant, and you knew everything there was to know about his entire life, including the women he slept with. Where were you the morning he was found?"

Her hands shook nervously as she said, "Luca sent me a text that instructed me to take some time off. I rarely get vacations, and with the drama between him and his wife, I was more than willing to go. I made plans to go to Mexico. When I returned, I saw that he had a heart attack on the news. I felt something wasn't right from the beginning. That was when I figured Luca wasn't the one who texted me. The message came from his phone, but it wasn't him."

"Do you still have these texts on your phone?"

She inhaled and blew out smoke as she scrolled through her phone. "I kept them because I figured I would be questioned eventually." She handed me her phone. "Luca doesn't text this way. He didn't use slang. I worked with him long enough to know his text message style."

"So, if you knew it wasn't him sending you on vacation, why'd you go?"

"I was looking for a break. Luca hadn't let me go on vacation for years."

I looked at the messages before handing back her phone. "Thank you. What do you think about Naomi? She was released."

"She loved that man too much to kill him. Plus, she had just lost her husband a few weeks before."

"Since it wasn't Naomi, who do you believe did this?"

She shook her head and replied, "I don't have a clue, but if there's anything else you need from me, I'm willing to provide you with everything I know." She handed me her business card. "I'll tell you more, but I don't want to get into it while I'm intoxicated. I'd rather talk when I'm sober."

I nodded as I took her card from her. "I'll be in touch," I said.

Jillian put out her cigarette and walked back inside to finish her evening with her friends.

I sighed heavily before returning inside and putting my glass on the bar. I decided to head home. I was exhausted, and my brain needed a break, but I wasn't going to be able to rest. Sand Cove wasn't off the hook just yet, and if the case was going to be reopened, I would stop at nothing until I found Luca Moretti's killer.